12/09

TALES TO FREEZE
THE BLOOD

Also Edited by Stephen Jones

Great Ghost Stories (with R. Chetwynd-Hayes)
The Mammoth Book of Best New Horror, Volumes 1-17
The Mammoth Book of Terror
The Mammoth Book of New Terror
The Mammoth Book of Vampire Stories by Women
The Mammoth Book of Vampires
The Mammoth Book of Dracula
Horror: 100 Best Books (with Kim Newman)
Horror: Another 100 Best Books (with Kim Newman)
Dancing With the Dark
The Best Horror from Fantasy Tales (with David Sutton)

TALES TO FREEZE THE BLOOD

Selected by R. Chetwynd-Hayes
and Stephen Jones

CARROLL & GRAF PUBLISHERS
NEW YORK

TALES TO FREEZE THE BLOOD:
More Great Ghost Stories

Carroll & Graf Publishers
An Imprint of Avalon Publishing Group, Inc.
245 West 17th Street
11th Floor
New York, NY 10011

AVALON
publishing group incorporated

The arrangement of this collection is copyright © Stephen Jones and the Estate of
Ronald Chetwynd-Hayes 2006.

First Carroll & Graf edition 2006

Library of Congress Cataloging-in-Publication Data is available.

ISBN-10: 0-7867-1679-7
ISBN-13: 978-0-78671-679-1

9 8 7 6 5 4 3 2 1

Interior design: *Ivelisse Robles Marrero*

Printed in the United States of America
Distributed by Publishers Group West

In Recognition of
SYD BOUNDS,
One of Britain's Masters of the Macabre

CONTENTS

ACKNOWLEDGEMENTS

Special thanks to Linda Smith, Herman Graf, Shaun Dillon, Mike Ashley, Chico Kidd and Dorothy Lumley for helping make this anthology possible.

The Editors gratefully acknowledge permission to publish the following copyright material:

FOREWORD

STEPHEN JONES

When he wasn't contributing his own, unique brand, of humorous horror to such classic anthologies as *The Pan Book of Horror Stories* and *The Fontana Book of Great Horror Stories,* Ronald Chetwynd-Hayes was editing his own successful series of ghost books from Britain's Fontana imprint.

Taking over with the eighth volume in 1973 when Robert Aickman tired of the role, Ron ably edited a further twelve volumes of *The Fontana Book of Great Ghost Stories* until that series was eventually discontinued in 1984. During that time, he not only decided to reprint classic and obscure stories of the macabre, but he also included a number of tales by more contemporary authors such as Ramsey Campbell, Brian Lumley, Sydney J. Bounds, Steve Rasnic Tem, Mary Williams, Tony Richards, Garry Kilworth, Tina Rath and others, including the first British publication of Stephen King's 'The Reaper's Image' in the 17th volume.

However, by the mid-1980s the horror field was going through one of its regular downturns in popularity and sales of anthologies—especially those containing Victorian and Edwardian reprints—were not as successful as they had been a decade before.

When Fontana decided to end the *Great Ghost Stories* series, although Ron did not agree with the decision, he understood what they were doing from a commercial viewpoint.

Oddly, in 1978 he had sold another volume, *Doomed to the Night: An Anthology of Ghost Stories,* to William Kimber & Co., his new hardcover publisher. Looking through the contents list of that title, which features W. Somerset Maugham, A. M. Burrage, Daphne Froome, Miss Braddon, J. S. Le Fanu, Mary E. Penn, Richard Middleton, Ambrose Bierce and other familiar names—including the ever-popular 'Anonymous' with two contributions—there is little doubt that this book could just as easily have been published as part of the Fontana series and may have even been originally compiled with that market in mind.

I have therefore decided to include some of its contents in this second omnibus of tales that I hope once again reflects the skill and knowledge that Ronald Chetwynd-Hayes brought to his editing more than a quarter of a century ago.

Although the traditional ghost story has enjoyed a revival recently—most notably in high-priced, limited editions from small imprints on both sides of the Atlantic—some of the following stories and authors will most probably be unfamiliar to those readers more used to the modern horrors of such authors as King and Koontz. However, I trust that you will find more than a few tales that will remain with you once you have closed the covers and turned off the light.

As Ron would have said all those years ago:

Happy shuddering.

Stephen Jones
London, England
September, 2005

INTRODUCTION

R. CHETWYND-HAYES

I wish I could say truthfully that I had seen a ghost.

I have read about reputedly haunted houses, listened to friends who knew someone who had experienced some kind of psychic phenomena, but as a professional horror-monger I really am ashamed to say that the dim world of the hereafter has, to date, given me the go-by.

This, I feel, is nothing short of a tragedy, because I would dearly love proof that some form of life exists beyond the grave. After all is said and done, one is dead longer than one is alive. Not that a ghost proves anything, one way or another. 'Time image', 'extension of personality', 'atmosphere', and 'fear-flamed imagination'—all can be responsible for the phenomena known as ghosts; and I have yet to meet anyone who has held an intelligent conversation with an apparition.

Of course, there may be people who think they have, and to those fortunate few doubt can no longer exist. The opinions of down-to-earth sceptics are of no importance; they, the lucky few, know, and knowledge is an asset which rises above belief, replaces mere faith and slaughters doubt.

It is my long-held contention that every room that has been used by a lot of people over a long number of years must be haunted. It would seem that O. Henry, that superb master of the short story, agreed with me. For in 'The Furnished Room' we sense the presence of numerous ghosts, but only one can make itself felt. Think about this story when you are next in a hotel bedroom.

Handsome, bitter, bad-tempered, brave, brilliant Ambrose Bierce was obsessed with the idea of people suddenly disappearing—and became one of the greatest vanishments of modern times himself. In 1914 he entered Mexico, then convulsed by civil war, and after writing one vague letter—disappeared. The logical explanation is of course that he was killed in some unreported skirmish, but there can be no doubt that the unsolved mystery helped to immortalise his name.

But 'The Night Doings at "Deadman's" ' really is a bit much. A haunted cabin where a dead Chinaman comes up from a hole in the floor, with the intention of getting his pigtail back.

Sydney J. Bounds allows his hero to do 'A Little Night Fishing' off the coast of Cornwall. As usual Mr. Bounds tells a story that has a nasty twist in the tail. The ghost of a wrecker who is still up to his old tricks of luring ships on to the rocks is not a pleasant prospect, and would put most of us off night—or day—fishing for life.

It gives me great pleasure to include two glorious oldies, found in some bound magazines dating back to 1886. First we have 'Not Yet Solved' by that indefatigable writer—so loved by Victorians—Anonymous; then 'The Grey Cottage' by Mrs. Claxton. I am not going to tell you anything about the story lines (that would spoil your enjoyment), but request you read them by candlelight. Better still, read them aloud to a group of friends.

Guy de Maupassant has inspired many modern writers, not least of whom is W. Somerset Maugham. 'The Hostelry' is probably one of his least known stories, which only goes to show that anthologists often do not do their homework. What could be more horrifying than this:

Aroused by the noise, the dog began to howl in terror, and ran hither and thither in the room, trying to find out whence the danger threatened. When he came to the door, he sniffed at the edge of it, and began howling, snorting, and snarling, his hair bristling, his tail erect.

A ghost trying to get in?

There can be no doubt that Mrs. Crowe was a Victorian lady who knew her ghosts and was not afraid to talk about them. In 'Round the Fire' we gather that a number of very polite, well-served people scared one another half to death by relating their supernatural experiences. And an exceedingly good job they made of it. One is inclined to wonder if Mrs. Crowe relied solely on her imagination, or was recording incidents that were at least purported to be true. Some readers will notice that I have omitted the early part of this story, being of the opinion that it rather hampered the narrative.

In *Great Ghost Stories* I used F. Marion Crawford's 'The Dead Smile' which, I am given to understand, gave at least two people nightmares. 'The Doll's Ghost' is not so much terrifying as disturbing—the ghost being small, with a penchant for saying 'Pa-pa', with a break between the syllables. But a useful phantom to have around when little Else gets lost.

Joseph Sheridan Le Fanu was, for most of his life, a recluse, refusing to see even close friends, and he gradually developed a deep melancholia. Perhaps this was why he was so interested in the supernatural and was able to turn out such soul-shaking ghost stories. Dissatisfaction with this world might engender an increasing curiosity as to the shadow-clad inhabitants of the next. 'Madam Crowl's Ghost' is related by an old woman who is recalling what took place at Applewale House when she first went there at the age of thirteen. She was to wait on Dame Crowl, who from being a great beauty seventy years before, was now:

I sid before me, stretched out like a painted lady on the tomb-stean in Lexhoe Church, the famous Dame Crowl, of Applewale House . . . A big powdered wig, half as high as herself, was a-top o' her head, and, wow—was there ever such wrinkles?—and her old baggy throat all powdered white, and her cheeks rouged, and mouseskin eyebrows

Then the old lady died.

'The Cold Embrace' by Miss Braddon was first published in 1862 and I have no doubt was intended to serve as a warning to young men who are:

handsome, studious, enthusiastic, metaphysical, reckless, unbelieving, heartless.

Such a complex character is worthy of our consideration, particularly when he leads a girl called Gertrude up the garden path and leaves her high and dry on the compost heap. I am speaking metaphorically of course, as I gravely doubt if Miss Braddon knew what a compost heap was. I suppose this could be classified as a Gothic ghost story, even though some passages are more inclined to merit a chuckle than a shudder. Of course this kind of thing might make the reader smile on the other side of his—or her—face.

His dead cousin's cold arms are around his neck—his dead cousin's wet hands are clasped upon his breast. He asks himself if he is mad. "Up Leo," he shouts. "Up, up boy!" and the Newfoundland leaps to his shoulders—the dog's paws are on the dead hands and the animal utters a terrific howl and springs away from his master.

Oh, wise and sagacious animal.

During the nineteenth century 'Anonymous' was an indefatigable writer of ghost tales, even though many of them were not worth reading. But I think you will agree that 'At Ravenholme Junction' could well have been written last week. The railways of yesteryear, with their fog-shrouded tracks, lonely signal-boxes, great steam-driven monsters, were a natural habitat for restless, conscience-stricken ghosts, that must have given the travellers something worse to think about than today's stale sausage rolls. On the other hand, to be a signalman in those far-off days was an extremely haphazard business, what with the managing director's son popping along without warning, the certain knowledge that a moment's inattention might result in a train crash and the possibility of a ghost taking his turn at the levers.

It is nice to know that Charles Dickens accepted 'How the Third Floor Knew the Potteries' by Amelia B. Edwards for inclusion in *All the Year Round* (1863), for it enables me to say: What was good enough for Boz is good enough for me. However, I hasten to add it is a well-told chilling story and the characters as real as a foggy Monday morning. Louis Laroche is a wonderful, subdued study in evil, for Miss Edwards does not (as did sometimes her famous editor) commit the crime of painting her villains jet black. Leah, so serious-minded, is a natural victim for the Frenchman's wiles, and poor George . . . No, I mustn't give the game away.

We all know (or should do) that Sir Richard Burton was the first Englishman to reach Mecca, had a go at discovering the source of the Nile and translated *The Arabian Nights* into English. He also discovered one of the strangest of ghost stories ever written. 'The Saving of a Soul' is reputed to be an authentic account of a haunting that took place in the Castle of Weixelstein in 1559. It would seem that the ghost was extremely garrulous and granted several interviews, a form of spectral behaviour that I find to be very unusual.

I understand that Fritz Hopman wrote 'The Bearer of the Message' some time towards the end of the 19th century, but that is all the information I can give you. His writing is uncomplicated for that period, which makes me wonder if this version is a translation as Mr. Hopman appears to have been a Frenchman. The plot is deceptively simple and therefore does not prepare the reader for the shock ending. But the author has drawn a realistic picture of Russia in 1869, which makes one assume that he must have been there around that time.

Altogether a nice, tight little story with disturbing undertones.

To have a full chilling effect a ghost should be heard and not seen. Possibly this is the reason that radio is such a perfect medium for the ghost story, because the listener is only permitted to hear approaching footsteps, creaking doors, a disembodied sigh—and his imagination does the rest. To actually meet a ghost face to face must be an anti-climax; merely confronting a man or woman who might be a little transparent round the edges.

Captain Marryat clearly thought so, for when he saw the famous Brown Lady of Raynham Hall coming towards him down a long passage, he promptly put a bullet through her. Not that it did much good, for she got herself photographed in 1926 and is in all probability roaming the corridors of Raynham to this day.

But to return to my contention that unseen ghosts are the only ones worth worrying about, 'Canon Alberic's Scrap-Book' by M. R. James illustrates what I am trying to convey very nicely. Or nastily. The most terrifying part of the tale is when Dennistoun hears a thin metallic voice laughing high up in the tower. The dreadful thing that appears in his bedroom is at first dismissed as being nothing more than a penwiper. Of course he soon realises it is *something* guaranteed to wipe the smile off the most sceptical face.

I have never completed reading a novel by E. and H. Heron, having long ago decided they are much too pedantic. But their occasional ghost story is another matter entirely, particularly when it includes the pompous psychologist Mr. Flaxman Low. 'The Story of Medhans Lea' is peopled by stout hearty men who say: "Don't you know! How ripping! It's a cursed creepy affair!" all of which is intended to inform us that here are some no-nonsense chaps who just don't believe in ghosts—or any of that rot. Which means we just can't wait for them to get their comeuppance. Which they do—in no uncertain terms.

Richard Middleton during his lifetime earned only five pounds from his writing and that was a literary prize. 'The Passing of Edward' is a prose poem and in my opinion a very beautiful one. A few weeks after completing this story Middleton committed suicide at the age of twenty-nine and, if I may coin a phrase, it shows. Purple melancholy tints every word and the reader is drawn into a mind that is preparing to welcome death as a long-awaited friend.

'An Unsolved Mystery' by E. Owens Blackburne is another oldie, written in 1886. Moreover it is purported to be true, a statement that does little to comfort a shivering reader. From the beginning we are left in no doubt as to what is in store for us.

> *Over all there hung a cloud of fear,*
> *A sense of mystery the spirit daunted,*
> *And said, as plain as whisper to the ear,*
> *'This house is haunted.'*

The Victorians were a tough lot. If I had witnessed half the goings-on that beset the Comyers family, there would have been a Hayes-shaped hole in the nearest window. But it was not until Mrs. Comyers was struck down by a *serious nervous illness* that the family decided to move out. Having said that, I must admit it would be the experience of a lifetime to spend a night in such an establishment.

'The Horrors of Sleep' is a poem by Emily Brontë. The author of *Wuthering Heights* was a mystic, one of those rare beings who are fully aware of a world that exists just beyond the frontiers of our lifetimes. 'The Horrors of Sleep' could have been nothing less than an account of some intense psychic experience. Like Richard Middleton, it would seem that this gifted, highly sensitive woman had a death wish that is stressed by her refusal to be treated by a doctor in her last illness.

Those readers who expressed their admiration of Tony Richards's 'Our Lady of the Shadows' in *Great Ghost Stories* will not be disappointed with his latest offering, 'Streets of the City'. I would like to think that Marshall Harris was haunted by a fear ghost, but the macabre events suggest a much more tangible enmity.

'In the Dark' by Mary E. Penn is an oldie (written around 1876) that is again set in an old house. A ghost-child is the most disturbing of phantoms, particularly when its voice can be heard crying piteously, "Let me out, let me out!" from the depths of a dark closet. I do not know who Mary E. Penn was, but am interested to learn she must have come from my stretch of the country, as we are told that John Dysart had rented a pretty, old-fashioned riverside villa between Richmond and Kew. I have no doubt that Miss Penn borrowed the name Dysart from the Dysart family who once owned Ham House.

I included 'Housewarming' by Steve Rasnic Tem in *Great Ghost Stories* and stated that the author had made quite a name for himself on both sides of the Atlantic as a fantasy writer of merit. 'Shadows on the Grass' will most certainly enhance that reputation. A subtle piece of writing that has much in common with the best work of Richard Middleton. A haunting story in more senses than one.

Rick Kennett, who hails from Australia, contributes 'The Roads of Donnington'. All about a ghost motorcyclist, which makes a nice change. Apparently the inhabitants of Donnington ignore it—the ghost motorcyclist—or pretend it does not exist. But of course there was an accident that transformed Barry into a ghost (together with his machine) and there is a suspicion that just maybe it was not all that much of an accident. I was interested to learn that the ghost of Lawrence of Arabia is reputed to have been seen riding his motorcycle through the country lanes of Dorset.

Last of all we come to my very own 'The Day That Father Brought

Something Home'. This first appeared in a collection of my stories which was published by Tandem Books under the title of *Cold Terror*. Since then the book has been published in the United States, Germany and Sweden and quite a few people have been kind enough to write to me and state how much they enjoyed this particular story and request that I explain how it came to be written.

So far I have been able to supply only one answer. I just don't know. I write all my stories blind. That is to say I sit down behind a typewriter and hope to hell that fingers and brain will come up with something readable. Believe it or not, usually this slap-dash procedure works, although the end result varies considerably. It is possible that the excitement of not knowing what is going to happen next keeps me going.

With regard to this particular specimen—having re-read it after a long period of time, made allowances for what I should have put in, what I should have left out, I had to admit it's not at all a bad story. Otherwise I would not have included it in this collection. Anyway, I hope you like it.

I sometimes like to think that long after I am dead and gone, these books of *Great Ghost Stories* will become collectors' items. Not impossible. If so—which stories will still be readable—and reprintable—in that, hopefully, far-off age? Obviously those that do not date, continue to entertain and scare. Make the reader say: 'They don't write 'em like that anymore'.

I do not write for posterity, but I always have it in mind. We all haunt the future and are of the stuff from which ghosts are made; often fit subjects for our own imaginative creations. Planting fantasy seedlings that, perhaps, will not be out of place in the literary landscape of a hundred years hence. Always supposing there is anyone left who can read.

So there we are. Twenty-three stories and one mystic poem. Some chilling, some humorous, a few down-right terrifying. May you never hear invisible footsteps following you down the stairs.

THE FURNISHED ROOM

O. HENRY

Restless, shifting, fugacious as time itself is a certain vast bulk of the population of the red brick district of the lower West Side. Homeless, they have a hundred homes. They flit from furnished room to furnished room, transients forever—transients in abode, transients in heart and mind. They sing 'Home, Sweet Home' in ragtime; they carry their *lares et penates* in a bandbox; their vine is entwined about a picture hat; a rubber plant is their fig tree.

Hence the houses of this district, having had a thousand dwellers, should have a thousand tales to tell, mostly dull ones, no doubt; but it would be strange if there could not be found a ghost or two in the wake of all these vagrant guests.

One evening after dark a young man prowled among these crumbling red mansions, ringing their bells. At the twelfth he rested his lean hand-baggage upon the step and wiped the dust from his hat-band and forehead. The bell sounded faint and far away in some remote, hollow depths.

To the door of this, the twelfth house whose bell he had rung, came a housekeeper who made him think of an unwholesome, surfeited worm that had eaten its nut to a hollow shell and now sought to fill the vacancy with edible lodgers.

He asked if there was a room to let.

'Come in,' said the housekeeper. Her voice came from her throat; her throat seemed lined with fur. 'I have the third-floor back, vacant since a week back. Should you wish to look at it?'

The young man followed her up the stairs. A faint light from no particular source mitigated the shadows of the halls. They trod noiselessly upon a stair carpet that its own loom would have forsworn. It seemed to have become vegetable; to have degenerated in that rank, sunless air to lush lichen or spreading moss that grew in patches to the staircase and was viscid under the foot like organic matter. At each turn of the stairs were vacant niches in the wall. Perhaps plants had once been set within them. If so they had died in that foul and tainted air. It may be that statues of the saints had stood there, but it was not difficult to conceive that imps and devils had dragged them forth in the darkness and down to the unholy depths of some furnished pit below.

'This is the room,' said the housekeeper, from her furry throat. 'It's a nice room. It ain't often vacant. I had some most elegant people in it last summer—no trouble at all, and paid in advance to the minute. The water's at the end of the hall. Sprowls and Mooney kept it three months. They done a vaudeville sketch. Miss B'retta Sprowls—you may have heard of her—Oh, that was just the stage names—right there over the dresser is where the marriage certificate hung, framed. The gas is here, and you see there is plenty of closet room. It's a room everybody likes. It never stays idle long.'

'Do you have many theatrical people rooming here?' asked the young man.

'They comes and goes. A good proportion of my lodgers is connected with the theatres. Yes, sir, this is the theatric district. Actor people never stays long anywhere. I get my share. Yes, they comes and they goes.'

He engaged the room, paying for a week in advance. He was tired, he said, and would take possession at once. He counted out the money. The room had been made ready, she said, even to towels and water. As the house-keeper moved away he put for the thousandth time, the question that he carried at the end of his tongue.

'A young girl—Miss Vashner—Miss Eloise Vashner—do you remember such a one among your lodgers? She would be singing on the stage, most likely. A fair girl, of medium height and slender, with reddish, gold hair and a dark mole near her left eyebrow.'

'No, I don't remember the name. Them stage people has names they change as often as their rooms. They comes and they goes. No, I don't call that one to mind.'

No. Always no. Five months of ceaseless interrogation and the inevitable negative. So much time spent by day in questioning managers, agents, schools and choruses; by night among the audiences of theatres from all-star casts down to music halls so low that he dreaded to find what he most hoped for. He who had loved her best had tried to find her. He was sure that since her disappearance from home this great, water-girt city held her somewhere, but it was like a monstrous quick-sand, shifting its particles constantly, with no foundation, its upper granules of today buried tomorrow in ooze and slime.

The furnished room received its latest guest with a first glow of pseudo-hospitality, a hectic, haggard, perfunctory welcome like the specious smile of a demirep. The sophistical comfort came in reflected gleams from the decayed furniture, the ragged brocade upholstery of a couch and two chairs, a foot-wide cheap pier glass between the two windows, from one or two gilt picture frames and a brass bedstead in a corner.

The guest reclined, inert, upon a chair, while the room, confused in speech as though it were an apartment in Babel, tried to discourse to him of its divers tenantry.

A polychromatic rug like some brilliant-flowered rectangular, tropical islet lay surrounded by a billowy sea of soiled matting. Upon the gay-papered wall were those pictures that pursue the homeless one from house to house—*The Huguenot Lovers, The First Quarrel, The Wedding Breakfast, Psyche at the Fountain*. The mantel's chastely severe outline was ingloriously veiled behind some pert drapery drawn rakishly askew like the sashes of the Amazonian ballet. Upon it was some desolate flotsam cast aside by the room's marooned when a lucky sail had borne them to a fresh port—a trifling vase or two, pictures of actresses, a medicine bottle, some stray cards out of a deck.

One by one, as the characters of a cryptograph become explicit, the little signs left by the furnished room's procession of guests developed a significance. The threadbare space in the rug in front of the dresser told that lovely women had marched in the throng. Tiny finger prints on the wall spoke of little prisoners trying to feel their way to sun and air. A splattered stain, raying like a shadow of a bursting bomb, witnessed where a hurled glass or bottle had splintered with its contents against the wall. Across the pier glass had been scrawled with a diamond in staggering letters the name 'Marie'. It seemed that the succession of dwellers in the furnished room had turned in fury—perhaps tempted beyond forbearance by its garish coldness—and wreaked upon it their passions. The furniture was chipped and bruised; the couch, distorted by bursting springs, seemed a horrible monster that had been slain during the stress of some grotesque convulsion. Some more potent upheaval had cloven a great slice from the marble mantel. Each plank in the floor owned its particular cant and shriek as from a separate and individual agony. It seemed incredible that all this malice and injury had been wrought upon the room by those who had called it for a time their home; and yet it may have been the cheated home instinct surviving blindly, the resentful rage at false household gods that had kindled their wrath. A hut that is our own we can sweep and adorn and cherish.

The young tenant in the chair allowed these thoughts to file, soft-shod, through his mind, while there drifted into the room furnished sounds and furnished scents. He heard in one room a tittering and incontinent, slack laughter; in others the monologue of a scold, the rattling of dice, a lullaby, and one crying dully; above him a banjo tinkled with spirit. Doors banged somewhere, the elevated trains roared intermittently; a cat yowled miserably upon a back fence. And he breathed the breath of the house—a dank savour rather than a smell—a cold, musty effluvium as from underground vaults mingled with the reeking exhalations of linoleum and mildewed and rotten woodwork.

Then, suddenly, as he rested there, the room was filled with the strong, sweet odour of mignonette. It came as upon a single buffet of wind with such sureness and fragrance and emphasis that it almost seemed a living visitant. And the man cried aloud: 'What, dear?' as if he had been called, and sprang up and faced about. The rich odour clung to him and wrapped him around. He reached out his arms for it, all his senses for the time confused and commingled. How could one be peremptorily called by an odour? Surely it must have been sound. But, was it not the sound that had touched, that had caressed him?

'She has been in this room,' he cried, and he sprang to wrest from it a token, for he knew he would recognize the smallest thing that had belonged to her or that she had touched. This enveloping scent of mignonette, the odour that she had loved and made her own—whence came it?

The room had been but carelessly set in order. Scattered upon the flimsy dresser scarf were half a dozen hairpins—those discreet, indistinguishable friends of womankind, feminine of gender, infinite of mood and uncommunicative of tense. These he ignored, conscious of their triumphant lack of identity. Ransacking the drawers of the dresser he came upon a discarded, tiny, ragged handkerchief. He pressed it to his face. It was racy and insolent with heliotrope; he hurled it to the floor. In another drawer he found odd buttons, a theater programme, a pawnbroker's card, two lost marshmallows, a book on the divination of dreams. In the last was a woman's black satin hair-bow, which halted him, poised between ice and fire. But the black satin hair-bow also is femininity's demure, impersonal, common ornament, and tells no tales.

And then he traversed the room like a hound on the scent, skimming the walls, considering the corners of the bulging matting on his hands and knees, rummaging mantel and tables, the curtains and hangings, the drunken cabinet in the corner, for a visible sign, unable to perceive that she was there beside, around, against, within, above him, clinging to him, wooing him, calling him so poignantly through the finer senses that even his grosser ones became cognisant of the call. Once again he answered loudly: 'Yes dear!' and turned, wild-eyed, to gaze on vacancy, for he could not yet discern form and colour and love and outstretched arms in the odour of mignonette. Oh, God! whence that odour, and since when have odours had a voice to call? Thus he groped.

He burrowed in crevices and corners, and found corks and cigarettes. These he passed in passive contempt. But once he found in a fold of the matting a half-smoked cigar, and this he ground beneath his heel with a green and trenchant oath. He sifted the room from end to end. He found dreary and ignoble small records of many a peripatetic tenant; but of her whom he sought, and who may have lodged there, and whose spirit seemed to hover there, he found no trace.

And then he thought of the housekeeper.

He ran from the haunted room downstairs and to a door that showed a crack of light. She came out to his knock. He smothered his excitement as best he could.

'Will you tell me, madam,' he besought her, 'who occupied the room I have before I came?'

'Yes, sir. I can tell you again. 'Twas Sprowls and Mooney, as I said. Miss

B'retta Sprowls it was in the theatres, but Missis Mooney she was. My house is well known for respectability. The marriage certificate hung, framed, on a nail over—'

'What kind of a lady was Miss Sprowls—in looks, I mean?'

'Why, black-haired, sir, short, and stout, with a comical face. They left a week ago Tuesday.'

'And before they occupied it?'

'Why, there was a single gentleman connected with the draying business. He left owing me a week. Before him was Missis Crowder and her two children, they stayed four months; and back of them was old Mr Doyle, whose sons paid for him. He kept the room six months. That goes back a year, sir, and further I do not remember.'

He thanked her and crept back to his room. The room was dead. The essence that had vivified it was gone. The perfume of mignonette had departed. In its place was the old, stale odour of mouldy house furniture, of atmosphere in storage.

The ebbing of his hope drained his faith. He sat staring at the yellow, singing gaslight. Soon he walked to the bed and began to tear the sheets into strips. With the blade of his knife he drove them tightly into every crevice around windows and door. When all was snug and taut he turned out the light, turned the gas full on again and laid himself gratefully upon the bed.

It was Mrs McCool's night to go with the can for beer. So she fetched it and sat with Mrs Purdy in one of those subterranean retreats where housekeepers forgather and the worm dieth seldom.

'I rented out my third floor, back, this evening,' said Mrs Purdy, across a fine circle of foam. 'A young man took it. He went up to bed two hours ago.'

'Now, did ye, Missis Purdy, ma'am?' said Mrs McCool, with intense admiration. 'You do be a wonder for rentin' rooms of that kind. And did ye tell him, then?' she concluded in husky whisper, laden with mystery.

'Rooms,' said Mrs Purdy, in her furriest tones, 'are furnished for to rent. I did not tell him, Mrs McCool.'

' 'Tis right ye are, ma'am; 'tis by renting rooms we kape alive. Ye have the rale sense for business, ma'am. There be many people will rayjict the rentin' of a room if they be tould a suicide has been after dyin' in the bed of it.'

'As you say, we has our living to be making,' remarked Mrs Purdy.

'Yis, ma'am, 'tis true. 'Tis just one wake ago this day I helped ye lay out the third floor, back. A pretty slip of colleen she was to be killin' herself wid the gas—a swate little face she had, Mrs Purdy, ma'am.'

'She'd a-been called handsome, as you say,' said Mrs Purdy, assenting but critical, 'but for that mole she had a-growin' by her left eyebrow. Do fill up your glass again, Missis McCool.'

THE NIGHT-DOINGS AT "DEADMAN'S"

AMBROSE BIERCE

It was a singularly sharp night, and clear as the heart of a diamond. Clear nights have a trick of being keen. In darkness you may be cold and not know it; when you see, you suffer. This night was bright enough to bite like a serpent. The moon was moving mysteriously along behind the giant pines crowning the South Mountain, striking a cold sparkle from the crusted snow, and bringing out against the black west the ghostly outlines of the Coast Range, beyond which lay the invisible Pacific. The snow had piled itself, in the open spaces along the bottom of the gulch, into long ridges that seemed to heave, and into hills that appeared to toss and scatter spray. The spray was sunlight, twice reflected: dashed once from the moon, once from the snow.

In this snow many of the shanties of the abandoned mining camp were obliterated (a sailor might have said they had gone down) and at irregular intervals it had overtopped the tall trestles which had once supported a river called a flume; for, of course, 'flume' is *flumen*. Among the advantages of which the mountains cannot deprive the gold hunter is the privilege of speaking Latin. He says of his dead neighbour, 'He has gone up the flume.' This is not a bad way to say, 'His life has returned to the Fountain of Life.'

While putting on its armour against the assaults of the wind, this snow had neglected no coign of vantage. Snow pursued by the wind is not wholly unlike a retreating army. In the open field it ranges itself in ranks and battalions; where it can get a foothold it makes a stand; where it can take cover it does so. You may see whole platoons of snow cowering behind a bit of broken wall. The devious old road, hewn out of the mountain-side, was full of it. Squadron upon squadron had struggled to escape by this line, when suddenly pursuit had ceased. A more desolate and dreary spot than Deadman's Gulch in a winter midnight it is impossible to imagine. Yet Mr Hiram Beeson elected to live there, the sole inhabitant.

Away up the side of the North Mountain his little pine-log shanty projected from its single pane of glass a long, thin beam of light, and looked not altogether unlike a black beetle fastened to the hillside with a bright new pin. Within it sat Mr Beeson himself, before a roaring fire, staring into its hot heart as if he had never before seen such a thing in all his life. He was not a comely man. He was grey; he was ragged and slovenly in his attire; his face was wan and haggard; his eyes were too bright. As to his age, if one had attempted to guess it, one might have said forty-seven, then corrected himself and said seventy-four. He was really twenty-eight. Emaciated he was; as much, perhaps, as he dared be, with a needy undertaker at Bentley's Flat and a new and enterprising coroner at Sonora. Poverty and zeal are an upper and a nether millstone. It is dangerous to make a third in that kind of sandwich.

As Mr Beeson sat there, with his ragged elbows on his ragged knees, his lean jaws buried in his lean hands, and with no apparent intention of going to bed, he looked as if the slightest movement would tumble him to pieces. Yet during the last hour he had winked no fewer than three times.

There was a sharp rapping at the door. A rap at that time of night and in that weather might have surprised an ordinary mortal who had dwelt two years in the Gulch without seeing a human face, and could not fail to know that the country was impassable; but Mr Beeson did not so much as pull his eyes out of the coals. And even when the door was pushed open he only shrugged a little more closely into himself, as one does who is expecting something that he would rather not see. You may observe this movement in women when, in a mortuary chapel, the coffin is borne up the aisle behind them.

But when a long old man in a blanket overcoat, his head tied up in a handkerchief and nearly his entire face in a muffler, wearing green goggles and with a complexion of glittering whiteness where it could be seen, strode silently into the room, laying a hard, gloved hand on Mr Beeson's shoulder, the latter so far forgot himself as to look up with an appearance of no small astonishment; whomever he may have been expecting, he had evidently not counted on meeting anyone like this. Nevertheless, the sight of this unexpected guest produced in Mr Beeson the following sequence: a feeling of astonishment; a sense of gratification; a sentiment of profound goodwill. Rising from his seat, he took the knotty hand from his shoulder, and shook it up and down with a fervour quite unaccountable; for in the old man's aspect was nothing to attract, much to repel. However, attraction is too general a property for repulsion to be without it. The most attractive object in the world is the face we instinctively cover with a cloth. When it becomes still more attractive—fascinating—we put seven feet of earth above it.

'Sir,' said Mr Beeson, releasing the old man's hand, which fell passively against his thigh with a quiet clack, 'it is an extremely disagreeable night. Pray be seated; I am very glad to see you.'

Mr Beeson spoke with an easy good breeding that one would hardly have expected, considering all things. Indeed, the contrast between his appearance and his manner was sufficiently surprising to be one of the commonest of social phenomena in the mines. The old man advanced a step toward the fire, glowing cavernously in the green goggles. Mr Beeson resumed:

'You bet your life I am!'

Mr Beeson's elegance was not too refined; it had made reasonable concessions to local taste. He paused a moment, letting his eyes drop from the muffled head of his guest, down along the row of mouldy buttons confining the blanket overcoat, to the greenish cowhide boots powdered with snow, which had begun to melt and run along the floor in little rills. He took an inventory of his guest, and appeared satisfied. Who would not have been? Then he continued:

'The cheer I can offer you is, unfortunately, in keeping with my surroundings; but I shall esteem myself highly favoured if it is your pleasure to partake of it, rather than seek better at Bentley's Flat.'

With a singular refinement of hospitable humility Mr Beeson spoke as if a sojourn in his warm cabin on such a night, as compared with walking fourteen miles up to the throat in snow with a cutting crust, would be an intolerable hardship. By way of reply, his guest unbuttoned the blanket overcoat. The host laid fresh fuel on the fire, swept the hearth with the tail of a wolf, and added:

'But *I* think you'd better skedaddle.'

The old man took a seat by the fire, spreading his broad soles to the heat without removing his hat. In the mines the hat is seldom removed except when the boots are. Without further remark Mr Beeson also seated himself in a chair which had been a barrel, and which, retaining much of its original character, seemed to have been designed with a view to preserving his dust if it should please him to crumble. For a moment there was silence; then, from somewhere among the pines, came the snarling yelp of a coyote; and simultaneously the door rattled in its frame. There was no other connection between the two incidents than that the coyote has an aversion to storms, and the wind was rising; yet there seemed somehow a kind of supernatural conspiracy between the two, and Mr Beeson shuddered with a vague sense of terror. He recovered himself in a moment and again addressed his guest.

'There are strange doings here. I will tell you everything, and then if you decide to go I shall hope to accompany you over the worst of the way; as far as where Baldy Peterson shot Ben Hike—I dare say you know the place.'

The old man nodded emphatically, as intimating not merely that he did, but that he did indeed.

'Two years ago,' began Mr Beeson, 'I, with two companions, occupied this house; but when the rush to the Flat occurred we left, along with the rest. In ten hours the Gulch was deserted. That evening, however, I discovered I had left behind me a valuable pistol (that is it) and returned for it, passing the night here alone, as I have passed every night since. I must explain that a few days before we left, our Chinese domestic had the misfortune to die while the ground was frozen so hard that it was impossible to dig a grave in the usual way. So, on the day of our hasty departure, we cut through the floor there, and gave him such burial as we could. But before putting him down I had the extremely bad taste to cut off his pigtail and spike it to that beam above his grave, where you may see it at this moment, or, preferably, when warmth has given you leisure for observation.

'I stated, did I not, that the Chinaman came to his death from natural causes? I had, of course, nothing to do with that, and returned through no irresistible attraction, or morbid fascination, but only because I had forgotten a pistol. This is clear to you, is it not, sir?'

The visitor nodded gravely. He appeared to be a man of few words, if any. Mr Beeson continued:

'According to the Chinese faith, a man is like a kite: he cannot go to heaven without a tail. Well, to shorten this tedious story—which, however, I thought it my duty to relate—on that night, while I was here alone and thinking of anything but him, that Chinaman came back for his pigtail.

'He did not get it.'

At this point Mr Beeson relapsed into blank silence. Perhaps he was fatigued by the unwonted exercise of speaking; perhaps he had conjured up a memory that demanded his undivided attention. The wind was now fairly abroad, and the pines along the mountain-side sang with singular distinctness. The narrator continued:

'You say you do not see much in that, and I must confess I do not myself.

'But he keeps coming!'

There was another long silence, during which both stared into the fire without the movement of a limb. Then Mr Beeson broke out, almost fiercely, fixing his eyes on what he could see of the impassive face of his auditor:

'Give it him? Sir, in this matter I have no intention of troubling anyone for advice. You will pardon me, I am sure—' here he became singularly persuasive—'but I have ventured to nail that pigtail fast, and have assumed the somewhat onerous obligation of guarding it. So it is quite impossible to act on your considerate suggestion.

'Do you play me for a Modoc?'

Nothing could exceed the sudden ferocity with which he thrust this indignant remonstrance into the ear of his guest. It was as if he had struck him on the side of the head with a steel gauntlet. It was a protest, but it was a challenge. To be mistaken for a coward—to be played for a Modoc: these two expressions are one. Sometimes it is a Chinaman. Do you play me for a Chinaman? is a question frequently addressed to the ear of the suddenly dead.

Mr Beeson's buffet produced no effect, and after a moment's pause, during which the wind thundered in the chimney like the sound of clods upon a coffin, he resumed:

'But, as you say, it is wearing me out. I feel that the life of the last two years has been a mistake—a mistake that corrects itself; you see how. The grave! No; there is no one to dig it. The ground is frozen, too. But you are very welcome. You may say at Bentley's—but that is not important. It was very tough to cut: they braid silk into their pigtails. Kwaagh.'

Mr Beeson was speaking with his eyes shut, and he wandered. His last word was a snore. A moment later he drew a long breath, opened his eyes with an effort, made a single remark, and fell into a deep sleep. What he said was this:

'They are swiping my dust!'

Then the aged stranger, who had not uttered one word since his arrival, arose from his seat and deliberately laid off his outer clothing, looking as angular in his flannels as the late Signorina Festorazzi, an Irish woman, six feet in height, and weighing fifty-six pounds, who used to exhibit herself in her chemise to the people of San Francisco. He then crept into one of the 'bunks', having first placed a revolver in easy reach, according to the custom of the country. This revolver he took from a shelf, and it was the one which Mr Beeson had mentioned as that for which he had returned to the Gulch two years before.

In a few moments Mr Beeson awoke, and seeing that his guest had retired he did likewise. But before doing so he approached the long, plaited wisp of pagan hair and gave it a powerful tug, to assure himself that it was fast and firm. The two beds—mere shelves covered with blankets not over-clean—faced each other from opposite sides of the room, the little square trap door that had given access to the Chinaman's grave being midway between. This, by the way, was crossed by a double row of spike-heads. In his resistance to the supernatural, Mr Beeson had not disdained the use of material precautions.

The fire was now low, the flames burning bluely and petulantly, with occasional flashes, projecting spectral shadows on the walls—shadows that moved mysteriously about, now dividing, now uniting. The shadow of the pendent queue, however, kept moodily apart, near the roof at the farther end of the room, looking like a note of admiration. The song of the pines outside had now risen to the dignity of a triumphal hymn. In the pauses the silence was dreadful.

It was during one of these intervals that the trap in the floor began to lift. Slowly and steadily it rose, and slowly and steadily rose the swaddled head of the old man in the bunk to observe it. Then, with a clap that shook the house to its foundation, it was thrown clean back, where it lay with its unsightly spikes pointing threateningly upward. Mr Beeson awoke, and without rising, pressed his fingers into his eyes. He shuddered; his teeth chattered. His guest was now reclining on one elbow, watching the proceedings with the goggles that glowed like lamps.

Suddenly a howling gust of wind swooped down the chimney, scattering ashes and smoke in all directions, for a moment obscuring everything. When the firelight again illuminated the room there was seen, sitting gingerly on the edge of a stool by the hearthside, a swarthy little man of prepossessing appearance and dressed with faultless taste, nodding to the old man with a friendly and engaging smile. 'From San Francisco, evidently,' thought Mr Beeson, who having somewhat recovered from his fright was groping his way to a solution of the evening's events.

But now another actor appeared upon the scene. Out of the square black hole in the middle of the floor protruded the head of the departed Chinaman, his glassy eyes turned upward in their angular slits and fastened on the dangling queue above with a look of yearning unspeakable. Mr Beeson groaned, and again spread his hands upon his face. A mild odour of opium pervaded the place. The phantom, clad only in a short blue tunic quilted and silken but covered with grave-mould, rose slowly, as if pushed by a weak spiral spring. Its knees were at the level of the floor, when with a quick upward impulse like the silent leaping of a flame it grasped the queue with both hands, drew up its body and took the tip in its horrible yellow teeth.

To this it clung in a seeming frenzy, grimacing ghastly, surging and plunging from side to side in its efforts to disengage its property from the beam, but uttering no sound. It was like a corpse artificially convulsed by means of a galvanic battery. The contrast between its superhuman activity and its silence was no less than hideous!

Mr Beeson cowered in his bed. The swarthy little gentleman uncrossed his legs, beat an impatient tattoo with the toe of his boot and consulted a heavy gold watch. The old man sat erect and quietly laid hold of the revolver. Bang!

Like a body cut from the gallows the Chinaman plumped into the black hole below, carrying his tail in his teeth. The trap door turned over, shutting down with a snap. The swarthy little gentleman from San Francisco sprang nimbly from his perch, caught something in the air with his hat, as a boy catches a butterfly, and vanished into the chimney as if drawn up by suction.

From away somewhere in the outer darkness floated in through the open door a faint, far cry—a long, sobbing wail, as of a child death-strangled in the desert, or a lost soul borne away by the Adversary. It may have been the coyote.

In the early days of the following spring a party of miners on their way to new diggings passed along the Gulch, and straying through the deserted shanties found in one of them the body of Hiram Beeson, stretched upon a bunk, with a bullet hole through the heart. The ball had evidently been fired from the opposite side of the room, for in one of the oaken beams overhead was a shallow blue dent, where it had struck a knot and been deflected downward to the breast of its victim. Strongly attached to the same beam was what appeared to be an end of a rope of braided horsehair, which had been cut by the bullet in its passage to the knot. Nothing else of interest was noted, excepting a suit of mouldy and incongruous clothing, several articles of which were afterwards identified by respectable witnesses as those in which certain deceased citizens of Deadman's had been buried years before. But it is not easy to understand how that could be, unless, indeed, the garments had been worn as a disguise by Death himself—which is hardly credible.

A LITTLE NIGHT FISHING

SYDNEY J. BOUNDS

'**H**ere is a gale warning. Sea areas Sole and Fastnet. Force eight, imminent.'

Robson switched off the wheelhouse radio and stepped on to the deck. The sky was clear and the sea calm. Well, the weathermen had been known to be wrong before, but there was no harm in checking with the locals. Not that it mattered; he had to go out tonight whatever the weather. Big Todd was not a man to accept excuses.

He studied the appearance of the cruiser before he left: everything looked all right, the fishing tackle was prominently displayed. He crossed the gangplank to the jetty and headed towards the Black Swan.

Robson was a heavy man with a perpetual scowl, dressed in roll-neck sweater, jeans and rope-soled shoes. He didn't like the sea or boats, he didn't like being away from the Smoke—but he liked the money.

Tregorrow, on the Cornish coast, was a scattering of grey stone houses, a small harbour and a pub. He crossed the quay in quick strides and went inside.

Four blue-jerseyed fishermen sat at a table with cards and a crib-board.

A giant of a man stood watching them. Behind the bar, the publican's wife polished glasses.

'Pint of bitter,' Robson called and, as the giant turned to look at him, added: 'Join me?'

'Aye, I can sink a pint. I'm Fletch.'

'Robbie.'

A big hand surrounded one of the two mugs pushed across the counter. 'Nice little boat you've got there, Robbie. Fast, I'd bet. You do a lot of fishing?'

'*Sweet Violet*? She's fast enough for what I want. I get my kicks night fishing—just an amateur, for sport, like.'

'You'll need to watch this coastline,' Fletch said in a warning tone.

'Yeah, more rocks than Hatton Garden. What d'you think to the weather just now?'

'Blowing up a storm I'd reckon.'

'What's a little storm?' Robson said, smiling. 'Adds zest to the job, and *Sweet Violet* can take it.'

Fletch didn't answer, just stared at the visitor, weighing him up.

Robson stared back. Fletch was blond with blue eyes, making him wonder if the Vikings had ever penetrated to this south-west corner of Britain. A big one, but he could take him. Robson was cockney and expert in the ways of back-street fighting.

'We get some bad storms on this coast,' Fletch said. 'In the past, that made a living for the wreckers. They'd use false lights to lure a ship on to the rocks, then plunder it. None o' that now, of course—but we still get the storms.'

He swallowed the rest of his pint and wiped the hairy back of a hand across his mouth. When he spoke again, his voice was soft, gentle almost.

'There's not so many wrecks now, either. Did you know this coast is haunted? 'Tis true as I stand at this bar—' His voice grew insistent. 'Too many have seen the ghost not to believe. Some say 'tis the phantom of some poor sailor murdered by wreckers. Come a storm, and fishermen see the grey wraith waving a lantern and warning them away from the rocks. Reckon it's saved a few lives.'

'Yeah? A real live ghost?'

'No, this un's been dead a hundred years. And if you happen to see it tonight, you'll do well to take notice, Robbie.'

The sea had an oily swell when Robson put out. The sun was a ball of fire sinking below the horizon and gulls wheeled and screamed beneath scudding cloud. On the jetty, Fletch stood beside drying nets, watching. Robson waved casually but the Cornishman ignored him.

The hell with you, friend, Robson thought and gave all his attention to the cruiser. *Sweet Violet* moved along easily, driven by two one-hundred-horse-power diesels, her bow parting the sea like a knife. No sign of ships on the grey water. Good. The last thing he wanted was a customs cutter nosing around. Robson checked his watch and compass, watching the receding cliffs for landmarks. There'd be a moon on his way back and he didn't want any foul-up, not with Todd waiting in a fast car. He had to know exactly where the shoals and reefs lay.

He motored at a steady speed, timing distance on a set course for the rendezvous. A huge tanker passed slowly in the distance. The lights of land faded and he seemed alone on a great grey ocean.

The swell increased and a wind began to keen. The moon went behind storm clouds.

Presently, on time and in the right place, a fishing boat showed. As he closed with it, he read the name on the bow: *Tante Marie*. He cruised parallel to the boat and a man in a beret flashed a torch: two short, pause, one long, repeated. Robson completed his half of the recognition signal and the Frenchman tossed a small package on a line to him. Robson caught it, cut the line and held up the packet to show he'd got it.

The two boats veered apart.

Robson placed the packet in a specially constructed compartment behind the chart locker and turned back for the English coast. That little packet was worth a few thou, but he never considered double-crossing Big Todd. Todd was the connection between a Paris mob specializing in jewel robberies and a fence in Hatton Garden. He also had a fancy way with a razor.

The French boat dropped from view as rain came gusting down. *Sweet Violet* began to rise and fall. At the wheel, Robson smiled. He wouldn't even have to pretend to catch fish now; the rising gale was a perfect excuse to run for harbour.

A dark sea merged with a dark sky and rain slanted down, effectively blocking any view he might have had. Mounting waves tossed the cruiser about like a cork; it was all Robson could do to stay on course. The wind howled and rain drummed on the wheelhouse roof.

He peered into the gloom with aching eyes, listening as waves slammed the hull like the blows of a sledge-hammer. He studied his watch and compass, timing himself. By now he was closing the shore, a shore infested with granite crags and shoal water.

Now he heard it, above the wind and the rain, the noise of surf breaking over rocks. There was not a glimmer of light anywhere and he cursed. The black night was a shroud covering him.

He had difficulty keeping the boat headed where he wanted, staring with suspicion at the compass. He felt uneasy; he wasn't used to relying solely on instruments. If he didn't see the lights of land soon he would be in trouble.

The crash of breakers sounded ominously close and he struggled into a life-jacket. A hell of a time to wish he'd learnt to swim . . .

Water poured across the wheelhouse window, though whether it was rain or sea he couldn't tell. *Sweet Violet* pitched and tossed as wind and waves battered her.

Then, through the darkness, a weak light winked at him. Robson stared in concentration. Had he imagined it? No, there was a light, swinging crazily. It might have been an oil lamp. As he neared the pin-point of yellow light, he saw a faint grey figure holding a lantern in one hand and swinging it to and fro.

The figure appeared to be a sailor in striped jersey, wearing a wool cap and standing atop a rock in the storming sea. It appeared so pale as to be unreal and did not look wet. Robson saw spray break over the figure . . . no, through it.

Paralysis gripped him. Sweat turned to ice. Fletch's ghost! He stared wild-eyed at the apparition with its swinging lantern, and trembled.

A ghostly voice lifted above the wind. 'Rocks . . . rocks ahead!'

Robson broke the grip of fear and wrenched desperately at the wheel, turning the cruiser away from the light. The hull juddered as she struck, throwing him off balance and he hit his head on the wall. He had a brief glimpse of a sharp-edged reef ripping along the hull, then water swirled at his feet.

In a daze, he scrambled through the doorway and clung to the deck-rail. An undertow caught the boat and swept her inshore. Robson clung to the rail, wet and cold, thinking of a fortune in diamonds hidden behind the chart locker. Big Todd would cut his heart out if he lost them—if he survived this.

Sweet Violet crashed against another rock, swung about and struck again. The wind hammered her, turning her over. Robson lost his grip and was washed overboard. He struggled weakly as his mouth filled with salt water. His feet touched bottom and he lurched upright, spluttering and gulping air.

The wind hurled him forward and he fell face-down on wet sand. A wave rolled over him as he lay gasping like a stranded fish. He could make out the dark shape of the cruiser, wedged between jutting crags, some twenty yards away. Get the diamonds, he thought, get out of here—but his legs were lead weights. It was just too much effort to stand against the gale. Rest a moment, then he'd—

Shadowy figures gathered about him. One, closer than the others, stooped over him. He recognized the blond Viking from the pub.

'Fletch! Thank God, help me . . .'

Fletch stared down, unsmiling. 'Still alive then, Robbie?' The giant selected a slab of rock and lifted it. 'See our ghost, did thee? As I said, it's real enough—but I told one lie. 'Tis not the ghost of a drowned sailor, but of a wrecker. One of the Brethren. Aye, and it still lures boats on to the rocks for us!'

He brought down the rock, cracking Robson's skull as neat as slicing an egg.

NOT YET SOLVED

ANONYMOUS

The following is a true ghost story. It is an account of some supernatural incidents which have recently taken place in a clergyman's house situated in a favourite London suburb. They are so strange as to be thought worthy of publication, and are here given by one of the daughters of the house.

What I am about to relate is quite true in all the main facts, and I make the story known as being another of the many instances which prove that links undeniably exist between the spiritual and the material world.

There neither was nor is anything gloomy about the house. It became our home many years ago on account of it being the only available house to suit us near my father's church. When my father took the house it had been built about three years. During that time it was occupied by a Captain somebody (whose name I forget), his wife and little child, a girl. But the child had then died suddenly, it was said under very painful circumstances, and the parents were so distressed that they threw up the lease of the house and went away, and my father took it.

There was nothing gloomy, I have said, about the house. Neither was there any apparent reason why all of us children should shun a particular bedroom in it, which stood on the first landing, immediately over the dining-room, looking out into the street. It was a spacious, airy room, nothing whatever to be seen amiss with it; nevertheless, we little ones, from the eldest to the youngest, felt an unaccountable fear of it. It was in vain that our nurse and Aunt Jane, who, between them, supplied the place of the mother we had lost, strove to reassure us, saying there was nothing to fear. We did fear the room, and could not help it.

This unreasonable fear was, no doubt, augmented by one curious fact, which had been observed from the time we first entered the house. Constantly, and more especially during the spring and autumn time, the stone staircase, of which the first flight was composed, and which led on to the landing of the before-mentioned bedroom, seemed to be perpetually promenaded at night by small, pattering feet, as of a small child ceaselessly toiling up and down. Indeed, on our instalment in the house, Nurse, who had reason to suspect one of my brothers of the bad habit of walking in his sleep, would rise from her bed, and descend, candle in hand, with a warm shawl ready to wrap round the little sleep-walker.

The first time, not finding him, and thinking she had somehow missed him, she talked to him the next day, saying: 'He might catch his death of cold, stepping up and down them bare stone stairs.' The stairs were not carpeted, owing to a whim of my father's.

But soon, to her amazement, Nurse found the sounds were not caused by him; on each occasion she found him asleep in bed. But the pattering footsteps continued to be heard by all of us. After many conjectures as to the cause of the sounds, Aunt Jane and Nurse ceased to talk of them, at least, in our hearing, apparently paying them no attention. Indeed, in time we all grew accustomed to them, and never gave them much thought, except when visitors were staying in the house. The sounds disturbed them, and they would now and then make a remark on the restless nature of the young members of the household, 'who appeared to prefer walking up and down stairs at night to resting in bed'.

But to the bedroom we never did get reconciled. As we grew older, Aunt Jane reasoned with us, saying how very wrong it was to give way to superstition and fears, especially when the fears were groundless. To this day the sensation remains with us.

Thus the years went on.

One afternoon, as we were all gathered together for afternoon tea, a message was brought to Aunt Jane that a workman, then employed on the premises, wished to speak with her. Aunt Jane still stayed with us, notwithstanding my being now old enough to take my mother's place, as far as the housekeeping was concerned. The man was engaged in cleaning out a cistern at the extreme top of the house. 'What does he want with me?' asked Aunt Jane, but the servant did not know.

So Aunt Jane went out to him. On her return, she held a very long, thin, and dirty-looking chain in her hand, which the workman had discovered in the cistern, it having, he said, in some extraordinary way, become wedged into a crack at one side, from which place he had extricated it. Aunt Jane rewarded the man for his honesty in bringing the chain to her; though whose it could possibly be and how it got there was an utter mystery. She thought the chain was gold.

My two brothers, both at the tea-table, pronounced the chain to be brass, and expressed their delight that Aunt Jane had been for once taken in, and had given five shillings for a worthless article. She strove to impress upon them that she had not given the man five shillings for the chain, which was none of his, but for his straightforward honesty.

Upon taking the chain to a jeweller's to be cleaned, we learned that it was a very fine Indian chain of pure gold, and of most delicate handicraft; which only served to increase the mystery of how it got into the place where it was found, and of how long it had lain there, hidden from the light of day.

When, a few days later, it was returned to us from the jeweller, glittering and clean, it was passed from one to another in wondering admiration, and shown to my father, who, until then, had only heard of its discovery, and had greatly pooh-poohed the idea of the chain being of any value.

'Found in the cistern at the top of the house!' he exclaimed, as we turned the beautiful thing about in our hands. 'That is most extraordinary!'

'I always said this was an uncanny house,' cried Ethel, the second of us, speaking upon impulse. 'All those unexplainable sounds of little footsteps for ever pattering up and down that stone staircase, and the curious feeling we have all had since we were little mites of shrinking from that front bedroom! It would not surprise me if a ghost were to turn up next.'

'Don't talk nonsense,' rebuked my father. 'We shall not keep a servant in the place if you begin to talk like that.'

'Well, at any rate,' went on the unabashed Ethel, 'how on earth did a fine long Indian chain, such as this, find its way into the top cistern?'

'That is the strange part of it,' said my brother Jack, who was minutely examining the chain. 'It is of value, this chain. What is to be done with it?'

'I shall wear it,' struck in Lily, the youngest of us, and consequently the most indulged. 'I've just got a watch given to me, you know, and as I want a chain to wear with it, I'll take this one. If any owner claims it later, I can give it up to him.'

'The question is, to whom *does* it belong?' cried Jack. 'The man thought it had been in the crack of that cistern for years.'

Aunt Jane, struck by a thought, laid down her knitting—she was always knitting—and turned to my father, to speak.

'I should think it must have belonged to those people who lived in the house before you took it. The chain is an Indian chain; and they were said, were they not, to have come from India.'

'Yes, I believe so,' he replied, 'if my memory serves me correctly.'

'What did you hear about them?'

'Not much,' he answered. 'They had taken a long lease of the house, and had been in it about three years when their little girl died suddenly. After that, they gave up the lease, and I took it.'

'How did she die? What of?' asked Aunt Jane.

'I do not know. It was said that the circumstances attending the death were painful, and that the parents were so cut up at the loss they could not stay in the place. Their grief would naturally be great, she having been an only child. I think they went abroad,' added he. 'Anyway, that is all I recollect to have heard of them.'

Aunt Jane took up her knitting again. She thought the chain must have belonged to those people: and she wondered what it was that had caused the death of the little girl.

Lily was allowed to take the chain to wear; and our busy conjectures respecting it and its mysterious discovery gradually died away.

Shortly afterwards, a cousin of ours, from the country, took up his abode with us for a time, for the purpose of studying medicine, being intended for the medical profession. He was a jolly young Englishman, not much more than a lad, with an excellent appetite, and no imagination at all. As to any superstitious tale, had he been told one, he would have laughed it to pieces.

When a certain shyness, attendant on his first arrival, had worn off, Charley became a great addition to our circle, and his proverbial good temper soon made him a general favourite.

One bright spring morning, however, he appeared at breakfast in a different mood. After sitting some time in grumpy silence, he, to our amazement, burst out with a vehement attack on practical jokes.

What absurd folly such jokes were, he said, as if *he* could ever be taken in by them! 'So mind, Lena,' he went on, pouncing suddenly round on me, 'don't you try it on again. You know how I hate young kids of children!'

I asked him what he meant. The rest of them, sitting round, gazed at him, wondering what had come to good-humoured Charley.

'Because you may happen to have a child staying in the house, it's no reason why you girls should send it into my room in the night, just to play a trick on me.'

We assured him we had done nothing of the kind.

'You must have done so,' said Charley. 'Dressed it up in white, with its golden hair round its face. Whose child is it? One comfort, it must have caught a jolly cold, standing all that time looking at itself in the glass!'

'My dear Charley!' exclaimed I. 'What on earth are you talking about? There's no child staying here.'

'Oh, isn't there!' grumbled he; 'and you didn't send her into my room, thinking to startle me?'

'A little girl, you say?'—humouring him.

'A little girl about four years old, all in white, with lots of golden hair,' he repeated. 'As if you wanted to be told!'

'Charley, believe me: there's no little girl staying in the house; nor was one sent into your room.'

'I dare say not! Why, Lena, I lay awake full half an hour, watching her. She stood by the dressing-table, looking at something in her hand.'

'Did you see her come in?' I asked. I could not understand this at all. Charley was in desperate earnest.

'No, I didn't,' he answered. 'What roused me suddenly, I don't know; something did, and I sat up to look at my watch. It was just five o'clock; light enough for me to see everything in the room distinctly; and my eyes at once fell upon the child standing at the dressing-table.'

30

'Charley, you must have had a dream—or a nightmare.'

'I wish you'd not talk nonsense,' he angrily returned, 'I was as wide awake as I am now. Didn't I tell you I watched the child for half an hour. When I got tired of sitting up in bed, I lay down, and watched her. She was still there when I fell asleep.'

'Did you speak to her?'

'Not I!' cried Charley. 'I'd not give you girls the satisfaction you were no doubt all listening for, outside. If you weren't there yourselves, you had posted old Nurse there, I know.'

Nothing more was said then, for Charley had to hasten away to his daily work at the hospital. In fact, we got no more out of him on the subject at all. Our suggestion, that it was a dream, he would not listen to; and it took the whole household several days to convince him, or, perhaps, try to, that no child was or had been in the house.

Charley's bedroom was the uncanny room on the first landing, but we had never told him our dread of it. Not only that it would have been wrong to do so, but that we had grown a little ashamed of the feeling which yet we could not conquer.

It was, I think, about a year afterwards—and we had forgotten the occurrence—that the figure was seen again. One evening, when Lily and I, having lingered a little behind the others in saying goodnight, were preparing to mount to our particular nest at the top of the house, Ethel called me into her little room, saying she wanted to speak to me. It was next to the one Charles had slept in, and faced my brother's room at the other end of the long, straight landing. The gas was burning brightly on the staircase. Jack's door stood half-open, showing that his gas was also fully on. I went into Ethel's room, Lily waiting for me outside; but a minute had hardly elapsed ere she called out quickly, in a low, sharp voice: 'Come here, Lena; make haste!'

I was reading a letter Ethel had just put into my hand, so I answered shortly: 'In a minute!'

'Make haste!' she cried again. 'Be quick!'

I ran out, rather impatiently, to find Lily gazing hard at Jack's door, with a strange, fixed look in her eyes.

'I have just seen the little girl Charles saw,' she said, solemnly. 'She was looking straight at me, dressed all in white, and she had such lovely golden hair! When you came, she vanished.'

Nothing was to be seen then. We looked around, no one stirring. Ethel had joined us.

'Lily,' spoke Ethel, presently, 'perhaps she was looking at the gold chain: you have it on.'

The chain was quite conspicuous outside Lily's dress. She repeated again that the little girl had stood gazing at her. Charles, we remembered, had said she did not look at him, but was all the time looking apparently at something in her hand. Lily had not felt any fear. The golden hair, she declared, was perfectly beautiful.

'This is really very strange,' exclaimed Aunt Jane, who, hearing our voices, had appeared on the scene to know what the talking was about. 'Are you quite sure, Lily, of what you say?'

'Of course I am sure,' returned Lily, who never could bear to be doubted, and was very matter-of-fact and truthful. 'The little girl stood there gazing at me, Aunt. She was as plainly to be seen as we are to one another.'

'We were wondering, Aunt, whether she could be looking at the chain which Lily has on,' said Ethel. 'Perhaps she recognized it? You know, when the chain was found, we thought it might possibly have belonged to the people who were in the house before us.' Which, of course, as Aunt Jane observed, was as much as to suggest that this little girl with the mass of golden hair might be the apparition of the child who had died in the house.

We talked of it as the days went on, suggesting all kinds of possibilities and impossibilities. As she had never appeared until after the discovery of the chain, we could but think the chain might in some way or other be connected with her, and that, if the chain had, indeed, belonged to the first occupiers of the house, the little spirit might well be that of the child who had died there. Another question we asked ourselves was: Could the chain, or its loss, have had aught to do with her death?

The story spread, and people came to see the room and passage where the little figure had appeared; but it was some time before it was seen again. Lily was married. She had left home and taken the chain with her.

Ethel was climbing slowly up the stone staircase one Sunday evening between seven and eight o'clock, when she saw the little white figure, crowned with its mass of golden curls, peeping through the banisters on the first landing, within three yards of her. It was a cold winter evening, and the gas was burning as usual on the staircase. The passages were always kept very bright. Ethel paused, and the little figure turned its head towards her, and then vanished. It was almost as though she had been looking out for someone, but not Ethel. Ethel, like Lily, felt no fear or surprise at the time. She noticed particularly the gloriously bright golden hair.

This last appearance was seen but a few months back, and it has revived all our curiosity, wonder and interest. Whether we shall ever learn the truth concerning the little dead maiden, and whether the gold chain is in any way connected with her mysterious visits, must remain for the present a mystery.

THE HOSTELRY

GUY DE MAUPASSANT

At the foot of the glaciers, in those naked and rock-bound *couloirs* which indent the snow-clad ranges of the High Alps, you will find every here and there a guest-house. These little hostelries are constructed of timber and are all built very much to the same pattern. The Schwarenbach Inn was one of them.

The Schwarenbach served as a refuge to travellers attempting the passage of the Gemmi. For the six summer months it remained open, with Jean Hauser's family in residence; but as soon as the early snows began to accumulate, filling the valley and rendering the descent to Loeche impracticable, Jean Hauser with his three sons and his wife and daughter quitted the house, leaving it in charge of the old guide Gaspard Hari and his companion, together with Sam, the big mountain-bred dog. The two men, with the dog, lived in their prison of snow until the spring arrived. They had nothing to look at, except the vast white slopes of the Balmhorn. Pale glistening mountain peaks rose all round them. They were shut in, blockaded, by the snow; it lay on them like a shroud, growing ever deeper and deeper until the little house was enveloped, closed in, obliterated. The snow piled itself upon the roof, blinded the windows and walled up the door.

On the day on which the Hauser family took their departure for Loeche, the winter was close at hand, and the descent was becoming dangerous. The three sons set off on foot leading three mules laden with household belongings. Behind them followed the mother, Jeanne Hauser, and her daughter Louise, both riding the same mule. Next and last came the father and the two caretakers. The latter were to accompany the family as far as the beginning of the track that leads down the mountain-side to Loeche.

The party first skirted the edge of the little lake, already frozen, in its rocky hollow in front of the inn; then they proceeded along the valley, which lay before them, a white sheet of snow, with icy peaks dominating it on every side. A flood of sunshine fell across the whiteness of this frozen wilderness, lighting it up with a cold, blinding brilliance. There was no sign of life in this sea of mountains; not a movement could be seen in the limitless solitude; not a sound disturbed the profound silence.

Gradually the younger of the guides, Ulrich Kunsi, a tall long-limbed Swiss, forged ahead of the two older men and overtook the mule on which the two women were riding. The daughter saw him as he approached and there was sadness in the glance with which she summoned him to her side.

She was a little peasant girl with a complexion like milk. Her flaxen hair was so pale that one would fancy it had been bleached by prolonged residence amongst the snows and glaciers.

On overtaking the mule on which Louise and her mother were riding, Ulrich Kunsi placed his hand on the crupper and slackened his pace. The mother began talking; she expounded in infinite detail her instructions for wintering. It was the first time that Ulrich had stayed behind. Old Hari, on the other hand, had already accomplished his fourteenth hibernation, under the snow that covered the Schwarenbach Inn.

Ulrich listened, but without any appearance of grasping what was said.

He never took his eyes off the daughter. Every now and then he would reply: 'Yes, Madame Hauser.' But his thoughts seemed far away, and his face remained calm and impassive.

They reached the Daubensee, which lies at the foot of the valley. Its surface was now a vast level sheet of ice. On the right, the rocks of the Daubenhorn, dark and precipitous, rose above the vast moraines of the Lemmern Glacier, and the Wildstrubel towered over all.

As they approached the Gemmi saddle, from which begins the descent to Loeche, they suddenly beheld, across the deep wide valley of the Rhone, the prodigious sky-line of the Valais Alps, a distant multitude of white peaks of unequal size, some pointed, some flattened, but all glistening in the rays of the sun.

There was the two-horned Mischabel, the majestic mass of the Weisshorn, the lumbering Brunegghorn, the lofty and fear-inspiring Cervin, which has killed so many men, and the Dent-Blanche, monstrous yet alluring. Below them, in an enormous hollow at the foot of terrifying precipices, they caught sight of Loeche, so far away from them that the houses seemed like a handful of sand, thrown down into the vast crevasse which has at one end the barrier of the Gemini, and at the other a wide exit to the Rhone valley.

They had reached the head of a path, which winds downwards in serpentine coils, fantastic and extraordinary, along the mountain-side, until it reaches the almost invisible village at the foot. The mule stopped and the two women jumped down into the snow. By this time the two older men had overtaken the rest of the party.

'Now, friends,' said old Hauser, 'we must say goodbye till next year. And keep your hearts up.'

'Till next year,' replied Hari.

The men embraced. Madame Hauser gave her cheek to be kissed and her daughter followed her example. When it was Ulrich Kunsi's turn to kiss Louise, he whispered in her ear:

'Don't forget us up on our heights.'

'No,' she replied in tones so low that he guessed, rather than heard, the word.

'Well, well, goodbye,' said old Hauser again. 'Take care of yourselves.'

He strode on past the women and led the way downwards. All three were lost to view at the first bend in the track. Gaspard and Ulrich turned back towards the Schwarenbach Inn. They walked slowly and in silence, side by side. They had seen the last of their friends. They were to be alone, with no other companionship, for four or five months.

Gaspard Hari began to tell Ulrich about the previous winter. His companion then had been Michael Carol; but accidents were likely to happen during the long solitude, and Michael had grown too old for the job. Still, they had had a pretty good time together. The secret of the whole thing was to make up your mind to it from the beginning. Sooner or later one invented distractions and games and things to while away the time.

With downcast eyes Ulrich Kunsi listened to his companion, but his thoughts were following the women, who were making their way to the village, down the zigzag path on the Gemmi mountain-side.

They soon caught sight of the distant inn. It looked very tiny, like a black dot at the base of the stupendous mountain of snow. When they opened the door of the house, Sam, the great curly-haired dog, gambolled round them joyfully.

'Well, Ulrich, my boy,' said old Gaspard, 'we have no women here now. We must get dinner ready ourselves. You can set to and peel the potatoes.'

They sat down on wooden stools and began to prepare the soup. The forenoon of the following day seemed long to Ulrich Kunsi. Old Hari smoked his pipe and spat into the fireplace. The younger man looked through the window at the superb mountain, which rose in front of the house. In the afternoon he went out, and pursuing the road he had taken the previous day, he followed the tracks of the mule on which the two women had ridden. He arrived at last at the saddle of the Gemmi, and lying prone on the edge of the precipice, gazed down on Loeche. The village, nestling in its rocky hollow, had not yet been obliterated by the snow. But there was snow very near it. Its advance had been arrested by the pine forests which guarded the environs of the hamlet. Seen from a height, the low houses of the village looked like paving-stones set in a field.

Ulrich reflected that Louise Hauser was now in one of those grey cottages. Which one was it, he wondered. They were too remote to be separately distinguished. He had a yearning to go down there while it was still possible. But the sun had disappeared behind the great peak of Wildstrubel, and Ulrich turned homewards. He found Hari smoking. On Ulrich's return Hari proposed a game of cards and the two men sat down on opposite sides of the table. They played for a long time at a simple game called brisque. Then they had supper and went to bed.

Subsequent days were like the first, clear and cold, without any fresh fall of snow. Gaspard passed his days watching the eagles and other rare birds, which adventure themselves in these frozen altitudes. For his part, Ulrich went regularly to the *col* to look down at the distant village. In the evening they played cards, dice and dominoes, staking small objects to lend an interest to the game.

One morning, Hari, who had been the first to rise, called out to Ulrich. A drifting cloud of white foam, deep yet ethereal, was sinking down on them and on all around them, spreading over them slowly, silently, a cover which grew ever thicker and heavier. The snowfall lasted four days and four nights. The door and windows had to be cleared, a passage dug, and steps cut, to enable them to climb out on to the surface of powdery snow, which twelve hours of frost had made harder than the granite of the moraines.

After that, they lived as in a prison, hardly ever venturing outside their dwelling. The household tasks were divided between them and were punctually performed. Ulrich Kunsi undertook the cleaning and washing up and keeping the house neat. He also split the firewood. Hari kept the fire going and did the cooking. These necessary and monotonous tasks were relieved by long contests at dice or cards. Being both of them of calm and placid temperament, they never quarrelled. They never went even as far as to display impatience or peevishness, or to speak sharply to each other, both having determined beforehand to make the best of their wintry sojourn on the heights. Occasionally Gaspard took his gun and went out hunting chamois, and when he had the good luck to kill one, it was high day and holiday in the Schwarenbach Inn and there was great feasting on fresh meat.

One morning Hari set forth on one of these expeditions. The thermometer outside the inn showed thirty degrees of frost. Hari started before sunrise, hoping to take the chamois by surprise on the lower slopes of the Wildstrubel.

Left to himself, Ulrich remained in bed until ten o'clock. He was by nature a good sleeper, but he would not have dared to give way to this proclivity in the presence of the old guide, who was an early riser and always full of energy. He lingered over his breakfast, which he shared with Sam, who passed his days and nights sleeping in front of the fire. After breakfast he felt his spirits oppressed, and almost daunted, by the solitude, and he longed for his daily game of cards with the unconquerable craving that comes of ingrained habit. Later, he went out to meet his comrade, who was due to return at four o'clock.

The whole valley was now of a uniform level under its thick covering of snow. The crevasses were full to the top; the two lakes could no longer be distinguished; the rocks lay hid under a snowy quilt. Lying at the foot of the immense peaks, the valley was now one immense basin, symmetrical, frozen, and of a blinding whiteness.

It was three weeks since Ulrich had been to the edge of the precipice from which he looked down at the village. He thought he would go there again, before climbing the slopes that led to the Wildstrubel. The snow had now reached Loeche, and the houses were lost under their white mantle.

Turning to the right, he reached the Lemmern glacier. He walked with the mountaineer's long stride, driving his iron-pointed stick down on to the snow, which was as hard as stone. With his far-sighted eyes he sought the small black dot which he expected to see moving, in the far distance, over this vast sheet of snow. On reaching the edge of the glacier he stopped, wondering whether old Hari had really come that way. Then, with increasing anxiety and quicker steps, he began to skirt the moraines.

The sun was sinking. The snow was suffused with a tinge of pink, and over its crystalline surface swept sharp gusts of a dry and icy breeze. Ulrich tried to reach his friend with a call, shrill, vibrant, prolonged. His voice took its flight into the deathless silence, in which the mountains slept. It rang far out over the deep motionless undulations of frozen foam, like the cry of a bird over the waves of the sea. Then it died away. And there was no reply.

He walked on and on. The sun had sunk behind the peaks, and the purple glow of sunset still lingered about them, but the depths of the valley were grey and shadowy, and Ulrich was suddenly afraid. He had an idea that the silence, the cold, the solitude were taking possession of him, were about to arrest his circulation and freeze his blood, stiffen his limbs and convert him into a motionless, frozen image. With all speed he could, he ran back towards the Inn. Hari, he thought, must have taken another way and reached home already. He would find him seated by the fire, with a dead chamois at his feet. He soon came in sight of the hostelry. There was no smoke issuing from the chimney. Ulrich ran yet faster, and when he opened the door of the house, Sam leaped up to greet him. But there was no Gaspard Hari.

In consternation Kunsi turned hither and thither, as though expecting to find his comrade hiding in a corner. Then he relighted the fire and made the soup, still hoping that he would look up and see the old man coming in. From time to time he went outside, in case there should be some sign of him. Night had fallen, that wan, livid night of the mountains, illumined only by the slender, yellow crescent of a new moon, which was sinking towards the skyline and would soon disappear behind the ridge.

Returning to the house, Ulrich sat down by the fire and while he was warming his hands and feet, his thoughts ran on possible accidents. Gaspard might have broken a leg, or fallen into a hollow, or made a false step, which had cost him a sprained ankle. He would be lying in the snow, helpless against the benumbing cold, in agony of mind, far from any other human soul, calling out for help, shouting with all the strength of his voice in the silence of the night.

How to discover where he was? So vast and craggy was the mountain, so dangerous the approaches to it, especially in the winter, that it would take ten or twenty guides searching for a week in all directions to find a man in that immensity. None the less Ulrich made up his mind to take Sam and set forth to look for Gaspard, if he had not come back by one in the morning.

He made his preparations. He put two days' provisions into a bag, took his cramp-irons, wound round his waist a long, strong, slender rope, and inspected thoroughly his spiked stick and his ice-axes. Then he waited. The fire was burning with a clear flame; the great dog lay snoring in its warmth; the steady ticking of the clock, in its resonant wooden case, sounded like the beating of a heart. Still he waited, his ears straining to catch any distant noise. When the light breeze whispered round roof and walls, he shivered.

The clock struck the hour of midnight. Feeling chilled and nervous, he put some water on the fire to boil, so that he might have some steaming coffee before setting out. When the clock struck one, he rose, called Sam, opened the door and struck out in the direction of the Wildstrubel. He climbed for five hours continuously. He scaled the rocks with the help of his irons, and cut steps in the ice with his axe, always advancing steadily and sometimes hauling the dog after him up some steep escarpment. It was about six o'clock when he reached one of the peaks to which Gaspard often came in search of chamois. There he waited for the day to break.

The sky above became gradually paler. Then suddenly that strange radiance, which springs no one knows whence, gleamed over the great ocean of snow-clad peaks, stretching for a hundred leagues around him. The vague light seemed to arise out of the snow itself and to diffuse itself in space. One by one, the highest and farthest pinnacles were suffused by a tender rosy hue and the red sun rose from behind the great masses of the Bernese Alps. Ulrich Kunsi set forth again. Like a hunter, he went down, searching for tracks and saying to his dog:

'Seek, old man, seek.'

He was now on his way down the mountain, investigating every chasm, and sometimes sending forth a prolonged call, which quickly died away in the dumb immensity. At times he put his ear close to the ground to listen. Once he thought he heard a voice and he ran in the direction of it, shouting as he ran, but he heard nothing more, and sat down, exhausted and despairing. About mid-day he shared some food with Sam, who was as weary as himself. And again he set out on his search. When evening came, he was still walking, having accomplished fifty kilometres among the mountains. He was too far from his house to think of returning there, and too tired to drag himself along any farther. Digging a hole in the snow, he curled up in it with his dog, under cover of a blanket which he had brought with him. Man and beast lay together, each body sharing the warmth of the other, but frozen to the marrow none the less. Ulrich's mind was haunted by visions, and his limbs were shaking with cold. He could not sleep at all. When he rose, day was on the point of breaking. His legs felt as rigid as bars of iron; his resolution was so enfeebled that he almost sobbed aloud in his distress, and his heart beat so violently that he nearly collapsed with emotion whenever he fancied that he heard a sound.

The thought suddenly came to him that he too might perish of cold amidst these solitudes, and the fear of such a death whipped up his energy and roused him to fresh vigour. He was now making the descent towards the Inn, and kept falling down from weariness and picking himself up again. His dog Sam, with one paw disabled, followed far behind, limping. It was four o'clock in the afternoon before they reached the Schwarenbach. Hari was not there. Ulrich lighted a fire, had something to eat, and then fell asleep, so utterly stupefied with fatigue that he could think of nothing. He slept for a long, a very long time. It seemed as if nothing could break his repose, when suddenly he heard a voice cry 'Ulrich.' He was shaken out of his profound torpor, and started up. Was it a dream? Was it one of those strange summonses that disturb the slumber of uneasy souls? No. He could hear it still. That quivering hail had pierced his ear, had taken possession of his body, right to the tips of his nervous fingers. Beyond all doubt, there had been a cry for help, an appeal for succour. Someone had called out 'Ulrich!' Then someone must be in the vicinity of the house. There could be no question about it. He opened the door and shouted with all his strength, 'Gaspard, is that you?'

There was no reply. The silence was not broken by sound, or whisper, or groan. It was night, and the snow lay all around, ghastly in its whiteness.

The wind had risen. It was that icy wind which splits the rocks and leaves nothing alive on these forsaken altitudes. It blew in sharp, withering gusts, dealing death more surely than even the fiery blasts of the desert. Again Ulrich called out:

'Gaspard, Gaspard, Gaspard!'

He waited a little, but silence still reigned on the mountainside, and he was forthwith stricken by a terror which shook him to the very bones. He leaped back into the inn, closed and bolted the door, and with chattering teeth collapsed into a chair. He was now sure that the appeal for help had come from his comrade, at the moment at which he was yielding up the ghost. He was as certain of that as one is of being alive or eating bread. For two days and three nights old Gaspard Hari had been wrestling with death in some hollow in one of those deep unsullied ravines, whose whiteness is more sinister than the darkness of underground caverns. For two days and three nights he had been dying, and at this very moment, while he lay in the article of death, his thoughts had turned to his comrade, and his soul, in the instant of gaining its freedom, had flown to the inn where Ulrich lay sleeping. It had exercised that mysterious and terrible power, possessed by the souls of the dead, to haunt the living. The voiceless spirit had called aloud in the overwrought soul of the sleeper, had uttered its last farewell, or, perhaps, its reproach, its curse on the man who had not searched diligently enough.

Ulrich felt its presence there, behind the walls of the house, behind the door, which he had just closed. The soul was prowling around. It was like a bird of night fluttering against a lighted window. Ulrich, distraught with terror, was ready to scream. He would have taken to flight, but dared not open the door. And never again, he felt, would he dare to open that door, for the spectre would be hovering, day and night, round the inn, until the corpse of the old guide had been recovered and laid in the consecrated earth of a cemetery.

When day broke, Ulrich regained a little confidence from the brilliance of the returning sun. He prepared his breakfast and made some soup for the dog, but after that he remained seated motionless in a chair. His heart was in agony; his thoughts turned ever to the old man, who was lying out there in the snow. When night again descended upon the mountains, new terrors assailed him. He paced to and fro in the smoke-blackened kitchen, by the dim light of a solitary candle. Up and down he strode, and always he was listening, listening, for that cry which had terrified him the night before. Might it not ring out again through the mournful silence of the outer world? He felt forlorn, poor wretch; forlorn, as never a man had been, here in this vast whiteness of snow, all alone, seven thousand feet above the inhabited world, above the dwellings of men, above the excitements, the hubbub, the noise, the thrills of life; alone in the frozen sky. He was torn by a mad desire to make his escape in whatsoever direction, by whatsoever means; to descend to Loeche, even if he had to hurl himself over the precipice. But he did not dare so much as to open the door; he felt sure that that thing outside, the dead man, would bar his passage and prevent him from leaving his comrade alone upon those heights.

As midnight approached his limbs grew weary, and fear and distress overcame him. He dreaded his bed, as one dreads a haunted spot, but yielding at last to drowsiness he sank into a chair.

Suddenly his ears were pierced by the same strident cry that he had heard the previous night. It was so shrill that Ulrich stretched out his hands to ward off the ghost, and losing his balance fell backwards on to the floor. Aroused by the noise, the dog began to howl in terror, and ran hither and thither in the room, trying to find out whence the danger threatened. When he came to the door, he sniffed at the edge of it, and began howling, snorting, and snarling, his hair bristling, his tail erect. Beside himself with terror, Kunsi rose and, grasping a stool by one leg, shouted:

'Don't come in. Don't come in. Don't come in or I'll kill you.'

Excited by his menacing tones, the dog barked furiously at the invisible enemy whom his master was challenging. Gradually Sam calmed down, and went back to lie on the hearth, but he was still uneasy; his eyes were gleaming and he was baring his fangs and growling. Ulrich, too, regained his wits; but, feeling faint with terror, he took a bottle of brandy from the sideboard and drank several glasses of it in quick succession. As his mind became duller his courage rose, and a feverish heat coursed along his veins. On the following day he ate hardly anything, confining himself to the brandy, and for some days after he lived in a state of brutish intoxication. The moment the thought of Gaspard Hari crossed his mind, he began drinking and he did not leave off until he collapsed to the ground in a drunken torpor, and lay there face downwards, snoring and helpless. Hardly had he recovered from the effects of the burning and maddening liquor, when the cry 'Ulrich!' roused him, as though a bullet had penetrated his skull. He started to his feet staggering to and fro, stretching out his hands to keep himself from falling, and calling to his dog to help him. Sam, too, appeared to be seized with his master's madness. He hurled himself against the door, scratching at it with his claws, gnawing it with his long white teeth, while Ulrich, with his head thrown back, his face turned upwards, swallowed brandy in great gulps, as though he were drinking cool water after a climb. Presently his thoughts, his memory, his terror, would be drowned in drunken oblivion.

In three weeks he had finished his entire stock of spirits. But the only effect of his inebriation was to lull his terror to sleep. When the means for this were no longer available, his fears returned with fresh ferocity. His fixed idea, aggravated by prolonged intoxication, gained force continually in that absolute solitude, and worked its way, like a gimlet, ever deeper into his spirit. Like a wild beast in a cage, he paced his room, every now and then putting his ear to the door to listen for the voice of Gaspard's ghost, and hurling defiance at it through the wall. And when, in utter weariness, he lay down, he would again hear the voice and leap once more to his feet. At last, one night, with the courage of a coward driven to bay, he flung himself at the door and opened it, to see who it was who was calling him, and to compel him to silence. But the cold air struck him full in the face, and froze him to the marrow. He slammed the door to again, and shot the bolts, never noticing that his dog had dashed out into the open. Shivering, he threw some more wood on to the fire and sat down to warm himself. Suddenly he started. There was someone scratching at the wall and moaning.

'Go away,' he said, terror-stricken.

The answer was a melancholy wail.

His last remaining vestiges of reason were swept away by fear.

'Go away,' he cried again, and he turned hither and thither in an effort to find some corner in which he could hide himself. But the creature outside continued to wail, and passed along the front of the house, rubbing itself against the wall. Ulrich dashed to the oaken sideboard, which was full of provisions and crockery, and with superhuman strength dragged it across the room and set it against the door to act as a barricade. Then he took all the remaining furniture, mattresses, palliasses, chairs, and blockaded the window, as if in a state of siege. But the thing outside went on groaning dismally, and Ulrich himself was soon replying with groans not less lugubrious. Days and nights passed, and still these two continued to answer each other's howls.

The ghost, as it seemed to Ulrich, moved unceasingly round the house, scratching at the walls with its nails in a fierce determination to break a way through. Within the house, Ulrich crouched with his ear close to the masonry, following every movement of the thing outside, and answering all its appeals with horrifying shrieks. Then came a night when Ulrich heard no more sounds from without. Overcome with fatigue, he dropped into a chair and fell asleep immediately. When he awoke, his mind and memory were a blank. It was as if that sleep of prostration had swept his brain clean of everything. He felt hungry and took some food . . .

The winter was over. The passage of the Gemmi became practicable; and the Hauser family set forth on its journey to the inn. At the top of the first long acclivity, the two women clambered up on to their mule. They spoke about the two men, whom they expected presently to meet again. They were surprised that neither of them had descended a few days earlier, as soon as the Loeche road was practicable, to give them the news of their long winter sojourn. When they came in sight of the inn, which was still covered with a thick mantle of snow, they saw that the door and window were closed, but old Hauser was reassured by a thin column of smoke which was rising from the chimney. As he drew nearer, however, he saw on the outer threshold the skeleton of an animal. It was a large skeleton, lying on its side, and the flesh had been torn off the bones by eagles.

All three examined it.

'That must be Sam,' Madame Hauser said.

Then she called out for Gaspard, and from the inside of the house came a shrill cry like that of an animal. Old Hauser, too, shouted Gaspard's name. A second cry came from within. The father and his two sons thereupon endeavoured to open the door, but it resisted their efforts. They took a long beam out of an empty stable and used it as a battering-ram. They dashed it with all their strength against the door, which gave way with the shriek of splintering planks. The sideboard fell over on the floor with a great crash which shook the house, and revealed, standing behind it, a man whose hair came down to his shoulders, and whose beard touched his chest. His eyes were bright; his clothing was in rags.

Louise alone recognized him.

'Mamma!' she gasped, 'it is Ulrich.'

And the mother saw that it was indeed Ulrich, although his hair had turned white.

He suffered them to come near him and touch him, but when they asked him questions he made no reply. He had to be taken down to Loeche, where the doctors certified that he was insane.

The fate of old Gaspard was never known.

During the following summer Louise Hauser came near to dying of a decline, which was attributed to the rigours of the mountain climate.

THE GREY COTTAGE

Mrs Claxton

The cottage was old and grey. A pear tree ran over the front of it; there was a wooden porch covered with jessamine and honeysuckle, which promised to be very sweet and delightful in the spring. It stood in a pretty garden, sloping down to a thick hedge; beyond this, and much below it, ran the lane leading up into the village. A large walnut tree and some tall fir trees shaded the cottage to the south; while the hill, on the side of which it was built, protected it from the north winds: they blew keenly enough at times. An orchard divided us from our neighbours at the back; from the front we looked over the thatched roofs of a few low dwellings to the wide valley beyond, where a lazy river wound in and out through clumps of pollards. A picturesque mill and loch lay to the left; to the right a graceful spire rose in the distance.

Such was my new home. It was chosen partly for its retirement and its pretty garden, chiefly on account of its low rental and the inexpensive neighbourhood. The nearest town was three miles off; more than that when the floods were out, as was often the case, for then the short cut across the fields was impassable.

This Grey Cottage—called so, possibly, from the old grey-stone of which it was built—had belonged to an aged man of the name of Vallyer. He had purchased it some fifty years before. By nature, as we heard, he had been close and miserly, saving up by little and little until he was reputed to be very rich. His wife he lost shortly after their marriage; and since that time he had led a most solitary life, the only other inmate of the cottage being an aged housekeeper, very deaf, and as eccentric as himself. Occasionally a married sister would come over to spend a few hours with him, but never stayed over the night. These visits were like angels' in being few and far between; but in another respect very unlike angels', for they never took place without a quarrel, and a declaration on the part of the sister, Mrs Bittern, that she would never enter the house again. People said her only reason for making these quarrels up, was the old man's money. Be that as it might, virtue proved to be its own reward, for when he died it was found he had left her nothing.

The old gentleman was wonderfully fond of his garden, working in it the greater part of the day, and seldom going beyond it. It was strange that with all his love for his flowers, he should never have cared to show them to his neighbours. On the contrary, he did what he could to keep them from their sight. During his life the place was unknown land; and, consequently, the subject of much curiosity, especially to the village children. Mr Vallyer always seemed to be on the lookout if they attempted to peer and pry through the hedge or over the gate, and he carried a thick stick, with which he would make sudden lunges and thrusts, scattering the young visitors ignominiously. It was not safe for juvenile eyes to gaze into Mr Vallyer's property. Another peculiarity he had. It was to stand by the garden gate in the gloaming leaning on his stick, and watching the few people who went up and down the lonely lane. No matter what the night was, under the bright frosty stars of winter, or in the mist following a heated day of summer, there would stand old Michael Vallyer.

It has been said that he was supposed to have saved money. None—save a few pounds—could be found after his death. It then became known that he had purchased a life annuity, which had died with him. The cottage and furniture were left to a nephew, a chemist in London. Not requiring to live in it himself, he advertised it to be let furnished. Two maiden ladies had taken it first by the month; but they had quickly given notice to leave, complaining of damp and other disagreeables. They had, however, always been considered rather crotchety people. I, with my two pretty nieces, Hilda and Cecily, took possession at Michaelmas, a few weeks after they left. We were pleased with our country home. The few neighbours were friendly and sociable. I began to look upon the little Grey Cottage as a haven of rest after a changeful and troubled life.

As our old servant, Martha, was not quite as active as she used to be, I enquired for a charwoman, to come in twice a week to assist her, and was recommended to a Mrs Briggs. She did not do her work amiss, but her propensity to gossip was irrepressible.

'You should see the place in the spring, ma'am, when the gillyflowers and stocks is out,' she said to me one day, when I was in the kitchen making a tart, and she stood at the other end of it cleaning brasses and tins. 'It looked beautiful when the Miss Jessops first came here.'

'I wonder what made them leave so soon?' I remarked. 'Damp, the agent told me: but I have discovered no damp about the cottage.'

'It weren't the damp, ma'am,' was Mrs Briggs's answer, and I thought her tone significant. 'At first they liked it—oh, so much: but in a little time they said they must leave. Doubtless,' lowering her voice, 'the ladies had their reasons.'

'Perhaps they found it too lonely?'

'No, and it weren't exactly the loneliness,' returned Mrs Briggs. 'Not that altogether, ma'am.'

I asked no more; for gossip, though Mrs Briggs's chief failing, is not one of mine; but went on with my pastry-making. She, rubbing fiercely at the copper tea-kettle, began again after an interlude.

'Did you chance to hear nothing about this cottage, ma'am?'

'Nothing particular. Why? What is there to hear?'

'Perhaps I ought not to tell it you, ma'am; you might be scared,' returned she, as she looked at me over the kettle.

'Scared! Not I. Pray tell what you have to tell—if it concerns the cottage.'

'Well, ma'am, it's a healthy place and a pretty place; that's for sure. But—it's about the old gentleman.'

'The old gentleman!'

'Old Mr Vallyer. They say he is in the house.'

'Why, what do you mean?' I asked, feeling somewhat as the woman had said—scared.

'It's said, ma'am, that he never went out of it, though his funeral did; that he stopped in to haunt it. Folks talk of something that happened here years and years ago; some friend of Mr Vallyer's came from over the seas to visit him. They used to quarrel, and one night the stranger was found dead in the garden. Some thought the death didn't come about by accident; that Vallyer knew more than he said. Anyway, it's pretty sure he can't rest now, but is about the place troubling it.'

I am not especially superstitious, but I confess I did not like the tale. Mrs Briggs continued. Her tongue, once oiled, would have gone on for ever.

'The first to see him was the Widow Munn's children; he had been dead about a month. I was at her place, helping her with a day's washing. "Mother," said they, running in at dusk, "we have seen the old gentleman at the Grey Cottage; he's leaning over the gate with his stick just as he used to be." They weren't frightened, those young children; they told it as a bit of news. The Widow Munn looked at me, and I at her, and then she whipped 'em all round, thinking it might be the best way to put it out of their heads.'

I laughed; and said the children might have been mistaken.

'So they might, ma'am,' assented Mrs Briggs. 'The next to see it was a stranger: a young man coming through the village one moonlight night on his way to London; he was walking it. He went into the public-house, down there in Greenford, and called for a glass of ale. While he was sitting by the fire drinking it, he began to talk. "What uncivil people you seem to have in these parts," says he. "I asked an old gentleman, standing at his garden gate half-way up the hill, whether there was a public-house near, and he would not answer me; he just stared straight in my face with his glassy-looking eyes, and never spoke." The company in the tap-room stopped talking at this, and looked at one another. "What sort of an old gentleman was it?" they asked; "how was he dressed?"

' "He wore a long grey coat, with a curious little cape to it," says the traveller, "and a spotted white kerchief, tied loose round his neck, with the ends hanging, and he had a stick in his hand. *Very* civil, I must say he was! I asked him the question again in a louder tone, thinking he might be deaf; but he never answered, only continued to stare at me." It was the dress of old Vallyer, ma'am; he never wore any other, and I'll leave you to judge what the company at the White Hart thought of it. A deal of talk went about Greenford next day.'

'Where is the old maid-servant?'

'She went away. They left her in the house to show it, but after a week or two she took the key to the agent, saying there was something she did not like about the place, and she shouldn't stop in it. Just before the Miss Jessops took it, that was.'

'No wonder the Miss Jessops were frightened away from the cottage if such tales were told to them,' I remarked. 'Why, you Greenford people must have driven them away!'

'Ah, well, I see, ma'am, you don't believe in it. It was said the ladies saw him in the house as well as out of it, though I can't speak for certain as to what happened. They went away all quiet and composed like; they didn't want to be laughed at.'

We found that Mr Vallyer's ghost was firmly believed in by the neighbourhood. Fortunately my nieces were sensible girls, and only laughed. The stories told were made a source of amusement to them, and their young friends. They treated the subject as a good joke; sometimes intruding irreverently near the confines of that strange and mysterious world beyond whose veil we know so little, and which, it has always seemed to me, should be treated with respect, if not with awe. On one occasion I felt obliged to expostulate.

'Why, Aunt Cameron,' exclaimed Hilda, laughing, 'I am almost sure you believe in the ghost!'

Cecily took the matter more seriously, and agreed with me that too much fun had been made. After that, it was a favourite joke of Hilda's to tell her friends confidentially that her aunt and Cecily believed in old Vallyer's reappearance.

Weeks passed away, during which we saw nothing, and the winter set in. A young nephew of mine, and cousin to my nieces, came to spend some days with us; chiefly, I believe, on account of the skating. His arrival made Hilda and Cecily think it high time to make a little return for the kindness and hospitality which had been shown to us; or, rather, to induce me to think it. I let myself be persuaded, and cards went out for a small evening party.

The weather was now intensely cold. The river had been flooded before the frost set in; not only that, but also the meadows were frozen over. We might almost have been at the North Pole, such an expanse of snow and ice did we overlook. The village seemed skating mad; and, not content with the day's amusement, our young people would remain on the ice until late at night, for the moon, nearing the full, shone brilliantly in a cloudless sky.

Leonard, my nephew, was a clever and amusing young fellow, holding strong views on many subjects, and propounding them with all the energy and decision of youth and inexperience. Old customs and old beliefs were not good enough for him—'*nous avons changé tout cela*' was his motto. I do not think he really believed, or rather disbelieved, all he pretended to do. He liked to startle us, and delighted in shocking the prejudices of his cousins, especially of Hilda, who was a warm partisan of that very ultra school of theology which is now so prevalent amongst the young and imaginative. On one point, however, they both agreed—a strong disbelief in the supernatural.

The evening of the party arrived, and brought our guests. Sixteen in all, including our own young people; I made the seventeenth. The time passed pleasantly, and lastly dancing was introduced. They had had a few quadrilles, when one gentleman had to leave, to catch a midnight train: and when a double set of Lancers was formed after his departure, one was lacking to make it up. There were only fifteen. You may think it strange I should enter into such particulars, but you will see.

'You must do double duty, Leonard,' I said.

'No, Aunt,' exclaimed Hilda, with a saucy smile. 'You shall invite old Mr Vallyer to join us. I wish he would!'

All laughed; and then our neighbour, Mrs Goldsmith, a tall, handsome woman, called out that she had no objection to dance with the old gentleman —should like to. 'See, here he is!' she went on, making a bow to the sofa cushion in her careless merriment, and taking it up in her arms. 'You are not accustomed to dancing, sir, so we will go to the side. Now let us begin.'

I had been so used to playing dance music, that I did it quite mechanically, often turning half round on the music stool to watch the dancers while my fingers were busy. My nieces were fine-looking girls, and I liked to follow Hilda's striking figure and Cecily's quiet grace as they moved through the mazes of the dance. After striking up the first inspiriting chords of the Lancers, I turned to see how Mrs Goldsmith was getting on with her 'partner'. She stood opposite to Cecily and young Kirby, a rising engineer, with whom she was dancing. Hilda and Leonard were at the bottom of the set.

There was a good deal of laughing at the cushion at first, but it soon subsided, and I was glad of it, for I had fatigued myself much in preparing for our little entertainment; my head ached now, and the mirth jarred upon my nerves. I began to feel in that stage of weariness when voices sound far off; when the hands work on at whatever occupies them, without help from the brain; when the thoughts roam away and the eye sees things mistily. It suddenly struck me that the room was growing very cold. Just as Mrs Goldsmith was passing me, cushion in arm, I felt a shiver.

'Ten degrees below freezing point last night, and colder tonight,' I thought to myself. 'What shall we come to?'

Turning round again to look at the dancing, I noticed how very pale they appeared, and how singularly quiet. Why had they ceased talking? As Cecily glided past me, I was struck by her face. It was white as marble, and her blue eyes were strangely distended and fixed with a puzzled kind of fascination on Mrs Goldsmith. Mine followed them. That lady was moving through the figure in her stately manner, the cushion still in her arms, and a fixed smile on her lips; and by her side—now, was it an overwrought brain or was I dreaming? Surely the latter, for I felt no surprise, no alarm—*there danced by her side a little old man!*

Everything seemed in a mist now, as though the night were foggy, and the fog had got into the room, so I could not see the stranger clearly. The music sounded muffled, and my thoughts went back to former nights in London, when the thick yellow vapour enveloped the streets, and link boys were out, and conductors led omnibuses, and people shouted with hollow voices. It seemed hours since I began to play that set of Lancers.

This old man was dressed in a long grey coat, with a little cape, and a white spotted neckerchief loosely tied, and he carried a thick stick in his hand. He danced in an old-world fashion, executing his steps with great precision, and making formal bows to his partner and the rest of the company. Just then Mrs Goldsmith laid the cushion back on the sofa; shivering apparently with cold, she took up a scarf and wrapped it closely round her, dancing all the time. It was now the grand chain in the last figure, and for a moment or two I lost sight of the old man. Suddenly there was a wild scream—the dance stopped—Cecily had fainted!

A medical man, Mr Brook, was of the party. He attributed Cecily's attack to the intense coldness of the weather, and to the morning's skating, when she must have over-fatigued herself. The depression most of them had felt during the last set of quadrilles he put down to the same cause—unusual cold.

Cecily continued very poorly the following day. She confided to me privately her extraordinary impressions of the previous evening. I found them to be similar to my own; but I mentioned nothing to her about myself, and laughed a little.

'But I did see the old man, Aunt Cameron,' she persisted. 'He was by Mrs Goldsmith's side.'

I would not listen. On the contrary, I treated the matter entirely from a common-sense point of view; endeavouring to persuade her that the whole thing was due to an overwrought imagination. Indeed I was by no means sure that such was not the case. It was more likely that our brains, hers and mine, should have worked in the same groove, been '*en rapport*', as the mesmerists would have expressed it, than that we should really have seen an apparition. We are all aware of those invisible magnetic wires which so often flash a message from one brain to another, those mysterious reminders which at times precede the arrival of an absent friend—the dream at night followed by the letter of the morrow. 'There are,' as Hamlet hath it, 'more things in heaven and earth than are dreamt of in our philosophy.' What we call the supernatural may be but the gleams of a hidden science some time to be revealed.

Cecily tried to take up my view of the case. We agreed not to mention the matter to Hilda, or to anyone else.

'Please, Mr Cameron, you are wanted,' said Martha to my nephew, interrupting us that same evening when we were all sitting together, young Kirby, the engineer, being with us.

'Who is it?' cried Leonard.

'Will you please come out, sir, he won't give any name.'

Leonard went out. He came back again in a minute or two, and beckoned to Kirby, who was playing chess with Hilda.

'It's nothing,' he said, as we all started up. 'Only Martha has been frightened at someone standing at the back door and then going away without speaking. We'll go round the garden to make sure no tramps are about.'

I left the room myself, thinking of tramps, and of nothing else. The cottage was so low and so covered by fruit trees and trellis that it would have been a very easy matter to climb into the bedrooms. My window, just over the porch, had especial facilities that way, and I went up to it. Opening the lattice very gently, I concealed myself behind the curtain and looked out. The moon was bright. The voices of the two young men reached me from below.

'It's queer, Kirby—after all the talk, you know. Martha says she opened the door to get some wood, and there the old man stood. She thought it was a real tramp, mind you, and she did not like his staring in her face and never speaking. I am sure I saw him; he was going round towards the orchard.'

'Very odd!' replied young Kirby. 'I saw him too. He was leaning over the front gate.'

'And, by Jove, there he is now!'

'Where?'

'At the gate.'

'I don't see him!'

'Nor do I now—he's gone.'

Yes, there was no mistake; *I* saw him too from my window; the old man leaning on his stick at the gate, where he used to stand so often in life. Presently the two young men came in, and I went down.

'Have you seen any tramp, Leonard?'

'No, Aunt. Not a tramp.'

'What then? Anything?'

'A little old man leaning on a stick.'

'I saw him too, Mrs Cameron,' added Mr Kirby.

'We had better say nothing to the girls,' whispered Leonard.

'No, nor to anyone else, Leonard. The whole place would be astir.'

'What—on account of old Vallyer?'

I nodded. Just then the girls came running out.

'What a long time you have been! Have you found him?'

'Of course not,' Leonard replied. 'He had got clear off: those tramps are cunning. Let us have supper—it's awfully cold!'

This second little episode put me very much out of conceit with my pretty cottage. My nieces had a pressing invitation from Leonard's mother, and were to return with him to London. I thought I would go away somewhere too.

It was the afternoon of the day before Leonard and they were to leave. We had had one heavy fall of snow, and the air was again thick with the feathery flakes. Strangely depressed, both mentally and bodily, I stood alone at the window and looked out over the valley, which lay so still under its great white shroud. At last Cecily came in and stood by me.

'You will be very lonely, Aunt, after we are gone'

'Aye.' And then we stood in silence.

Suddenly the girl laid her hand on my arm, as though to attract my attention. A chilly draught of wind seemed to blow through the room, raising the hair off my forehead with a pricking sensation.

A feeble, bent figure, leaning heavily on a stick, passed slowly and silently from the door to the other window. A coal falling in the grate, the flame flickered up, showing distinctly the old man whom I had twice before seen!

The apparition, for such I now felt it to be, stood looking out of the window, with a worn, sad expression, such as his face might often have borne in the lonely, loveless life he had chosen for himself. After a moment or two of perfect stillness I could bear it no longer. Springing to the fire I stirred it vigorously; the flames rose up into the chimney and the little room was in a blaze of light.

The old man was gone! Cecily grasped my hands in both her own, for she had seen it too; every trace of the usual bright colour had vanished from her lips and face, and she was trembling from head to foot.

I went up with them the next day, and took old Martha with me. I could not stay in the place any more. The agent was informed of these facts, and he let me off easily, and made no remonstrance; so we thought mine could not have been the first complaint of the sort.

It is said the grey cottage is to be a cottage no longer; that it is to be pulled down. And I sincerely hope it will be.

ROUND THE FIRE

MRS CROWE

'I have travelled a great deal,' said our next speaker, the Chevalier de La C. G., 'and, certainly, I have never been in any country where instances of these spiritual appearances were not adduced on apparently credible authority. I have heard numerous stories of the sort, but the one that most readily occurs to me at present was told to me not long ago, in Paris, by Count P.—the nephew of the celebrated Count P. whose name occurs in the history of the remarkable incidents connected with the death of the Emperor Paul.

'Count P., my authority for the following story, was attached to the Russian embassy; and he told me, one evening, when the conversation turned on the inconveniences of travelling in the East of Europe, that on one occasion, when in Poland, he found himself about seven o'clock in an autumn evening on a forest road, where there was no possibility of finding a house of public entertainment within many miles. There was a frightful storm; the road, not good at the best, was almost impracticable from the weather, and his horses were completely knocked up. On consulting his people about what was best to be done, they said that to go back was as impossible as to go forward; but that by turning a little out of the main road, they should soon reach a castle where possibly shelter might be procured for the night. The count gladly consented, and it was not long before they found themselves at the gate of what appeared a building on a very splendid scale. The courier quickly alighted and rang at the bell, and while waiting for admission he enquired who the castle belonged to, and was told that it was Count X's.

'It was some time before the bell was answered, but at length an elderly man appeared at a wicket, with a lantern, and peeped out. On perceiving the equipage, he came forward and stepped up to the carriage, holding the light aloft to discover who was inside. Count P. handed him his card, and explained his distress.

' "There is no one here, my lord," replied the man, "but myself and my family; the castle is not inhabited."

' "That's bad news," said the count, "but nevertheless, you can give me what I am most in need of and that is—shelter for the night."

' "Willingly," said the man, "if your lordship will put up with such accommodation as we can hastily prepare."

' "So," said the count, "I alighted and walked in, and the old man unbarred the great gates to admit my carriages and people. We found ourselves in an immense *cour,* with the castle *en face,* and stables and offices on each side. As we had a *fourgon* with us, with provender for the cattle and provisions for ourselves, we wanted nothing but beds and a good fire; and as the only one lighted was in the old man's apartments, he first took us there. They consisted of a suite of small rooms in the left wing, that had probably been formerly occupied by the upper servants. They were comfortably furnished, and he and his large family appeared to be very well lodged. Besides the wife, there were three sons, with their wives and children, and two nieces; and in a part of the offices, where I saw a light, I was told there were labourers and women servants for it was a valuable estate, with a fine forest, and the sons acted as *gardes chasse*.

' "Is there much game in the forest?" I asked.

' "A great deal of all sorts," they answered.

' "Then I suppose during the season the family live here?"

' "Never," they replied. "None of the family ever reside here."

' "Indeed!" I said, "how is that? It seems a very fine place."

' "Superb," answered the wife of the custodian; "but the castle is haunted."

'She said this with a simple gravity that made me laugh, upon which they all stared at me with the most edifying amazement.

' "I beg your pardon," I said, "but you know, perhaps, in great cities, such as I usually inhabit, there are no ghosts."

' "Indeed!" said they. "No ghosts!"

' "At least," I said, "I never heard of any; and we don't believe in such things."

'They looked at each other with surprise, but said nothing, not appearing to have any desire to convince me. "But do you mean to say," said I, "that that is the reason the family don't live here, and that the castle is abandoned on that account?"

' "Yes," they replied, "that is the reason nobody has resided here for many years."

' "But how can you live here then?"

' "We are never troubled in this part of the building," said she. "We hear noises, but we are used to that."

' "Well, if there is a ghost, I hope I shall see it," said I.

' "God forbid!" said the woman, crossing herself. "But we shall guard against that; your seigneurie will sleep not far from this, where you will be quite safe."

' "Oh! but," said I, "I am quite serious: if there is a ghost I should particularly like to see him, and I should be much obliged to you to put me in the apartments he most frequents."

'They opposed this proposition earnestly, and begged me not to think of it; besides, they said if anything was to happen to my lord, how should they answer for it; but as I insisted, the women went to call the members of the family who were lighting fires and preparing beds in some rooms on the same floor as they occupied themselves. When they came they were as earnest against the indulgence of my wishes as the women had been. Still I insisted.

' "Are you afraid," I said, "to go yourselves in the haunted chambers?"

' "No," they answered. "We are the custodians of the castle and have to keep the rooms clean and well aired lest the furniture be spoiled—my lord talks always of removing it, but it has never been removed yet—but we would not sleep up there for all the world."

' "Then it is the upper floors that are haunted?"

' "Yes, especially the long room, no one could pass a night there; the last that did is in a lunatic asylum now at Warsaw," said the custodian.

' "What happened to him?"

' "I don't know," said the man; "he was never able to tell."

' "Who was he?" I asked.

' "He was a lawyer. My lord did business with him; and one day he was speaking of this place, and saying that it was a pity he was not at liberty to pull it down and sell the materials; but he cannot, because it is family property and goes with the title; and the lawyer said he wished it was his, and that no ghost should keep him out of it. My lord said that it was easy for anyone to say that who knew nothing about it, and that he must suppose the family had not abandoned such a fine place without good reasons. But the lawyer said it was some trick, and that it was coiners, or robbers, who had got a footing in the castle, and contrived to frighten people away that they might keep it to themselves; so my lord said if he could prove that he should be very much obliged to him, and more than that, he would give him a great sum—I don't know how much. So the lawyer said he would; and my lord wrote to me that he was coming to inspect the property, and I was to let him do anything he liked.

' "Well, he came, and with him his son, a fine young man and a soldier. They asked me all sorts of questions, and went over the castle and examined every part of it. From what they said, I could see that they thought the ghost was all nonsense, and that I and my family were in collusion with the robbers or coiners. However, I did not care for that; my lord knew the castle had been haunted before I was born.

' "I had prepared rooms on this floor for them—the same I am preparing for your lordship, and they slept there, keeping the keys of the upper rooms to themselves, so I did not interfere with them. But one morning, very early, we were awakened by someone knocking at our bedroom door, and when we opened it we saw Mr Thaddeus—that was the lawyer's son—standing there half-dressed and as pale as a ghost; and he said his father was very ill and he begged us to go to him; to our surprise he led us upstairs to the haunted chamber, and there we found the poor gentleman speechless, and we thought they had gone up there early and that he had had a stroke. But it was not so; Mr Thaddeus said that after we were all in bed they had gone up there to pass the night. I know they thought that there was no ghost but us, and that's why they would not let us know their intention. They laid down upon some sofas, wrapped up in their fur cloaks, and resolved to keep awake, and they did so for some time, but at last the young man was overcome by drowsiness; he struggled against it, but could not conquer it, and the last thing he recollects was his father shaking him and saying, 'Thaddeus, Thaddeus, for God's sake keep awake!' But he could not, and he knew no more till he woke and saw that day was breaking, and found his father sitting in a corner of the room speechless, and looking like a corpse; and there he was when we went up. The young man thought he'd been taken ill or had a stroke, as we supposed at first; but when we found they had passed the night in the haunted chambers, we had no doubt what had happened—he had seen some terrible sight and so lost his senses."

' "He lost his senses, I should say, from terror when his son fell asleep," said I, "and he felt himself alone. He could have been a man of no nerve. At all events, what you tell me raises my curiosity. Will you take me upstairs and show me these rooms?"

' "Willingly," said the man, and fetching a bunch of keys and a light, and calling one of his sons to follow him with another, he led the way up the great staircase to a suite of apartments on the first floor. The rooms were lofty and large, and the man said the furniture was very handsome, but old. Being all covered with canvas cases, I could not judge of it.

' "Which is the long room?" I said.

'Upon which he led me into a long narrow room that might rather have been called a gallery. There were sofas along each side, something like a dais at the upper end, and several large pictures hanging on the walls.

'I had with me a bulldog, of a very fine breed, that had been given me in England by Lord F. She had followed me upstairs—indeed, she followed me everywhere—and I watched her narrowly as she went smelling about, but there were no indications of her perceiving anything extraordinary. Beyond this gallery there was only a small octagonal room, with a door that led out upon another staircase. When I had examined it all thoroughly, I returned to the long room and told the man as that was the place especially frequented by the ghost, I should feel much obliged if he would allow me to pass the night there. I could take upon myself to say that Count X would have no objection.

' "It is not that," replied the man, "but the danger to your lordship," and he conjured me not to insist on such a perilous experiment.

'When he found I was resolved, he gave way, but on condition that I signed a paper, stating that in spite of his representations I had determined to sleep in the long room.

'I confess the more anxious these people seemed to prevent my sleeping there, the more curious I was; not that I believed in the ghost the least in the world. I thought that the lawyer had been right in his conjecture, but that he hadn't nerve enough to investigate whatever he saw or heard, and that they succeeded in frightening him out of his senses. I saw what an excellent place these people had got, and how much it was their interest to maintain the idea that the castle was uninhabitable. Now, I have pretty good nerves—I have been in situations that have tried them severely—and I did not believe that any ghost, if there was such a thing, or any jugglery by which a semblance of one might be contrived, would shake them. As for any real danger, I did not apprehend it; the people knew who I was, and any mischief happening to me would have led to consequences they well understood. So they lighted fires in both the grates of the gallery, and as they had an abundance of dry wood they soon blazed up. I was determined not to leave the room after I was once in it, lest, if my suspicions were correct, they might have time to make their arrangements; so I desired my people to bring up my supper, and I ate it there.

'My courier said he had always heard the castle was haunted, but he dare say there was no ghost but the people below, who had a very comfortable berth of it; and he offered to pass the night with me, but I declined any companion and preferred trusting to myself and my dog. My valet, on the contrary, strongly advised me against the enterprise, assuring me that he had lived with a family in France whose chateau was haunted, and had left his place in consequence.

'By the time I had finished my supper it was ten o'clock, and everything was prepared for the night. My bed, though an impromptu, was very comfortable, made of amply stuffed cushions and thick coverlets, placed in front of the fire. I was provided with light and plenty of wood; and I had my regimental cutlass, and a case of excellent pistols, which I carefully primed and loaded in presence of the custodian, saying, "You see I am determined to fire at the ghost, so if he cannot stand a bullet he had better not pay me a visit."

'The old man shook his head calmly, but made no answer. Having desired the courier, who said he should not go to bed, to come upstairs immediately if he heard the report of firearms, I dismissed my people and locked the doors, barricading each with a heavy ottoman besides. There was no arras or hangings of any sort behind which a door could he concealed; and I went round the room, the walls of which were panelled with white and gold, knocking every part, but neither the sound, nor Dido, the dog, gave any indications of there being anything unusual. Then I undressed and lay down with my sword and my pistols beside me; and Dido at the foot of my bed, where she always slept.

'I confess I was in a state of pleasing excitement; my curiosity and my love of adventure were roused; and whether it was ghost, or robber, or coiner, I was to have a visit from, the interview was likely to be equally interesting. It was half-past ten when I lay down; my expectations were too vivid to admit of much sleep; and after an attempt at a French novel, I was obliged to give it up; I could not fix my attention to it. Besides, my chief care was not to be surprised. I could not help thinking the custodian and his family had some secret way of getting into the room, and I hoped to detect them in the act; so I lay with my eyes and ears open in a position that gave me a view of every part of it, till my travelling clock struck twelve, which being pre-eminently the ghostly hour, I thought the critical moment was arrived. But no, no sound, no interruption of any sort to the silence and solitude of the night occurred. When half-past twelve and one struck, I pretty well made up my mind that I should be disappointed in my expectations, and that the ghost, whoever he was, knew better than to encounter Dido and a brace of well-charged pistols; but just as I arrived at this conclusion an unaccountable *frisson* came over me, and I saw Dido, who tired with her day's journey had lain till now quietly curled up asleep, begin to move, and slowly get upon her feet. I thought she was only going to turn, but, instead of lying down, she stood still with her ears erect and her head towards the dais, uttering a low growl.

'The dais, I should mention, was but the skeleton of a dais, for the draperies were taken off. There was only remaining a canopy covered with crimson velvet, and an arm-chair covered with velvet too, but cased in canvas like the rest of the furniture. I had examined this part of the room thoroughly, and had moved the chair aside to ascertain that there was nothing under it.

'Well, I sat up in bed and looked steadily in the same direction as the dog, but I could see nothing at first, though it appeared that she did: but as I looked I began to perceive something like a cloud in the chair, while at the same time a chill which seemed to pervade the very marrow in my bones crept through me, yet the fire was good; and it was not the chill of fear, for I cocked my pistols with perfect self-possession and abstained from giving Dido the signal to advance, because I wished eagerly to see the denouement of the adventure.

'Gradually this cloud took a form, and assumed the shape of a tall white figure that reached from the ceiling to the floor of the dais, which was raised by two steps. "At him, Dido! At him!" I said, and away she dashed to the steps, but instantly turned and crept back completely cowed. As her courage was undoubted, I own this astonished me, and I should have fired, but that I was perfectly satisfied that what I saw was not a substantial human form, for I had seen it grow into its present shape and height from the undefined cloud that first appeared in the chair. I laid my hand on the dog, who had crept up to my side, and I felt her shaking in her skin. I was about to rise myself and approach the figure, though I confess I was a good deal awestruck, when it stepped majestically from the dais, and seemed to be advancing. "At him!" I said. "At him, Dido!" and I gave the dog every encouragement to go forward; she made a sorry attempt, but returned when she had got half-way and crouched beside me whining with terror. The figure advanced upon me; the cold became icy; the dog crouched and trembled; and I, as it approached, honestly confess,' said Count P., 'that I hid my head under the bedclothes and did not venture to look up till morning. I know not what it was—as it passed over me I felt a sensation of undefinable horror, that no words can describe—and I can only say that nothing on earth would tempt me to pass another night in that room, and I am sure if Dido could speak you'd find her of the same opinion.

'I had desired to be called at seven o'clock, and when the custodian, who accompanied my valet, found me safe and in my perfect senses, I must say the poor man appeared greatly relieved; and when I descended the whole family seemed to look upon me as a hero. I thought it only just to them to admit that something had happened in the night that I felt impossible to account for, and that I should not recommend anybody who was not very sure of their nerves to repeat the experiment.'

When the Chevalier had concluded this extraordinary story, I suggested that the apparition of the castle very much resembled that mentioned by the late Professor Gregory, in his letters on mesmerism, as having appeared in the Tower of London some years ago, and, from the alarm it created, having occasioned the death of a lady, the wife of an officer quartered there, and one of the sentries. Every one who had read that very interesting publication was struck by the resemblance.

THE DOLL'S GHOST

F. MARION CRAWFORD

I t was a terrible accident, and for one moment the splendid machinery of Cranston House got out of gear and stood still. The butler emerged from the retirement in which he spent his elegant leisure, two grooms of the chambers appeared simultaneously from opposite directions, there were actually housemaids on the grand staircase, and those who remember the facts most exactly assert that Mrs Pringle herself positively stood upon the landing. Mrs Pringle was the housekeeper. As for the head nurse, the under nurse and the nursery-maid, their feelings cannot be described.

The Lady Gwendolen Lancaster-Douglas-Scroop, youngest daughter of the ninth Duke of Cranston, and aged six years and three months, picked herself up quite alone, and sat down on the third step of the grand staircase in Cranston House.

'Oh!' ejaculated the butler, and he disappeared again.

'Ah!' responded the grooms of the chambers, as they also went away.

'It's only that doll,' Mrs Pringle was distinctly heard to say, in a tone of contempt.

The under nurse heard her say it. Then the three nurses gathered round Lady Gwendolen and patted her, and gave her unhealthy things out of their pockets, and hurried her out of Cranston House as fast as they could, lest it should be found out upstairs that they had allowed the Lady Gwendolen Lancaster-Douglas-Scroop to tumble down the grand staircase with her doll in her arms. And as the doll was badly broken, the nursery-maid carried it, with the pieces, wrapped up in Lady Gwendolen's little cloak. It was not far to Hyde Park, and when they had reached a quiet place they took means to find out that Lady Gwendolen had no bruises. For the carpet was very thick and soft, and there was thick stuff under it to make it softer.

Lady Gwendolen Lancaster-Douglas-Scroop sometimes yelled, but she never cried. It was because she had yelled that the nurse had allowed her to go downstairs alone with Nina, the doll, under one arm, while she steadied herself with her other hand on the balustrade, and trod upon the polished marble steps beyond the edge of the carpet. So she had fallen, and Nina had come to grief.

Mr Bernard Puckler and his little daughter lived in a little house in a little alley, which led out off a quiet little street not very far from Belgrave Square. He was the great doll doctor, and his extensive practice lay in the most aristocratic quarter. He mended dolls of all sizes and ages, boy dolls and girl dolls, baby dolls in long clothes, and grown-up dolls in fashionable gowns, talking dolls and dumb dolls, those that shut their eyes when they lay down, and those whose eyes had to be shut for them by means of a mysterious wire. His daughter Else was only just over twelve years old, but she was already very clever at mending dolls' clothes, and at doing their hair, which is harder than you might think, though the dolls sit quite still while it is being done.

Mr Puckler had originally been a German, but he had dissolved his nationality in the ocean of London many years ago, like a great many foreigners. He still had one or two German friends, however, who came on

Saturday evenings and smoked with him and played picquet or 'skat' with him for farthing points, and called him 'Herr Doktor', which seemed to please Mr Puckler very much.

He looked older than he was, for his beard was rather long and ragged, his hair was grizzled and thin, and he wore horn-rimmed spectacles.

As for Else, she was a thin, pale child, very quiet and neat, with dark eyes and brown hair that was plaited down her back and tied with a bit of black ribbon. She mended the dolls' clothes and took the dolls back to their homes when they were quite strong again.

The house was a little one, but too big for the two people who lived in it. There was a small sitting-room on the street, and the workshop was at the back, and there were three rooms upstairs. But the father and daughter lived most of their time in the workshop, because they were generally at work, even in the evenings.

Mr Puckler laid Nina on the table and looked at her a long time, till the tears began to fill his eyes behind the horn-rimmed spectacles. He was a very susceptible man, and he often fell in love with the dolls he mended, and found it hard to part with them when they had smiled at him for a few days. They were real little people to him, with characters and thoughts and feelings of their own, and he was very tender with them all. But some attracted him especially from the first, and when they were brought to him maimed and injured, their state seemed so pitiful to him that the tears came easily. You must remember that he had lived among dolls during a great part of his life, and understood them.

'How do you know that they feel nothing?' he went on to say to Else. 'You must be gentle with them. It costs nothing to be kind to the little beings, and perhaps it makes a difference to them.'

And Else understood him, because she was a child, and she knew that she was more to him than all the dolls.

He fell in love with Nina at first sight, perhaps because her beautiful brown glass eyes were something like Else's own, and he loved Else first and best, with all his heart. And, besides, it was a very sorrowful case. Nina had evidently not been long in the world, for her complexion was perfect, her hair was smooth where it should be smooth, and curly where it should be curly, and her silk clothes were perfectly new. But across her face was that frightful gash, like a sabre-cut, deep and shadowy within, but clean and sharp at the edges. When he tenderly pressed her head to close the gaping wound, the edges made a fine, grating sound, that was painful to hear, and the lids of the dark eyes quivered and trembled as though Nina were suffering dreadfully.

'Poor Nina!' he exclaimed sorrowfully. 'But I shall not hurt you much, though you will take a long time to get strong.'

He always asked the names of the broken dolls when they were brought to him, and sometimes the people knew what the children called them, and told him. He liked 'Nina' for a name. Altogether and in every way she pleased him more than any doll he had seen for many years, and he felt drawn to her, and made up his mind to make her perfectly strong and sound, no matter how much labour it might cost him.

Mr Puckler worked patiently a little at a time, and Else watched him. She could do nothing for poor Nina, whose clothes needed no mending. The longer the doll doctor worked the more fond he became of the yellow hair and the beautiful brown glass eyes. He sometimes forgot all the other dolls that were waiting to be mended, lying side by side on a shelf and sat for an hour gazing at Nina's face, while he racked his ingenuity for some new invention by which to hide even the smallest trace of the terrible accident.

She was wonderfully mended. Even he was obliged to admit that; but the scar was still visible to his keen eyes, a very fine line right across the face, downwards from right to left. Yet all the conditions had been most favourable for a cure, since the cement had set quite hard at the first attempt and the weather had been fine and dry, which makes a great difference in a dolls' hospital.

At last he knew that he could do no more, and the under nurse had already come twice to see whether the job was finished, as she coarsely expressed it.

'Nina is not quite strong yet,' Mr Puckler had answered each time, for he could not make up his mind to face the parting.

And now he sat before the square deal table at which he worked, and Nina lay before him for the last time with a big brown-paper box beside her. It stood there like her coffin, waiting for her, he thought. He must put her into it, and lay tissue paper over her dear face, and then put on the lid, and at the thought of tying the string his sight was dim with tears again. He was never to look into the glassy depths of the beautiful brown eyes any more, nor to hear the little wooden voice say 'Pa-pa' and 'Ma-ma'. It was a very painful moment.

In the vain hope of gaining time before the separation, he took up the little sticky bottles of cement and glue and gum and colour, looking at each one in turn, and then at Nina's face. And all his small tools lay there, neatly arranged in a row, but he knew that he could not use them again for Nina. She was quite strong at last, and in a country where there should be no cruel children to hurt her she might live a hundred years, with only that almost imperceptible line across her face, to tell of the fearful thing that had befallen her on the marble steps of Cranston House.

Suddenly Mr Puckler's heart was quite full, and he rose abruptly from his seat and turned away.

'Else,' he said unsteadily, 'you must do it for me. I cannot bear to see her go into the box.'

So he went and stood at the window with his back turned, while Else did what he had not the heart to do. 'Is it done?' he asked, not turning round. Then take her away, my dear. Put on your hat, and take her to Cranston House quickly, and when you are gone I will turn round.'

Else was used to her father's queer ways with the dolls, and though she had never seen him so much moved by a parting, she was not much surprised.

'Come back quickly,' he said, when he heard her hand on the latch. 'It is growing late, and I should not send you at this hour. But I cannot bear to look forward to it any more.'

When Else was gone, he left the window and sat down in his place before the table again, to wait for the child to come back. He touched the place where Nina had lain, very gently, and he recalled the softly-tinted pink face, and the glass eyes, and the ringlets of yellow hair, till he could almost see them.

The evenings were long, for it was late in the spring. But it began to grow dark soon, and Mr Puckler wondered why Else did not come back. She had been gone an hour and a half, and that was much longer than he had expected, for it was barely half a mile from Belgrave Square to Cranston House. He reflected that the child might have been kept waiting, but as the twilight deepened he grew anxious, and walked up and down in the dim workshop, no longer thinking of Nina, but of Else, his own living child, whom he loved.

An indefinable, disquieting sensation came upon him by fine degrees, a chilliness and a faint stirring of his thin hair, joined with a wish to be in any company rather than to be alone much longer. It was the beginning of fear.

He told himself in strong German-English that he was a foolish old man, and he began to feel about for the matches in the dusk. He knew just where they should be, for he always kept them in the same place, close to the little tin box that held bits of sealing-wax of various colours, for some kinds of mending. But somehow he could not find the matches in the gloom.

Something had happened to Else, he was sure, and as his fear increased, he felt as though it might be allayed if he could get a light and see what time it was. Then he called himself a foolish old man again, and the sound of his own voice startled him in the dark. He could not find the matches. The window was grey still; he might see what time it was if he went close to it, and he could go and get matches out of the cupboard afterwards. He stood back from the table, to get out of the way of the chair, and began to cross the board floor.

Something was following him in the dark. There was a small pattering, as of tiny feet upon the boards. He stopped and listened, and the roots of his hair tingled. It was nothing and he was a foolish old man. He made two steps more, and he was sure that he heard the little pattering again. He turned his back to the window, leaning against the sash so that the panes began to crack, and he faced the dark. Everything was quite still, and it smelt of paste and cement and wood-filings as usual.

'Is that you, Else?' he asked, and he was surprised by the fear in his voice.

There was no answer in the room, and he held up his watch and tried to make out what time it was by the grey dusk that was just not darkness. So far as he could see, it was within two or three minutes of ten o'clock. He had been a long time alone. He was shocked, and frightened for Else, out in London, so late, and he almost ran across the room to the door. As he fumbled for the latch, he distinctly heard the running of the little feet after him.

'Mice!' he exclaimed feebly, just as he got the door open.

He shut it quickly behind him, and felt as though some cold thing had settled on his back and was writhing upon him. The passage was quite dark, but he found his hat and was out in the alley in a moment, breathing more freely, and surprised to find how much light there still was in the open air. He could see the pavement clearly under his feet, and far off in the street to which the alley led he could hear the laughter and calls of children, playing some game out of doors. He wondered how he could have been so nervous, and for an instant he thought of going back into the house to wait quietly for Else. But instantly he felt that nervous fright of something stealing over him again. In any case it was better to walk up to Cranston House and ask the servants about the child. One of the women had perhaps taken a fancy to her, and was even now giving her tea and cake.

He walked quickly to Belgrave Square, and then up the broad streets, listening as he went, whenever there was no other sound, for the tiny footsteps. But he heard nothing, and was laughing at himself when he rang the servants' bell at the big house. Of course, the child must be there.

The person who opened the door was quite an inferior person—for it was a back door—but affected the manners of the front, and stared at Mr Puckler superciliously.

No little girl had been seen, and he knew 'nothing about no dolls'.

'She is my little girl,' said Mr Puckler tremulously, for all his anxiety was returning tenfold, 'and I am afraid something has happened.'

The inferior person said rudely that 'nothing could have happened to her in that house, because she had not been there, which was a jolly good reason why'; and Mr Puckler was obliged to admit that the man ought to know, as it was his business to keep the door and let people in. He wished to be allowed to speak to the under nurse, who knew him; but the man was ruder than ever, and finally shut the door in his face.

When the doll doctor was alone in the street, he steadied himself by the railing, for he felt as though he were breaking in two, just as some dolls break, in the middle of the backbone.

Presently he knew that he must be doing something to find Else, and that gave him strength. He began to walk as quickly as he could through the streets, following every highway and byway which his little girl might have taken on her errand. He also asked several policemen in vain if they had seen her, and most of them answered him kindly, for they saw that he was a sober man and in his right senses, and some of them had little girls of their own.

It was one o'clock in the morning when he went up to his own door again, worn out and hopeless and broken-hearted. As he turned the key in the lock, his heart stood still, for he knew that he was awake and not dreaming, and that he really heard those tiny footsteps pattering to meet him inside the house along the passage.

But he was too unhappy to be much frightened any more, and his heart went on again with a dull regular pain, that found its way all through him with every pulse. So he went in, and hung up his hat in the dark, and found the matches in the cupboard and the candlestick in its place in the corner.

Mr Puckler was so much overcome and so completely worn out that he sat down in his chair before the work-table and almost fainted, as his face dropped forward upon his folded hands. Beside him the solitary candle burned steadily with a low flame in the still warm air.

'Else! Else!' he moaned against his yellow knuckles. And that was all he could say, and it was no relief to him. On the contrary, the very sound of the name was a new and sharp pain that pierced his ears and his head and his very soul. For every time he repeated the name it meant that little Else was dead, somewhere out in the streets of London in the dark.

He was so terribly hurt that he did not even feel something pulling gently at the skirt of his old coat, so gently that it was like the nibbling of a tiny mouse. He might have thought that it was really a mouse if he had noticed it.

'Else! Else!' he groaned, right against his hands.

Then a cool breath stirred his thin hair, and the low flame of the one candle dropped down almost to a mere spark, not flickering, as though a draught were going to blow it out, but just dropping down as if it were tired out. Mr Puckler felt his hands stiffening with fright under his face; and there was a faint rustling sound, like some small silk thing blown in a gentle breeze. He sat up straight, stark and scared, and a small wooden voice spoke in the stillness.

'Pa-pa,' it said, with a break between the syllables.

Mr Puckler stood up in a single jump, and his chair fell over backwards with a smashing noise upon the wooden floor. The candle had almost gone out.

It was Nina's doll-voice that had spoken, and he should have known it among the voices of a hundred other dolls. And yet there was something more in it, a little human ring, with a pitiful cry and a call for help, and the wail of a hurt child. Mr Puckler stood up, stark and stiff, and tried to look round, but at first he could not, for he seemed to be frozen from head to foot.

Then he made a great effort, and he raised one hand to each of his temples, and pressed his own head round as he would have turned a doll's. The candle was burning so low that it might as well have been out altogether, for any light it gave, and the room seemed quite dark at first. Then he saw something. He would not have believed that he could be more frightened than he had been just before that. But he was, and his knees shook, for he saw the doll standing in the middle of the floor, shining with a faint and ghostly radiance, her beautiful glassy brown eyes fixed on his. And across her face the very thin line of the break he had mended shone as though it were drawn in light with a fine point of white flame.

Yet there was something more in the eyes, too; there was something human, like Else's own, but as if only the doll saw him through them, and not Else. And there was enough of Else to bring back all his pain and to make him forget his fear.

'Else! My little Else!' he cried aloud.

The small ghost moved, and its doll-arm slowly rose and fell with a stiff, mechanical motion.

'Pa-pa,' it said.

It seemed this time that there was even more of Else's tone echoing somewhere between the wooden notes that reached his ears so distinctly and yet so far away. Else was calling him, he was sure.

His face was perfectly white in the gloom, but his knees did not shake any more, and he felt that he was less frightened.

'Yes, child! But where? Where?' he asked. 'Where are you, Else?'

'Pa-pa!'

The syllables died away in the quiet room.

There was a low rustling of silk, the glassy brown eyes turned slowly away, and Mr Puckler heard the pitter-patter of the small feet in the bronze kid slippers as the figure ran straight to the door. Then the candle burned high again, the room was full of light, and he was alone.

Mr Puckler passed his hand over his eyes and looked about him. He could see everything quite clearly, and he felt that he must have been dreaming, though he was standing instead of sitting down, as he should have been if he had just waked up. The candle burned brightly now. There were the dolls to be mended, lying in a row with their toes up. The third one had lost her right shoe, and Else was making one. He knew that, and he was certainly not dreaming now. He had not been dreaming when he had come in from his fruitless search and had heard the doll's footsteps running to the door. He had not fallen asleep in his chair. How could he possibly have fallen asleep when his heart was breaking? He had been awake all the time.

He steadied himself, set the fallen chair upon its legs, and said to himself again very emphatically that he was a foolish old man. He ought to be out in the streets looking for his child, asking questions, and enquiring at the police stations, where all accidents were reported as soon as they were known, or at the hospitals.

'Pa-pa!'

The longing, wailing, pitiful little wooden cry rang from the passage, outside the door, and Mr Puckler stood for an instant with white face, transfixed and rooted to the spot. A moment later his hand was on the latch. Then he was in the passage, with the light streaming from the open door behind him.

Quite at the other end he saw the little phantom shining clearly in the shadow, and the right hand seemed to beckon to him as the arm rose and fell once more. He knew all at once that it had not come to frighten him but to lead him, and when it disappeared, and he walked boldly towards the door, he knew that it was in the street outside, waiting for him. He forgot that he was tired and had eaten no supper, and had walked many miles, for a sudden hope ran through and through him, like a golden stream of life.

And sure enough, at the corner of the alley, and at the corner of the street, and out in Belgrave Square, he saw the small ghost flitting before him. Sometimes it was only a shadow, where there was other light, but then the glare of the lamps made a pale green sheen on its little Mother Hubbard frock of silk; and sometimes, where the streets were dark and silent, the whole figure shone out brightly with its yellow curls and rosy neck. It seemed to trot along like a tiny child, and Mr Puckler could hear the pattering of the bronze kid slippers on the pavement as it ran. But it went very fast, and he could only just keep up with it, tearing along with his hat on the back of his head and his thin hair blown by the night breeze, and his horn-rimmed spectacles firmly set upon his broad nose.

On and on he went, and he had no idea where he was. He did not even care, for he knew certainly that he was going the right way.

Then at last, in a wide, quiet street, he was standing before a big, sober-looking door that had two lamps on each side of it, and a polished brass bell-handle, which he pulled.

And just inside, when the door was opened, in the bright light, there was the little shadow, and the pale green sheen on the little silk dress, and once more the small cry came to his ears, less pitiful, more longing.

'Pa-pa!'

The shadow turned suddenly bright, and out of the brightness the beautiful brown glass eyes were turned up happily to his, while the rosy mouth smiled so divinely that the phantom doll looked almost like a little angel just then.

'A little girl was brought in soon after ten o'clock,' said the quiet voice of the hospital doorkeeper. 'I think they thought she was only stunned. She was holding a big brown-paper box against her, and they could not get it out of her arms. She had a long plait of brown hair that hung down as they carried her.'

'She is my little girl,' said Mr Puckler, but he hardly heard his own voice.

He leaned over Else's face in the gentle light of the children's ward, and when he had stood there a minute the beautiful brown eyes opened and looked up to his.

'Pa-pa!' cried Else softly, 'I knew you would come!'

Then Mr Puckler did not know what he did or said for a moment, and what he felt was worth all the fear and terror and despair that had almost killed him that night. But by and by Else was telling her story, and the nurse let her speak, for there were only two other children in the room, who were getting well and were sound asleep.

'They were big boys with bad faces,' said Else, 'and they tried to get Nina away from me, but I held on and fought as well as I could till one of them hit me with something, and I don't remember any more, for I tumbled down and I suppose the boys ran away, and somebody found me there. But I'm afraid Nina is all smashed.'

'Here is the box,' said the nurse. 'We could not take it out of her arms till she came to herself. Would you like to see if the doll is broken?'

And she undid the string cleverly, but Nina was all smashed to pieces. Only the gentle light of the children's ward made a pale green sheen in the folds of the little Mother Hubbard frock.

MADAM CROWL'S GHOST

J. SHERIDAN LE FANU

'I'm an ald woman now, and I was but thirteen, my last birthday, the night I came to Applewale House. My aunt was the housekeeper there, and a sort o' one-horse carriage was down at Lexhoe waitin' to take me and my box up to Applewale.

'I was a bit frightened by the time I got to Lexhoe, and when I saw the carriage and horse, I wished myself back again with my mother at Hazelden. I was crying when I got into the "shay"—that's what we used to call it—and old John Mulbery that drove it, and was a good-natured fellow, brought me a handful of apples at the Golden Lion to cheer me up a bit; and he told me that there was a currant-cake, and tea, and pork chops, waiting for me, all hot, in my aunt's room at the great house. It was a fine moonlight night, and I eat the apples, lookin' out o' the shay winda.

'It's a shame for gentlemen to frighten a poor foolish child like I was. I sometimes think it might be tricks. There was two on 'em on the tap o' the coach beside me. And they began to question me after nightfall, when the moon rose, where I was going to. Well, I told them it was to wait on Dame Arabella Crowl, of Applewale House, near by Lexhoe.

' "Ho, then," says one of them, "you'll not be long there!"

'And I looked at him as much as to say "Why not?" for I had spoken out when I told them where I was goin', as if 'twas something clever I hed to say.

' "Because," says he, "and don't you for your life tell no one, only watch her and see—she's possessed by the devil, and more an half a ghost. Have you got a Bible?"

' "Yes, sir," says I. For my mother put my little Bible in my box, and I knew it was there: and by the same token, though the print's too small for my ald eyes, I have it in my press to this hour.

'As I looked up at him saying "Yes, sir," I thought I saw him winkin' at his friend; but I could not be sure.

' "Well," says he, "be sure you put it under your bolster every night, it will keep the ald girl's claws aff ye."

'And I got such a fright when he said that, you wouldn't fancy! And I'd a liked to ask him a lot about the ald lady, but I was too shy, and he and his friend began talkin' together about their own consarns, and dowly enough I got down, as I told ye, at Lexhoe. My heart sank as I drove into the dark avenue. The trees stand very thick and big, as ald as the ald house almost, and four people, with their arms out and fingertips touchin', barely girds round some of them.

'Well, my neck was stretched out o' the winda, looking for the first view o' the great house; and all at once we pulled up in front of it.

'A great white-and-black house it is, wi' great black beams across and right up it, and gables lookin' out, as white as a sheet, to the moon, and the shadows o' the trees, two or three up and down in front, you could count the leaves on them, and all the little diamond-shaped winda-panes, glimmering on the great hall winda, and great shutters, in the old fashion, hinged on the wall outside, boulted across all the rest o' the windas in front, for there was but three or four servants, and the old lady in the house, and most o' t'rooms was locked up.

'My heart was in my mouth when I sid the journey was over, and this the great house afoore me, and I sa near my aunt that I never sid till noo, and Dame Crowl, that I was come to wait upon, and was afeard on already.

'My aunt kissed me in the hall, and brought me to her room. She was tall and thin, wi' a pale face and black eyes, and long thin hands wi' black mittins on. She was past fifty, and her word was short; but her word was law. I hev no complaints to make of her, but she was a hard woman, and I think she would hev bin kinder to me if I had bin her sister's child in place of her brother's. But all that's o' no consequence noo.

'The squire—his name was Mr Chevenix Crowl, he was Dame Crowl's grandson—came down there, by way of seeing that the old lady was well treated, about twice or thrice in the year. I sid him but twice all the time I was at Applewale House.

'I can't say but she was well taken care of, notwithstanding; but that was because my aunt and Meg Wyvern, that was her maid, had a conscience, and did their duty by her.

'Mrs Wyvern—Meg Wyvern my aunt called her to herself, and Mrs Wyvern to me—was a fat, jolly lass of fifty, a good height and a good breadth, always good-humoured and walked slow. She had fine wages, but she was a bit stingy, and kept all her fine clothes under lock and key, and wore, mostly, a twilled chocolate cotton, wi' red, and yellow, and green sprigs and balls on it, and it lasted wonderful.

'She never gave me nout, not the vally o' a brass thimble, all the time I was there; but she was good-humoured, and always laughin', and she talked no end o' proas over her tea; and, seeing me sa sackless and dowly, she roused me up wi' her laughin' and stories; and I think I liked her better than my aunt—children is so taken wi' a bit o' fun or a story—though my aunt was very good to me, but a hard woman about some things, and silent always.

'My aunt took me into her bed-chamber, that I might rest myself a bit while she was settin' the tea in her room. But first, she patted me on the shouther, and said I was a tall lass o' my years, and had spired up well, and asked me if I could do plain work and stitchin'; and she looked in my face, and said I was like my father, her brother, that was dead and gone, and she hoped I was a better Christian, and wad na du a' that lids.*

'It was a hard sayin' the first time I set foot in her room, I thought.

'When I went into the next room, the housekeeper's room—very comfortable, yak** all round—there was a fine fire blazin' away, wi' coal, and peat, and wood, all in a low together, and tea on the table, and hot cake, and smokin' meat; and there was Mrs Wyvern, fat, jolly, and talkin' away, more in an hour than my aunt would in a year.

'While I was still at my tea my aunt went upstairs to see Madam Crowl.

' "She's agone up to see that old Judith Squailes is awake," says Mrs Wyvern. "Judith sits with Madam Crowl when me and Mrs Shutters"— that was my aunt's name—"is away. She's a troublesome old lady. Ye'll hev to be sharp wi' her, or she'll be into the fire, or out o' t' winda. She goes on wires, she does, old though she be."

' "How old, ma'am?" says I.

' "Ninety-three her last birthday, and that's eight months gone," says she; and she laughed. "And don't be askin' questions about her before your aunt—mind, I tell ye; just take her as you find her, and that's all."

' "And what's to be my business about her, please, ma'am?" says I.

' "About the old lady? Well," says she, "your aunt, Mrs Shutters, will tell you that; but I suppose you'll hev to sit in the room with your work, and see she's at no mischief, and let her amuse herself with her things on the table, and get her her food or drink as she calls for it, and keep her out o' mischief, and ring the bell hard if she's troublesome."

* Would not do anything of that sort.
** Oak.

' "Is she deaf, ma'am?"

' "No, nor blind," says she; "as sharp as a needle, but she's gone quite aupy, and can't remember nout rightly; and Jack the Giant Killer, and Goody Twoshoes will please her as well as the king's court, or the affairs of the nation."

' "And what did the little girl go away for, ma'am, that went on Friday last? My aunt wrote to my mother she was to go."

' "Yes; she's gone."

' "What for?" says I again.

' "She didn't answer Mrs Shutters, I do suppose," says she. "I don't know. Don't be talkin'; your aunt can't abide a talkin' child."

' "And please, ma'am, is the old lady well in health?" says I.

' "It ain't no harm to ask that," says she. "She's torflin a bit lately, but better this week past, and I dare say she'll last out her hundred years yet. Hish! Here's your aunt coming down the passage."

'In comes my aunt, and begins talkin' to Mrs Wyvern, and I, beginnin' to feel more comfortable and at home like, was walkin' about the room lookin' at this thing and at that. There was pretty old china things on the cupboard, and pictures again the wall; and there was a door open in the wainscot, and I sees a queer old leathern jacket, wi' straps and buckles to it, and sleeves as long as the bed-post hangin' up inside.

' "What's that you're at, child?" says my aunt, sharp enough, turning about when I thought she least minded. "What's that in your hand?"

' "This, ma'am?" says I, turning about with the leathern jacket. "I don't know what it is, ma'am."

'Pale as she was, the red came up in her cheeks, and her eyes flashed wi' anger, and I think only she had half a dozen steps to take, between her and me, she'd a gev me a sizzup. But she did gie me a shake by the shouther, and she plucked the thing out o' my hand, and says she, "While ever you stay here, don't ye meddle wi' nout that don't belong to ye," and she hung it up on the pin that was there, and shut the door wi' a bang and locked it fast.

'Mrs Wyvern was liftin' up her hands and laughin' all this time, quietly, in her chair, rolling herself a bit in it, as she used when she was kinkin'.

The tears was in my eyes, and she winked at my aunt, and says she, dryin' her own eyes that was wet wi' the laughin', "Tut, the child meant no harm—come here to me, child. It's only a pair o' crutches for lame ducks, and ask us no questions mind, and we'll tell ye no lies; and come here and sit down, and drink a mug o' beer before ye go to your bed."

'My room, mind ye, was upstairs, next to the old lady's, and Mrs Wyvern's bed was near hers in her room, and I was to be ready at call, if need should be.

'The old lady was in one of her tantrums that night and part of the day before. She used to take fits o' the sulks. Sometimes she would not let them dress her, and at other times she would not let them take her clothes off. She was a great beauty, they said, in her day. But there was no one about Applewale that remembered her in her prime. And she was dreadful fond o' dress, and had thick silks, and stiff satins, and velvets, and laces, and all sorts, enough to set up seven shops at the least. All her dresses was old-fashioned and queer, but worth a fortune.

'Well, I went to my bed. I lay for a while awake; for a' things was new to me; and I think the tea was in my nerves, too, for I wasn't used to it, except now and then on a holiday, or the like. And I heard Mrs Wyvern talkin', and I listened with my hand to my ear; but I could not hear Mrs Crowl, and I don't think she said a word.

'There was great care took of her. The people at Applewale knew that when she died they would every one get the sack; and their situations was well paid and easy.

'The doctor came twice a week to see the old lady, and you may be sure they all did as he bid them. One thing was the same every time; they were never to cross or frump her, any way, but to humour and please her in everything.

'So she lay in her clothes all that night, and next day, not a word she said, and I was at my needlework all that day, in my own room, except when I went down to my dinner.

'I would a liked to see the ald lady, and even to hear her speak. But she might as well a' bin in Lunnon a' the time for me.

'When I had my dinner my aunt sent me out for a walk for an hour. I was glad when I came back, the trees was so big, and the place so dark and lonesome, and 'twas a cloudy day, and I cried a deal, thinkin' of home, while I was walkin' alone there. That evening, the candles bein' alight, I was sittin' in my room, and the door was open into Madam Crowl's chamber, where my aunt was. It was, then, for the first time I heard what I suppose was the ald lady talking.

'It was a queer noise like, I couldn't well say which, a bird, or a beast, only it had a bleatin' sound in it, and was very small.

'I pricked my ears to hear all I could. But I could not make out one word she said. And my aunt answered:

' "The evil one can't hurt no one, ma'am, bout the Lord permits."

'Then the same queer voice from the bed says something more that I couldn't make head nor tail on.

'And my aunt med answer again: "Let them pull faces, ma'am, and say what they will; if the Lord be for us, who can be against us?"

'I kept listenin' with my ear turned to the door, holdin' my breath, but not another word or sound came in from the room. In about twenty minutes, as I was sittin' by the table, lookin' at the pictures in the old Aesop's Fables, I was aware o' something moving at the door, and lookin' up I sid my aunt's face lookin' in at the door, and her hand raised.

' "Hish!" says she, very soft, and comes over to me on tiptoe, and she says in a whisper: "Thank God, she's asleep at last, and don't ye make no noise till I come back, for I'm goin' down to take my cup o' tea, and I'll be back i' noo—me and Mrs Wyvern, and she'll be sleepin' in the room, and you can run down when we come up, and Judith will gie ye yaur supper in my room."

'And with that she goes.

'I kep' looking at the picture-book, as before, listenin' every noo and then, but there was no sound, not a breath, that I could hear; an' I began whisperin' to the picture and talkin' to myself to keep my heart up, for I was growin' feared in that big room.

'And at last up I got, and began walkin' about the room, lookin' at this and peepin' at that, to amuse my mind, ye'll understand. And at last what sud I do but peeps into Madam Crowl's bedchamber.

'A grand chamber it was, wi' a great four-poster, wi' flowered silk curtains as tall as the ceilin', and foldin' down on the floor, and drawn close all round. There was a lookin'-glass, the biggest I ever sid before, and the room was a blaze o' light. I counted twenty-two wax candles, all alight. Such was her fancy, and no one dared say her nay.

'I listened at the door, and gaped and wondered all round. When I heard there was not a breath, and did not see so much as a stir in the curtains, I took heart, and walked into the room on tiptoe, and looked round again. Then I takes a keek at myself in the big glass; and at last it came in my head, "Why couldn't I ha' a keek at the ald lady herself in the bed?"

'Ye'd think me a fule if ye knew half how I longed to see Dame Crowl, and I thought to myself if I didn't peep now I might wait many a day before I got so gude a chance again.

'Well, my dear, I came to the side o' the bed, the curtains bein' close, and my heart a'most failed me. But I took courage, and I slips my finger in between the thick curtains, and then my hand. So I waits a bit, but all was still as death. So, softly, softly I draws the curtain, and there, sure enough, I sid before me, stretched out like the painted lady on the tomb-stean in

Lexhoe Church, the famous Dame Crowl, of Applewale House. There she was, dressed out. You never sid the like in they days. Satin and silk, and scarlet and green, and gold and pint lace; by Jen! 'twas a sight! A big powdered wig, half as high as herself, was a-top o' her head, and, wow!—was ever such wrinkles?—and her old baggy throat all powdered white, and her cheeks rouged, and mouse-skin eyebrows, that Mrs Wyvern used to stick on, and there she lay proud and stark, wi' a pair o' clocked silk hose on, and heels to her shoon as tall as ninepins. Lawk! But her nose was crooked and thin, and half the whites o' her eyes was open. She used to stand, dressed as she was, gigglin' and dribblin' before the lookin'-glass, wi' a fan in her hand and a big nosegay in her bodice. Her wrinkled little hands was stretched down by her sides, and such long nails, all cut into points, I never sid in my days. Could it even a bin the fashion for grit fowk to wear their fingernails so?

'Well, I think ye'd a-bin frightened yourself if ye'd a sid such a sight. I couldn't let go the curtain, nor move an inch, nor take my eyes off her; my very heart stood still. And in an instant she opens her eyes and up she sits, and spins herself round, and down wi' her, wi' a clack on her two tall heels on the floor, facin' me, ogglin' in my face wi' her two great glassy eyes, and a wicked simper wi' her wrinkled lips, and lang fause teeth.

'Well, a corpse is a natural thing; but this was the dreadfullest sight I ever sid. She had her fingers straight out pointin' at me, and her back was crooked, round again wi' age. Says she:

' "Ye little limb! what for did ye say I killed the boy? I'll tickle ye till ye're stiff."

'If I'd a thought an instant, I'd a turned about and run. But I couldn't take my eyes off her, and I backed from her as soon as I could; and she came clatterin' after like a thing on wires, with her fingers pointing to my throat, and she makin' all the time a sound with her tongue like zizz-zizz-zizz.

'I kept backin' and backin' as quick as I could, and her fingers was only a few inches away from my throat, and I felt I'd lose my wits if she touched me.

'I went back this way, right into the corner, and I gev a yellock, ye'd think saul and body was partin', and that minute my aunt, from the door, calls out wi' a blare, and the ald lady turns round on her, and I turns about, and ran through my room, and down the stairs, as hard as my legs could carry me.

'I cried hearty, I can tell you, when I got down to the housekeeper's room. Mrs Wyvern laughed a deal when I told her what had happened. But she changed her key when she heard the ald lady's words.

' "Say them again," says she.

'So I told her.

' "Ye little limb! What for did ye say I killed the boy? I'll tickle ye till ye're stiff."

' "And did ye say she killed a boy?" says she.

' "Not I, ma'am," says I.

'Judith was always up with me, after that, when the two elder women was away from her. I would a jumped out a winda, rather than stay alone in the same room wi' her.

'It was about a week after, as well as I can remember, Mrs Wyvern, one day when me and her was alone, told me a thing about Madam Crowl that I did not know before.

'She being young and a great beauty, full seventy year before, had married Squire Crowl, of Applewale. But he was a widower, and had a son about nine years old.

'There never was tale or tidings of this boy after one mornin'. No one could say where he went to. He was allowed too much liberty, and used to be off in the morning, one day, to the keeper's cottage and breakfast wi' him, and away to the warren, and not home, mayhap, till evening; and another time down to the lake, and bathe there, and spend the day fishin' there, or paddlin' about in the boat. Well, no one could say what was gone wi' him; only this, that his hat was found by the lake, under a haathorn that grows thar to this day, and 'twas thought he was drowned bathin'. And the squire's son, by his second marriage, with this Madam Crowl that lived sa dreadful lang, came in far the estates. It was his son, the ald lady's grandson, Squire Chevenix Crowl, that owned the estates at the time I came to Applewale.

'There was a deal o' talk lang before my aunt's time about it; and 'twas said the step-mother knew more than she was like to let out. And she managed her husband, the ald squire, wi' her white-heft and flatteries. And as the boy was never seen more, in course of time the thing died out of fowks' minds.

'I'm goin' to tell ye noo about what I sid wi' my own een.

'I was not there six months, and it was winter time, when the ald lady took her last sickness.

'The doctor was afeard she might a took a fit o' madness, as she did fifteen years befoore, and was buckled up, many a time, in a strait-waistcoat, which was the very leathern jerkin I sid in the closet, off my aunt's room.

'Well, she didn't. She pined, and windered, and went off, torflin', torflin', quiet enough, till a day or two before her flittin', and then she took to rabblin', and sometimes skirlin' in the bed, ye'd think a robber had a knife to her throat, and she used to work out o' the bed, and not being strong enough, then, to walk or stand, she'd fall on the flure, wi' her ald wizened hands stretched before her face, and skirlin' still for mercy.

'Ye may guess I didn't go into the room, and I used to be shiverin' in my bed wi' fear, at her skirlin' and scrafflin' on the flure, and blarin' out words that id make your skin turn blue.

'My aunt, and Mrs Wyvern, and Judith Squailes, and a woman from Lexhoe, was always about her. At last she took fits, and they wore her out.

'"T" sir was there, and prayed for her; but she was past praying with. I suppose it was right, but none could think there was much good in it, and sa at lang last she made her flittin', an a' was over, and old Dame Crowl was shrouded and coffined, and Squire Chevenix was wrote for. But he was away in France, and the delay was sa lang, that t' sir and doctor both agreed it would not du to keep her langer out o' her place, and no one cared but just them two, and my aunt and the rest o' us, from Applewale, to go to the buryin'. So the old lady of Applewale was laid in the vault under Lexhoe Church; and we lived up at the great house till such time as the squire should come to tell his will about us, and pay off such as he chose to discharge.

'I was put into another room, two doors away from what was Dame Crowl's chamber, after her death, and this thing happened the night before Squire Chevenix came to Applewale.

'The room I was in now was a large square chamber, covered wi' yak panels, but unfurnished except for my bed, which had no curtains to it, and a chair and a table, or so, that looked nothing at all in such a big room. And the big looking-glass, that the old lady used to keek into and admire herself from head to heel, now that there was na mair o' that wark, was put out of the way, and stood against the wall in my room, for there was shiftin' o' many things in her chamber ye may suppose, when she came to be coffined.

'The news had come that day that the squire was to be down next morning at Applewale; and not sorry was I, for I thought I was sure to be sent home again to my mother. And right glad was I, and I was thinkin' of a' at hame, and my sister Janet, and the kitten and the pymag, and Trimmer the tike, and all the rest, and I got sa fidgetty, I couldn't sleep, and the clock struck twelve, and me wide awake, and the room as dark as pick. My back was turned to the door, and my eyes towards the wall opposite.

'Well, it could na be a full quarter past twelve, when I sees a lightin' on the wall befoore me, as if something took fire behind, and the shadas o' the bed, and the chair, and my gown, that was hangin' from the wall, was dancin' up and down on the ceilin' beams and the yak panels; and I turns my head ower my shouther quick, thinkin' something must a gone a' fire.

'And what sud I see, by Jen! but the likeness o' the ald beldame, bedizened out in her satins and velvets, on her dead body, simperin', wi' her eyes as wide as saucers, and her face like the fiend himself. 'Twas a red light that rose about her in a fuffin low, as if her dress round her feet was blazin'. She was drivin' on right for me, wi' her ald shrivelled hands crooked as if she was goin' to claw me. I could not stir, but she passed me straight by, wi' a blast o' cald air, and I sid her, at the wall, in the alcove as my aunt used to call it, which was a recess where the state bed used to stand in ald times wi' a door open wide, and her hands gropin' in at somethin' was there. I never sid that door befoore. And she turned round to me, like a thing on a pivot, flyrin', and all at once the room was dark, and I standin' at the far side o' the bed; I don't know how I got there, and I found my tongue at last, and if I did na blare a yellock, rennin' down the gallery and almost pulled Mrs Wyvern's door off t' hooks, and frighted her half out o' wits.

'Ye may guess I did na sleep that night; and wi' the first light, down wi' me to my aunt, as fast as my two legs cud carry me.

'Well, my aunt did na frump or flite me, as I thought she would, but she held me by the hand, and looked hard in my face all the time. And she telt me not to be feared; and says she:

' "Hed the appearance a key in its hand?"

' "Yes," says I, bringin' it to mind; "a big key in a queer brass handle."

' "Stop a bit," says she, lettin' go ma hand, and openin' the cupboard-door. "Was it like this?" says she, takin' one out in her fingers, and showing it to me, with a dark look in my face.

' "That was it," says I, quick enough.

' "Are ye sure?" she says, turnin' it round.

' "Sart," says I, and I felt like I was gain' to faint when I sid it.

' "Well that will do, child," says she, saftly thinkin', and she locked it up again.

' "The squire himself will be here today, before twelve o'clock, and ye must tell him all about it," says she, thinkin', "and I suppose I'll be leavin' soon, and so the best thing for the present is, that ye should go home this afternoon, and I'll look out another place for you when I can."

'Fain was I, ye may guess, at that word.

'My aunt packed up my things for me, and the three pounds that was due to me, to bring home, and Squire Crowl himself came down to Applewale that day, a handsome man, about thirty years ald. It was the second time I sid him. But this was the first time he spoke to me.

'My aunt talked wi' him in the housekeeper's room, and I don't know what they said. I was a bit feared on the squire, he bein' a great gentleman down in Lexhoe, and I darn't go near till I was called. And says he, smilin':

' "What's a' this ye a sen, child? It mun be a dream, for ye know there's na sic a thing as a bo or a freet in a' the world. But whatever it was, ma little maid, sit ye down and tell all about it from first to last."

'Well, so soon as I made an end, he thought a bit, and says he to my aunt:

' "I mind the place well. In old Sir Olivur's time lame Wyndel told me there was a door in that recess, to the left, where the lassie dreamed she saw my grandmother open it. He was past eighty when he told me that, and I but a boy. It's twenty year sen. The plate and jewels used to be kept there, long ago, before the iron closet was made in the arras chamber, and he told me the key had a brass handle, and this ye say was found in the bottom o' the kist where she kept her old fans. Now, would not it be a queer thing if we found some spoons or diamonds forgot there? Ye mun come up wi' us, lassie, and point to the very spot."

'Loth was I, and my heart in my mouth, and fast I held by my aunt's hand as I stept into that awesome room, and showed them both how she came and passed me by, and the spot where she stood, and where the door seemed to open.

'There was an ald empty press against the wall then, and shoving it aside, sure enough there was the tracing of a door in the wainscot, and a keyhole stopped with wood, and planed across as smooth as the rest, and the joining of the door all stopped wi' putty the colour o' yak, and, but for the hinge that showed a bit when the press was shoved aside, ye would not consayt there was a door there at all.

' "Ha!" says he, wi' a queer smile, "this looks like it."

'It took some minutes wi' a small chisel and hammer to pick the bit o' wood out o' the keyhole. The key fitted, sure enough, and, wi' a strang twist and a lang skreak, the boult went back and he pulled the door open.

'There was another door inside, stranger than the first, but the lacks was gone, and it opened easy. Inside was a narrow floor and walls and vault o' brick; we could not see what was in it, for 'twas dark as pick.

'When my aunt had lighted the candle, the squire held it up and stept in.

'My aunt stood on tiptoe tryin' to look over his shouther, and I did na see nout.

' "Ha! ha!" says the squire, steppin' backward. "What's that? Gi' ma the poker—quick!' says he to my aunt. And as she went to the hearth I peeps beside his arm, and I sid squat down in the far corner a monkey or a flayin' on the chest, or else the maist shrivelled up, wizzened ald wife that ever was sen on yearth.

' "By Jen!" says my aunt, as puttin' the poker in his hand she keeked by his shouther, and sid the ill-favoured thing, "hae a care, sir, what ye're doin'. Back wi' ye, and shut to the door!"

'But in place o' that he steps in saftly, wi' the poker pointed like a swoord, and he gies it a poke, and down it a' tumbles together, head and a', in a heap o' bayans and dust, little meyar an' a hatful.

' 'Twas the bayans o' a child; a' the rest went to dust at a touch. They said nout for a while, but he turns round the skull, as it lay on the floor.

'Young as I was, I consayted I knew well enough what they was thinkin' on.

' "A dead cat!" says he, pushin' back and blowin' out the candle, and shuttin' to the door. "We'll come back, you and me, Mrs Shutters, and look on the shelves by-and-bye. I've other matters first to speak to ye about; and this little girl's goin' hame, ye say. She has her wages, and I mun mak' her a present," says he, pattin' my shouther wi' his hand.

'And he did gimma a goud pound and I went aff to Lexhoe about an hour after, and sa hame by the stage-coach, and fain was I to be at hame again; and I never sid Dame Crowl o' Applewale, God be thanked, either in appearance or in dream, at-efter. But when I was grown to be a woman, my aunt spent a day and night wi' me at Littleham, and she telt me there was no doubt it was the poor little boy that was missing sa lang sen, that was shut up to die thar in the dark by that wicked beldame, whar his skirls, or his prayers, or his thumpin' cud na be heard, and his hat was left by the water's edge, whoever did it, to mak' belief he was drowned. The clothes, at the first touch, a' ran into a snuff o' dust in the cell whar the bayans was found. But there was a handful o' jet buttons, and a knife with a green heft, together wi' a couple o' pennies the poor little fella had in his pocket. I suppose, when he was decoyed in thar, and sid his last o' the light. And there was, amang the squire's papers, a copy o' the notice that was prented after he was lost, when the ald squire thought he might 'a run away, or bin took by gipsies, and it said he had a green-hefted knife wi' him, and that his buttons were o' cut jet. Sa that is a' I hev to say consarnin' ald Dame Crowl, o' Applewale House.'

THE COLD EMBRACE

MARY ELIZABETH BRADDON

He was an artist—such things as happened to him happen sometimes to artists.

He was a German—such things as happened to him happen sometimes to Germans.

He was young, handsome, studious, enthusiastic, metaphysical, reckless, unbelieving, heartless.

And being young, handsome, and eloquent, he was beloved.

He was an orphan, under the guardianship of his dead father's brother, his uncle Wilhelm, in whose house he had been brought up from a little child; and she who loved him was his cousin—his cousin Gertrude, whom he swore he loved in return.

Did he love her? Yes, when he first swore it. It soon wore out, this passionate love; how threadbare and wretched a sentiment it became at last in the selfish heart of the student! But in its first golden dawn, when he was only nineteen, and had just returned from his apprenticeship to a great painter at Antwerp, and they wandered together in the most romantic outskirts of the city at rosy sunset, by holy moonlight, or bright and joyous morning, how beautiful a dream!

They keep it a secret from Wilhelm, as he has the father's ambition of a wealthy suitor for his only child—a cold and dreary vision beside the lover's dream.

So they are betrothed; and standing side by side, when the dying sun and the pale rising moon divide the heavens, he puts the betrothal ring upon her finger, the white and tapered finger whose slender shape he knows so well. This ring is a peculiar one, a massive golden serpent, its tail in its mouth, the symbol of eternity; it had been his mother's, and he would know it amongst a thousand. If he were to become blind tomorrow, he could select it from amongst a thousand by the touch alone.

He places it on her finger, and they swear to be true to each other for ever and ever—through trouble and danger—in sorrow and change—in wealth and poverty. Her father must needs be won to consent to their union by and by, for they were now betrothed, and death alone could part them.

But the young student, the scoffer at revelation, yet the enthusiastic adorer of the mystical asks:

'Can death part us? I would return to you from the grave, Gertrude. My soul would come back to be near my love. And you—you, if you died before me—the cold earth would not hold you from me; if you loved me, you would return, and again these fair arms would be clasped round my neck as they are now.'

But she told him, with a holier light in her deep-blue eyes than had ever shone in his—she told him that the dead who die at peace with God are happy in heaven, and cannot return to the troubled earth; and that it is only the suicide—the lost wretch on whom sorrowful angels shut the door of Paradise—whose unholy spirit haunts the footsteps of the living.

The first year of their betrothal is passed, and she is alone, for he has gone to Italy, on a commission for some rich man, to copy Raphaels, Titians, Guidos, in a gallery at Florence. He has gone to win fame, perhaps; but it is not the less bitter—he is gone!

Of course her father misses his young nephew, who has been as a son to him; and he thinks his daughter's sadness no more than a cousin should feel for a cousin's absence.

In the meantime, the weeks and months pass. The lover writes—often at first, then seldom—at last, not at all.

How many excuses she invents for him! How many times she goes to the distant little post-office, to which he is to address his letters! How many times she hopes, only to be disappointed! How many times she despairs only to hope again!

But real despair comes at last, and will not be put off any more. The rich suitor appears on the scene, and her father is determined. She is to marry at once. The wedding-day is fixed—the fifteenth of June.

The date seems burnt into her brain.

The date, written in fire, dances for ever before her eyes.

The date, shrieked by the Furies, sounds continually in her ears.

But there is time yet—it is the middle of May—there is time for a letter to reach him at Florence; there is time for him to come to Brunswick, to take her away and marry her, in spite of her father—in spite of the whole world.

But the days and weeks fly by, and he does not write—he does not come. This is indeed despair which usurps her heart, and will not be put away.

It is the fourteenth of June. For the last time she goes to the little post-office; for the last time she asks the old question, and they give her for the last time the dreary answer, 'No; no letter.'

For the last time—for tomorrow is the day appointed for her bridal. Her father will hear no entreaties; her rich suitor will not listen to her prayers. They will not be put off a day—an hour; tonight alone is hers—this night, which she may employ as she will.

She takes another path than that which leads home; she hurries through some by-streets of the city, out on to a lonely bridge, where he and she had stood so often in the sunset, watching the rose-coloured light glow, fade, and die upon the river.

He returns from Florence. He had received her letter. That letter, blotted with tears, entreating, despairing—he had received it, but he loved her no longer. A young Florentine, who has sat to him for a model, had bewitched his fancy—that fancy which with him stood in place of a heart—and Gertrude had been half-forgotten. If she had a richer suitor, good; let her marry him; better for her, better far for himself. He had no wish to fetter himself with a wife. Had he not his art always?—his eternal bride, his unchanging mistress.

Thus he thought it wiser to delay his journey to Brunswick, so that he should arrive when the wedding was over—arrive in time to salute the bride.

And the vows—the mystical fancies—the belief in his return, even after death, to the embrace of his beloved? O, gone out of his life; melted away for ever, those foolish dreams of his boyhood.

So on the fifteenth of June he enters Brunswick, by that very bridge on which she stood, the stars looking down on her, the night before. He strolls across the bridge and down by the water's edge, a great rough dog at his heels, and the smoke from his short meerschaum-pipe curling in blue wreaths fantastically in the pure morning air. He has his sketch-book under his arm, and attracted now and then by some object that catches his artist's eye, stops to draw; a few weeds and pebbles on the river's brink—a crag on the opposite shore—a group of pollard willows in the distance. When he has done, he admires his drawing, shuts his sketch-book, empties the ashes from his pipe, refills from this tobacco-pouch, sings the refrain of a gay drinking-song, calls to his dog, smokes again, and walks on. Suddenly he opens his sketch-book again; this time that which attracts him is a group of figures: but what is it?

It is not a funeral, for there are no mourners.

It is not a funeral, but it is a corpse lying on a rude bier, covered with an old sail, carried between two bearers.

It is not a funeral, for the bearers are fishermen—fishermen in their everyday garb.

About a hundred yards from him they rest their burden on a bank—one stands at the head of the bier, the other throws himself down at the foot of it.

And thus they form a perfect group; he walks back two or three paces, selects his point of sight, and begins to sketch a hurried outline. He has finished it before they move; he hears their voices, though he cannot hear their words, and wonders what they can be talking of. Presently he walks on and joins them.

'You have a corpse there, my friends?' he says.

'Yes; a corpse washed ashore an hour ago.'

'Drowned?'

'Yes, drowned. A young girl, very handsome.'

'Suicides are always handsome,' says the painter; and then he stands for a little while idly smoking and meditating, looking at the sharp outline of the corpse and the stiff folds of the rough canvas covering.

Life is such a golden holiday for him—young, ambitious, clever—that it seems as though sorrow and death could have no part in his destiny.

At last he says that, as this poor suicide is so handsome, he should like to make a sketch of her.

He gives the fishermen some money, and they offer to remove the sail-cloth that covers her features.

No; he will do it himself. He lifts the rough, coarse, wet canvas from her face. What face?

The face that shone on the dreams of his foolish boyhood; the face which once was the light of his uncle's home. His cousin Gertrude—his betrothed!

He sees, as in one glance, while he draws one breath, the rigid features—the marble arms—the hands crossed on the cold bosom; and, on the third finger of the left hand, the ring which had been his mother's—the golden serpent; the ring which, if he were to become blind, he could select from a thousand others by the touch alone.

But he is a genius and a metaphysician—grief, true grief, is not for such as he. His first thought is flight—flight anywhere out of that accursed city—anywhere far from the brink of that hideous river—anywhere away from memory, away from remorse—anywhere to forget.

He is miles on the road that leads away from Brunswick before he knows that he has walked a step.

It is only when his dog lies down panting at his feet that he feels how exhausted he is himself, and sits down upon a bank to rest. How the landscape spins round and round before his dazzled eyes, while his morning's sketch of the two fishermen and the canvas-covered bier glares redly at him out of the twilight!

At last, after sitting a long time by the roadside, idly playing with his dog, idly smoking, idly lounging, looking as any idle, light-hearted travelling student might look, yet all the while acting over that morning's scene in his burning brain a hundred times a minute; at last he grows a little more composed, and tries presently to think of himself as he is, apart from his cousin's suicide. Apart from that, he was no worse off than he was yesterday. His genius was not gone; the money he had earned at Florence still lined his pocket-book; he was his own master, free to go whither he would.

And while he sits on the roadside, trying to separate himself from the scene of that morning—trying to put away the image of the corpse covered with the damp canvas sail—trying to think of what he should do next, where he should go, to be farthest away from Brunswick and remorse, the old diligence comes rumbling and jingling along. He remembers it; it goes from Brunswick to Aix-la-Chapelle.

He whistles to his dog, shouts to the postillion to stop, and springs into the *coupé*.

During the whole evening, through the long night, though he does not once close his eyes, he never speaks a word; but when morning dawns, and the other passengers awake and begin to talk to each other, he joins in the conversation. He tells them that he is an artist, that he is going to Cologne and to Antwerp to copy the Rubenses, and the great picture by Quentin Matsys, in the museum. He remembered afterwards that he talked and laughed boisterously, and that when he was talking and laughing loudest, a passenger, older and graver than the rest, opened the window near him, and told him to put his head out. He remembered the fresh air blowing in his face, the singing of the birds in his ears, and the flat fields and roadside reeling before his eyes. He remembered this, and then falling in a lifeless heap on the floor of the diligence.

It is a fever that keeps him for six long weeks laid on a bed at a hotel in Aix-la-Chapelle.

He gets well, and, accompanied by his dog, starts on foot for Cologne. By this time he is his former self once more. Again the blue smoke from his short meerschaum curls upwards in the morning air—again he sings some old university drinking-song—again stops here and there, meditating and sketching.

He is happy, and has forgotten his cousin—and so on to Cologne.

It is by the great cathedral he is standing, with his dog at his side. It is night, the bells have just chimed the hour, and the clocks are striking eleven; the moonlight shines full upon the magnificent pile, over which the artist's eye wanders, absorbed in the beauty of form.

He is not thinking of his drowned cousin, for he has forgotten her and is happy.

Suddenly someone, something from behind him, puts two cold arms round his neck, and clasps its hands on his breast.

And yet there is no one behind him, for on the flags bathed in the broad moonlight there are only two shadows, his own and his dog's. He turns quickly round—there is no one—nothing to be seen in the broad square but himself and his dog; and though he feels, he cannot see the cold arms clasped round his neck.

It is not ghostly, this embrace, for it is palpable to the touch—it cannot be real, for it is invisible.

He tries to throw off the cold caress. He clasps the hands in his own to tear them asunder, and to cast them off his neck. He can feel the long delicate fingers cold and wet beneath his touch, and on the third finger of the left hand he can feel the ring which was his mother's—the golden serpent—the ring which he has always said he would know among a thousand by the touch alone. He knows it now!

His dead cousin's cold arms are round his neck—his dead cousin's wet hands are clasped upon his breast. He asks himself if he is mad. 'Up, Leo!' he shouts. 'Up, up, boy!' and the Newfoundland leaps to his shoulders—the dog's paws are on the dead hands, and the animal utters a terrific howl, and springs away from his master.

The student stands in the moonlight, the dead arms around his neck, and the dog at a little distance moaning piteously.

Presently a watchman, alarmed by the howling of the dog, comes into the square to see what is wrong.

In a breath the cold arms are gone.

He takes the watchman home to the hotel with him and gives him money; in his gratitude he could have given that man half his little fortune.

Will it ever come to him again, this embrace of the dead?

He tries never to be alone; he makes a hundred acquaintances, and shares the chamber of another student. He starts up if he is left by himself in the public room at the inn where he is staying, and runs into the street. People notice his strange actions, and begin to think that he is mad.

But, in spite of all, he is alone once more; for one night the public room being empty for a moment, when on some idle pretence he strolls into the street, the street is empty too, and for the second time he feels the cold arms round his neck, and for the second time, when he calls his dog, the animal slinks away from him with a piteous howl.

After this he leaves Cologne, still travelling on foot—of necessity now, for his money is getting low. He joins travelling hawkers, he walks side by side with labourers, he talks to every foot-passenger he falls in with, and tries from morning till night to get company on the road.

At night he sleeps by the fire in the kitchen of the inn at which he stops; but do what he will, he is often alone, and it is now a common thing for him to feel the cold arms around his neck.

Many months have passed since his cousin's death—autumn, winter, early spring. His money is nearly gone, his health is utterly broken, he is the shadow of his former self, and he is getting near Paris. He will reach that city at the time of the Carnival. To this he looks forward. In Paris, in Carnival time, he need never, surely, be alone, never feel that deadly caress; he may even recover his lost gaiety, his lost health, once more resume his profession, once more earn fame and money by his art.

How hard he tries to get over the distance that divides him from Paris, while day by day he grows weaker, and his step slower and more heavy!

But there is an end at last; the long dreary roads are passed. This is Paris, which he enters for the first time—Paris, of which he has dreamed so much—Paris, whose million voices are to exorcise his phantom.

To him tonight Paris seems one vast chaos of lights, music, and confusion—lights which dance before his eyes and will not be still—music that rings in his ears and deafens him—confusion which makes his head whirl round and round.

But, in spite of all, he finds the opera-house, where there is a masked ball. He has enough money left to buy a ticket of admission, and to hire a domino to throw over his shabby dress. It seems only a moment after his entering the gates of Paris that he is in the very midst of all the wild gaiety of the opera-house ball.

No more darkness, no more loneliness, but a mad crowd, shouting and dancing, and a lovely Debardeuse hanging on his arm.

The boisterous gaiety he feels surely is his old light-heartedness come back. He hears the people round him talking of the outrageous conduct of some drunken student, and it is to him they point when they say this—to him, who has not moistened his lips since yesterday at noon, for even now he will not drink; though his lips are parched, and his throat burning, he cannot drink. His voice is thick and hoarse, and his utterance indistinct; but still this must be his old light-heartedness come back that makes him so wildly gay.

The little Debardeuse is wearied out—her arm rests on his shoulder heavier than lead—the other dancers one by one drop off.

The lights in the chandeliers one by one die out.

The decorations look pale and shadowy in that dim light which is neither night nor day.

A faint glimmer from the dying lamps, a pale streak of cold grey light from the new-born day, creeping in through half-opened shutters.

And by this light the bright-eyed Debardeuse fades sadly. He looks her in the face. How the brightness of her eyes dies out! Again he looks her in the face. How white that face has grown! Again—and now it is the shadow of a face alone that looks in his.

Again—and they are gone—the bright eyes, the face, the shadow of the face. He is alone; alone in that vast saloon.

Alone, and, in the terrible silence, he hears the echoes of his own footsteps in that dismal dance which has no music.

No music but the beating of his heart against his breast. For the cold arms are round his neck—they whirl him round, they will not be flung off, or cast away; he can no more escape from their icy grasp than he can escape from death. He looks behind him—there is nothing but himself in the great empty *salle;* but he can feel—cold, deathlike, but oh, how palpable!—the long slender fingers, and the ring which was his mother's.

He tries to shout, but he has no power in his burning throat. The silence of the place is only broken by the echoes of his own footsteps in the dance from which he cannot extricate himself. Who says he has no partner? The cold hands are clasped on his breast, and now he does not shun their caress. No! One more polka, if he drops down dead.

The lights are all out, and, half an hour after, the *gendarmes* come in with a lantern to see that the house is empty; they are followed by a great dog that they have found seated howling on the steps of the theatre. Near the principal entrance they stumble over—

The body of a student, who has died from want of food, exhaustion, and the breaking of a blood-vessel.

AT RAVENHOLME JUNCTION

ANONYMOUS

'Were you ever out in a more wretched night in your life?' asked Harry Luscombe in a tone of disgust, as we were trudging wearily along after a full half-hour of absolute silence.

The rain was certainly coming down 'with a vengeance', as people say. We had been out all day fishing in some private waters about ten miles from home. A friend had given us a lift in his trap the greater part of the way in going, and we had arranged to walk back, never dreaming that the sunny day would resolve itself into so wet an evening. Fortunately, each of us had taken a light mackintosh, and we had on our thick fishing-boots, otherwise our plight would have been much worse than it was.

'Wretched night!' again ejaculated Harry, whose pipe the rain would persist in putting out.

'But surely we cannot be far from the Grange now?' I groaned.

'A good four miles yet, old fellow,' answered my friend. 'We must grin and bear it.'

For ten more minutes we paced the slushy road in moist silence.

'I wouldn't have cared so much,' growled Harry at last, 'if we had only a decent lot of fish to take home. Won't Gerty and the governor chaff us in the morning!'

I winced. Harry had touched a sore point. I rather prided myself on my prowess with rod and line; yet here was I, after eight hours' patient flogging of the water, going back to the Grange with a creel that I should blush to open when I got there. It was most annoying.

By-and-by we came to a stile, crossing which we found a footpath through the meadows, just faintly visible in the dark. The footpath, in time, brought us to a level crossing over the railway. But instead of crossing the iron road to the fields beyond, as I expected he would do, Harry turned half round and began to walk along the line. 'Where on earth are you leading me to?' I asked, as I stumbled and barked my shins over a heap of loose sleepers by the side of the rails, 'Seest thou not yonder planets that flame so brightly in the midnight sky?' he exclaimed, pointing to two railway signals clearly visible some quarter of a mile away. 'Thither are we bound. Disturb not the meditations of a great mind by further foolish questionings.'

I was too damp to retort as I might otherwise have done, so I held my peace and stumbled quietly after him. Little by little we drew nearer to the signal lamps, till at last we stood close under them. They shone far and high above our heads, being, in fact, the crowning points of two tall semaphore posts. But we were not going quite so far skyward as the lamps, our destination being the signalman's wooden hut from which the semaphores were worked. This of itself stood some distance above the ground, being built on substantial posts driven firmly into the embankment. It was reached by a flight of wooden steps, steep and narrow. We saw by the light shining from its windows that it was not without an occupant. Harry put a couple of fingers to his mouth and whistled shrilly. 'Jim Crump,' he shouted, 'Jim Crump—Hi! Where are you?'

'Is that you, Mr Harry?' said a voice, and then the door above us was opened. 'Wait a moment, sir, till I get my lantern. The steps are slippery with the rain, and one of them is broken.'

'You see, my governor is one of the managing directors of this line,' said Harry, in explanation, while we were waiting for the lantern, 'so that I can come and go, and do pretty much as I like about here.'

'But why have you come here at all?' I asked.

'For the sake of a rest and a smoke, and a talk with Jim Crump about his dogs.'

Two minutes later and we had mounted the steps, and for the first time in my life I found myself in a signalman's box.

It was a snug little place enough, but there was not much room to spare. There were windows on three sides of it, so that the man on duty might have a clear view both up and down the line. Five or six long iron levers were fixed in a row below the front window. The due and proper manipulation of these levers, which were connected by means of rods and chains with the points and signals outside, and the working of the simple telegraphic apparatus which placed him *en rapport* with the stations nearest to him, up and down, were the signalman's sole but onerous duties. Both the box and the lamps overhead were lighted with gas brought from the town, two miles away.

'I have been wanting to see you for the last two or three weeks, Mr Harry,' said Crump, a well-built man of thirty, with clear resolute eyes and a firm-set mouth.

'Ay, ay. What's the game now, Crump? Got some more of that famous tobacco?'

'Something better than the tobacco, Mr Harry. I've got a bull terrier pup for you. Such a beauty!'

'The dickens you have!' cried Harry, his eyes all a-sparkle with delight. 'Crump, you are a brick. A bull terrier pup is the very thing I've been hankering after for the last three months. Have you got it here?'

'No, it's at home. You see, I didn't know that you were coming tonight.'

Harry's countenance fell. 'That's a pity now, isn't it?'

'It don't rain near so fast as it did,' said Crump, 'and if you would like to take the pup with you, I'll just run home and fetch it. I can go there and back in twenty minutes. It's agen the rules to leave my box, I know, and I wouldn't leave it for anybody but you; and not even for you, Mr Harry, if I didn't know that you knew how to work the levers and the telly a'most as well as I do myself. Besides all that, there will be nothing either up or down till twelve-thirty. What say you, sir?'

'I say go by all means, Crump. You may depend on my looking well after the signals while you are away.'

'Right you are, sir.' And Crump proceeded to pull on his overcoat.

'I wish I could make you more comfortable, sir,' said Crump to me. 'But this is only a roughish place.'

Harry and I sat down on a sort of bunk or locker at the back of the box. Harry produced his flask, which he had filled with brandy before leaving the hotel. Crump declined any of the proffered spirit, but accepted a cigar. Then he pulled up the collar of his coat and went. In the pauses of our talk we could hear the moaning of the telegraph wires outside as the invisible fingers of the wind touched them in passing.

'This is Ravenholme Junction,' said Harry to me.

'Is it, indeed? Much obliged for the information,' I answered drily.

'About two years ago a terrible accident happened close to this spot. No doubt you read about it at the time.'

'Possibly so. But if I did, the facts have escaped my memory.'

'The news was brought to the Grange, and I was on the spot in less than three hours after the smash. I shall never forget what I saw that night.' He smoked in grave silence for a little while, and then he spoke again. 'I don't know whether you are acquainted with the railway geography of this district, but Ravenholme—I am speaking of the village, which is nearly two miles away—is on a branch line, which diverges from the main line some six miles north of this box, and after zigzagging among various busy townships and hamlets, joins the main line again about a dozen miles south of the point where it diverged; thus forming what is known as the Ravenholme Loop Line. None of the main line trains run over the loop. Passengers from it going to any place on the main line have to change from the local trains at either the north or south junction, according to the direction they intend to travel.'

I wondered why he was telling me this.

'You will understand from this that the junction where we are now is rather an out-of-the-way spot—out of the way, that is, of any great bustle of railway traffic. It forms, in fact, the point of connection between the Ravenholme Loop and a single line of rails which turns off to the left about a hundred yards from here, and gives access to a cluster of important collieries belonging to Lord Exbrooke; and the duty of Crump is, by means of his signals, to guard against the possibility of a collision between the coal trains coming off the colliery line and the ordinary trains passing up and down the loop. You will readily comprehend that, at a quiet place like this, a signalman has not half the work to do, nor half the responsibility to labour under, of a man in a similar position at some busy junction on the main line. In fact, a signalman at Ravenholme Junction may emphatically be said to have an easy time of it.'

I nodded.

'Some two years ago, however, it so fell out that an abutment of one of the bridges on the main line was so undermined by heavy floods that instructions had to be given for no more trains to pass over it till it had been thoroughly repaired. In order to prevent any interruption of traffic, it was decided that till the necessary repairs could be effected all main line trains should work, for the time being, over the Ravenholme Loop. As it was arranged so it was carried out.'

'Well?'

'The signalman at that time in charge of this box was named Dazeley—a shy, nervous sort of man, as I have been told, lacking in self-confidence, and not to be depended upon in any unforeseen emergency. Such as he was, however, he had been at Ravenholme for three years, and had always performed the duties of his situation faithfully and well. As soon as the main line trains began to travel by the new route, another man was sent from headquarters to assist Dazeley—there had been no night-work previously. The men came on duty turn and turn about, twelve hours on and twelve hours off, the man who was on by day one week being on by night the following week.'

'Go on.'

'It is said that Dazeley soon began to look worn and depressed, and that he became more nervous and wanting in self-confidence than ever. Be that as it may, he never spoke a complaining word to anyone, but went on doing his duty in the silent depressed way habitual with him. One morning when he was coming off duty—it was his turn for night-work that week—his mate was taken suddenly ill and was obliged to go home again. There was no help for it: Dazeley was obliged to take the sick man's place for the day. When evening came round, his mate sent word that he was somewhat better, but not well enough to resume work before morning; so Dazeley had to take his third consecutive spell of twelve hours in the box. You see, Ravenholme is a long way from headquarters, and in any case it would have taken some time to get assistance; besides which, Dazeley expected that a few hours at the very most would see his mate thoroughly recovered. So nothing was said or done.'

I was growing interested.

'The night mail from south to north was timed to pass Ravenholme Junction, without stopping, at 11.40. On the particular night to which we now come—the night of the accident—it is supposed that poor Dazeley, utterly worn out for want of rest, had lain down for a minute or two on this very bunk, and had there dropped off to sleep, his signals, as was usual at that hour, standing at 'all clear.' Had he remained asleep till after the mail had passed all would have been well, everything being clear for its safe transit past the junction; but unfortunately the night was somewhat foggy, and the engine-driver, not being able to see the lamps at the usual distance, blew his whistle loudly. Roused by the shrill summons, Dazeley, as it is supposed, started suddenly to his feet, and his brain being still muddled with sleep, he grasped one of the familiar levers, and all unconscious of what he was doing, he turned the mail train on to the single line that led to the collieries.'

'Oh!'

'The consequences were terrible. Some two or three hundred yards down the colliery line a long coal train was waiting for the mail to pass before proceeding on its journey. Into this train the mail dashed at head-long speed. Two people were killed on the spot, and twenty or thirty more or less hurt.'

'How dreadful!'

'When they came to look for Dazeley he was not to be found. Horror-stricken at the terrible consequences of his act he had fled. A warrant for his arrest was obtained. He was found four days afterwards in a wood, hanging to the bough of a tree, dead. One of his hands clasped a scrap of paper on which a few half-illegible words had been scrawled, the purport of which was that after what had happened he could no longer bear to live.'

'A sad story, truly,' I said, as Harry finished. 'It seems to me that the poor fellow was to be pitied more than blamed.

'Crump's twenty minutes are rather long ones,' said Harry, as he looked at his watch. 'It is now thirty-eight minutes past eleven. No chance of getting home till long after midnight.'

The rain was over and the wind had gone with it. Not a sound was audible save now and again the faint moaning of the telegraph wires overhead. Harry crossed to the window and opened one of the three casements. 'A breath of fresh air will be welcome,' he said. 'The gas makes this little place unbearable.' Having opened the window he came back again and sat down beside me on the bunk.

Hardly had Harry resumed his seat, when all at once the gas sank down as though it were going out, but next moment it was burning as brightly as before. An icy shiver ran through me from head to foot. I turned my head to glance at Harry, and as I did so I saw, to my horror, that we were no longer alone. There had been but two of us only a moment before: the door had not been opened, yet now we were three. Sitting in a low wooden chair close to the levers, and with his head resting on them, was a stranger, to all appearance fast asleep!

I never before experienced the feeling of awful dread that crept over me at that moment, and I hope never to do so again. I knew instinctively that the figure before me was no corporeal being, no creature of flesh and blood like ourselves. My heart seemed to contract, my blood to congeal: my hands and feet turned cold as ice: the roots of my hair were stirred with a creeping horror that I had no power to control. I could not move my eyes from that sleeping figure. It was Dazeley come back again: a worn, haggard-looking man, restless, and full of nervous twitchings even in his sleep.

'Listen!' said Harry, almost inaudibly, to me. I wanted to look at him, I wanted to see whether he was affected in the same way that I was, but for the life of me I could not turn my eyes away from that sleeping phantom.

Listening as he bade me, I could just distinguish the first low dull murmur made by an on-coming train while it is still a mile or more away. It was a murmur that grew and deepened with every second, swelling gradually into the hoarse inarticulate roar of an express train coming towards us at full speed. Suddenly the whistle sounded its loud, shrill, imperative summons. For one moment I tore my eyes away from the sleeping figure. Yonder, a quarter, or it might be half a mile away, but being borne towards us in a wild rush of headlong fury, was plainly visible the glowing Cyclopean eye of the coming train. Still the whistle sounded, painful, intense—agonised, one might almost fancy.

Louder and louder grew the heavy thunderous beat of the train. It was close upon us now. Suddenly the sleeping figure started to its feet—pressed its hands to its head for a moment as though lost in doubt—gave one wild, frenzied glance round—and then seizing one of the levers with both hands, pulled it back and there held it.

A sudden flash—a louder roar—and the phantom train had passed us and was plunging headlong into the darkness beyond. The figure let go its hold of the lever, which fell back to its original position. As it did so, a dreadful knowledge seemed all at once to dawn on its face. Surprise, horror, anguish unspeakable—all were plainly depicted on the white, drawn features of the phantom before me. Suddenly it flung up its arms as if in wild appeal to Heaven, then sank coweringly on its knees, and buried its face in both its hands with an expression of misery the most profound.

Next moment the gas gave a flicker as though it were going out, and when I looked again Harry and I were alone. The phantom of the unhappy signalman had vanished: the noise of the phantom train had faded into silence. No sound was audible save the unceasing monotone of the electric wires above us. Harry was the first to break the spell.

'Today is the eighth of September,' he said, 'and it was on the eighth of September, two years ago, that the accident happened, I had forgotten the date till this moment.'

At this instant the door opened, and in came Jim Crump with the puppy under his arm. Struck with something in our faces he looked from one to the other of us, and did not speak for a few seconds, 'Here be the pup, sir,' he said at last, 'and a reg'lar little beauty I call her.'

'Was it not two years ago this very night that the accident took place?' asked Harry, as he took the puppy out of Crump's arms into his own.

Crump reflected for a few moments. 'Yes, sir, that it was though I'd forgotten it. It was on the eighth of September, I ought to know, because it was on that very night my youngster was born.'

'Were you signalman here on the eighth of September last year—the year after the accident?'

'No, sir, a man of the name of Moffat was here then, I came on the twentieth of September. Moffat was ordered to be moved. They said he had gone a little bit queer in his head. He went about saying that Dazeley's ghost had shown itself to him in this very box, and that he saw and heard a train come past that wasn't a train, and I don't know what bosh; so it was thought best to remove him.'

'We thought just now—my friend and I—that we heard a train coming,' said Harry as he gently stroked the puppy. 'Did you hear anything as you came along?'

'Nothing whatever, sir. Had a train been coming I must have heard it, because I walked from my house up the line. Besides, there's no train due yet for some time.'

Harry glanced at me. He was evidently not minded to enlighten Crump as to anything we had seen or heard.

Five minutes later we left, carrying the dog with us. Whether or not Harry said anything to his father I don't know. This, however, I do know, that within six months from that time certain alterations were made on the line which necessitated the removal of the signalman's box at Ravenholme Junction to a point half a mile further south. But I have never visited it since that memorable night.

HOW THE THIRD FLOOR KNEW THE POTTERIES

AMELIA B. EDWARDS

I am a plain man, Major, and you may not dislike to hear a plain statement of facts from me. Some of those facts lie beyond my understanding. I do not pretend to explain them. I only know that they happened as I relate them, and that I pledge myself for the truth of every word of them.

I began life roughly enough, down among the Potteries. I was an orphan; and my earliest recollections are of a great porcelain manufactory in the country of the Potteries, where I helped about the yard, picked up what halfpence fell in my way, and slept in a harness-loft over the stable. Those were hard times; but things bettered themselves as I grew older and stronger, especially after George Barnard had come to be foreman of the yard.

George Barnard was a Wesleyan—we were mostly dissenters in the Potteries—sober, clear-headed, somewhat sulky and silent, but a good fellow every inch of him, and my best friend at the time when I most needed a good friend. He took me out of the yard, and set me to the furnace-work. He entered me on the books at a fixed rate of wages. He helped me to pay for a little cheap schooling four nights a week; and he let me go with him on Sundays to the chapel down by the river-side, where I first saw Leah Payne. She was his sweetheart, and so pretty that I used to forget the preacher and everybody else, when I looked at her. When she joined in the singing, I heard no voice but hers. If she asked me for the hymn-book, I used to blush and tremble. I believe I worshipped her, in my stupid igno-rant way; and I think I worshipped Barnard almost as blindly, though after a different fashion. I felt I owed him everything. I knew that he had saved me, body and mind; and I looked up to him as a savage might look up to a missionary.

Leah was the daughter of a plumber, who lived close by the chapel. She was twenty, and George about seven or eight-and-thirty. Some captious folks said there was too much difference in their ages; but she was so serious-minded, and they loved each other so earnestly and quietly, that, if nothing had come between them during their courtship, I don't believe the question of disparity would ever have troubled the happiness of their mar-ried lives. Something did come, however; and that something was a Frenchman, called Louis Laroche. He was a painter on porcelain, from the famous works at Sèvres; and our master, it was said, had engaged him for three years certain, at such wages as none of our own people, however skilful, could hope to command. It was about the beginning or middle of September when he first came among us. He looked very young; was small, dark, and well made; had little white soft hands, and a silky moustache; and spoke English nearly as well as I do. None of us liked him; but that was only natural, seeing how he was put over the head of every Englishman in the place. Besides, though he was always smiling and civil, we couldn't help seeing that he thought himself ever so much better than the rest of us; and that was not pleasant. Neither was it pleasant to see him strolling about the town, dressed just like a gentleman, when working hours were over; smoking good cigars, when we were forced to be content with a pipe of common tobacco; hiring a horse on Sunday afternoons, when we were trudging a-foot; and taking his pleasure as if the world was made for him to enjoy, and us to work in.

'Ben, boy,' said George, 'there's something wrong about that Frenchman.'

It was on a Saturday afternoon, and we were sitting on a pile of empty seggars against the door of my furnace-room, waiting till the men should all have cleared out of the yard. Seggars are deep earthen boxes in which the pottery is put, while being fired in the kiln.

I looked up, inquiringly.

'About the Count?' said I, for that was the nickname by which he went in the pottery.

George nodded, and paused for a moment with his chin resting on his palms.

'He has an evil eye,' said he, 'and a false smile. Something wrong about him.'

I drew nearer, and listened to George as if he had been an oracle.

'Besides,' added he, in his slow quiet way, with his eyes fixed straight before him as if he was thinking aloud, 'there's a young look about him that isn't natural. Take him just at sight, and you'd think he was almost a boy; but look close at him—see the little fine wrinkles under his eyes, and the hard lines about his mouth, and then tell me his age, if you can! Why, Ben boy, he's as old as I am, pretty near; ay, and as strong, too. You stare; but I tell you that, slight as he looks, he could fling you over his shoulder as if you were a feather. And as for his hands, little and white as they are, there are muscles of iron inside them, take my word for it.'

'But, George, how can you know?'

'Because I have a warning against him,' replied George, very gravely. 'Because, whenever he is by, I feel as if my eyes saw clearer, and my ears heard keener, than at other times. Maybe it's presumption, but I sometimes feel as if I had a call to guard myself and others against him. Look at the children,

Ben, how they shrink away from him; and see there, now! Ask Captain what he thinks of him! Ben, that dog likes him no better than I do.'

I looked, and saw Captain crouching by his kennel with his ears laid back, growling audibly, as the Frenchman came slowly down the steps leading from his own workshop at the upper end of the yard. On the last step he paused; lighted a cigar; glanced round, as if to see whether anyone was by; and then walked straight over to within a couple of yards of the kennel. Captain gave a short angry snarl, and laid his muzzle close down upon his paws, ready for a spring. The Frenchman folded his arms deliberately, fixed his eyes on the dog, and stood calmly smoking. He knew exactly how far he dared go, and kept just that one foot out of harm's way. All at once he stooped, puffed a mouthful of smoke in the dog's eyes, burst into a mocking laugh, turned lightly on his heel, and walked away; leaving Captain straining at his chain, and barking after him like a mad creature.

Days went by, and I, at work in my own department, saw no more of the Count. Sunday came—the third, I think, after I had talked with George in the yard. Going with George to chapel, as usual, in the morning, I noticed that there was something strange and anxious in his face, and that he scarcely opened his lips to me on the way. Still I said nothing. It was not my place to question him; and I remember thinking to myself that the cloud would all clear off as soon as he found himself by Leah's side, holding the same book, and joining in the same hymn. It did not, however, for no Leah was there. I looked every moment to the door, expecting to see her sweet face coming in; but George never lifted his eyes from his book, or seemed to notice that her place was empty. Thus the whole service went by, and my thoughts wandered continually from the words of the preacher. As soon as the last blessing was spoken, and we were fairly across the threshold, I turned to George, and asked if Leah was ill?

'No,' said he, gloomily. 'She's not ill.'

'Then why wasn't she—?'

'I'll tell you why,' he interrupted, impatiently. 'Because you've seen her here for the last time. She's never coming to chapel again.'

'Never coming to the chapel again?' I faltered, laying my hand on his sleeve in the earnestness of my surprise. 'Why, George, what is the matter?'

But he shook my hand off, and stamped with his iron heel till the pavement rang again.

'Don't ask me,' said he, roughly. 'Let me alone. You'll know soon enough.'

And with this he turned off down a by-lane leading towards the hills, and left me without another word.

I had had plenty of hard treatment in my time; but never, until that moment, an angry look or syllable from George. I did not know how to bear it. That day my dinner seemed as if it would choke me; and in the afternoon I went out and wandered restlessly about the fields till the hour for evening prayers came round. I then returned to the chapel, and sat down on a tomb outside, waiting for George. I saw the congregation go in by twos and threes; I heard the first psalm-tune echo solemnly through the evening stillness; but no George came. Then the service began, and I knew that, punctual as his habits were, it was of no use to expect him any longer. Where could he be? What could have happened? Why should Leah Payne never come to chapel again? Had she gone over to some other sect, and was that why George seemed so unhappy?

Sitting there in the little dreary churchyard with the darkness fast gathering around me, I asked myself these questions over and over again, till my brain ached; for I was not much used to thinking about anything in those times. At last, I could bear to sit quiet no longer. The sudden thought struck me that I would go to Leah, and learn what the matter was, from her own lips. I sprang to my feet, and set off at once towards her home.

It was quite dark, and a light rain was beginning to fall. I found the garden-gate open, and a quick hope flashed across me that George might be there. I drew back for a moment, hesitating whether to knock or ring, when a sound of voices in the passage, and the sudden gleaming of a bright line of light under the door, warned me that someone was coming out. Taken by surprise, and quite unprepared for the moment with anything to say, I shrank back behind the porch, and waited until those within should have passed out. The door opened, and the light streamed suddenly upon the roses and the wet gravel.

'It rains,' said Leah, bending forward and shading the candle with her hand.

'And is as cold as Siberia,' added another voice, which was not George's, and yet sounded strangely familiar. 'Ugh! what a climate for such a flower as my darling to bloom in!'

'Is it so much finer in France?' asked Leah, softly.

'As much finer as blue skies and sunshine can make it. Why, my angel, even your bright eyes will be ten times brighter, and your rosy cheeks ten times rosier, when they are transplanted to Paris. Ah! I can give you no idea of the wonders of Paris—the broad streets planted with trees, the palaces, the shops, the gardens!—it is a city of enchantment.'

'It must be, indeed!' said Leah. 'And you will really take me to see all those beautiful shops?'

'Every Sunday, my darling—Bah! don't look so shocked. The shops in Paris are always open on Sunday, and everybody makes holiday. You will soon get over these prejudices.'

'I fear it is very wrong to take so much pleasure in the things of this world,' sighed Leah.

The Frenchman laughed, and answered her with a kiss.

'Goodnight, my sweet little saint!' and he ran lightly down the path, and disappeared in the darkness. Leah sighed again, lingered a moment, and then closed the door.

Stupefied and bewildered, I stood for some seconds like a stone statue, unable to move; scarcely able to think. At length, I roused myself, as it were mechanically, and went towards the gate. At that instant a heavy hand was laid upon my shoulder, and a hoarse voice close beside my ear, said:

'Who are you? What are you doing here?'

It was George. I knew him at once, in spite of the darkness, and stammered his name. He took his hand quickly from my shoulder.

'How long have you been here?' said he, fiercely. 'What right have you to lurk about, like a spy in the dark? God help me, Ben—I'm half mad. I don't mean to be harsh to you.'

'I'm sure you don't,' I cried, earnestly.

'It's that cursed Frenchman,' he went on, in a voice that sounded like the groan of one in pain. 'He's a villain. I know he's a villain; and I've had a warning against him ever since the first moment he came among us. He'll make her miserable, and break her heart some day—my pretty Leah—and I loved her so! But I'll be revenged—as sure as there's a sun in heaven, I'll be revenged!'

His vehemence terrified me. I tried to persuade him to go home; but he would not listen to me. 'No, no,' he said. 'Go home yourself, boy, and let me be. My blood is on fire: this rain is good for me, and I am better alone.'

'If I could only do something to help you—'

'You can't,' interrupted he. 'Nobody can help me. I'm a ruined man, and I don't care what becomes of me. The Lord forgive me! my heart is full of wickedness, and my thoughts are the promptings of Satan. There go—for Heaven's sake, go. I don't know what I say, or what I do!'

I went, for I did not dare refuse any longer; but I lingered a while at the corner of the street, and watched him pacing to and fro, to and fro in the driving rain. At length I turned reluctantly away, and went home.

I lay awake that night for hours, thinking over the events of the day, and hating the Frenchman from my very soul. I could not hate Leah. I had worshipped her too long and too faithfully for that; but I looked upon her as a creature given over to destruction. I fell asleep towards morning, and woke again shortly after daybreak. When I reached the pottery, I found George there before me, looking very pale, but quite himself, and setting the men to their work the same as usual. I said nothing about what had happened the day before. Something in his face silenced me; but seeing him so steady and composed, I took heart, and began to hope he had fought through the worst of his trouble. By-and-by the Frenchman came through the yard, gay and off-hand, with his cigar in his mouth, and his hands in his pockets. George turned sharply away into one of the workshops, and shut the door. I drew a deep breath of relief. My dread was to see them come to an open quarrel; and I felt that as long as they kept clear of that, all would be well.

Thus the Monday went by, and the Tuesday; and still George kept aloof from me. I had sense enough not to be hurt by this. I felt he had a good right to be silent, if silence helped him to bear his trial better; and I made up my mind never to breathe another syllable on the subject, unless he began.

Wednesday came. I had overslept myself that morning, and came to work a quarter after the hour, expecting to be fined; for George was very strict as foreman of the yard, and treated friends and enemies just the same. Instead of blaming me, however, he called me up, and said:

'Ben, whose turn is it this week to sit up?'

'Mine, sir,' I replied. (I always called him 'Sir' in working hours.)

'Well, then, you may go home today, and the same on Thursday and Friday; for there's a large batch of work for the ovens tonight, and there'll be the same tomorrow night and the night after.'

'All right, sir,' said I. 'Then I'll be here by seven this evening.'

'No, half-past nine will be soon enough. I've some accounts to make up, and I shall be here myself till then. Mind you are true to time, though.'

'I'll be as true as the clock, sir,' I replied, and was turning away when he called me back again.

'You're a good lad, Ben,' said he. 'Shake hands.'

I seized his hand, and pressed it warmly.

'If I'm good for anything, George,' I answered with all my heart, 'it's you who have made me so. God bless you for it!'

'Amen!' said he, in a troubled voice, putting his hand to his hat.

And so we parted.

In general, I went to bed by day when I was attending to the firing by night; but this morning I had already slept longer than usual, and wanted exercise more than rest. So I ran home; put a bit of bread and meat in my pocket; snatched up my big thorn stick; and started off for a long day in the country. When I came home, it was quite dark and beginning to rain, just as it had begun to rain at about the same time that wretched Sunday evening: so I changed my wet boots, had an early supper and a nap in the chimney-corner, and went down to the works at a few minutes before half-past nine. Arriving at the factory-gate, I found it ajar, and so walked in and closed it after me. I remember thinking at the time that it was unlike George's usual caution to leave it so; but it passed from my mind next moment. Having slipped in the bolt, I then went straight over to George's little counting-house, where the gas was shining cheerfully in the window. Here also, somewhat to my surprise, I found the door open, and the room empty. I went in. The threshold and part of the floor was wetted by the driving rain. The wages-book was open on the desk, George's pen stood in the ink, and his hat hung on its usual peg in the corner. I concluded, of course, that he had gone round to the ovens; so, following him, I took down his hat and carried it with me, for it was now raining fast.

The baking-houses lay just opposite, on the other side of the yard. There were three of them, opening one out of the other; and in each, the great furnace filled all the middle of the room. These furnaces are, in fact, large kilns built of brick, with an oven closed in by an iron door in the centre of each, and a chimney going up through the roof. The pottery, enclosed in seggars, stands round inside on shelves, and has to be turned from time to time while the firing is going on. To turn these seggars, test the heat, and keep the fires up, was my work at the period of which I am now telling you, Major.

Well! I went through the baking-houses one after the other, and found all empty alike. Then a strange, vague, uneasy feeling came over me, and I began to wonder what could have become of George. It was possible that he might be in one of the workshops; so I ran over to the counting-house, lighted a lantern, and made a thorough survey of the yards. I tried the doors; they were all locked as usual. I peeped into the open sheds; they were all vacant. I called 'George! George!' in every part of the outer premises; but the wind and rain drove back my voice, and no other voice replied to it. Forced at last to believe that he was really gone, I took his hat back to the counting-house, put away the wages-book, extinguished the gas, and prepared for my solitary watch.

The night was mild, and the heat in the baking-rooms intense. I knew, by experience, that the ovens had been overheated, and that none of the porcelain must go in at least for the next two hours; so I carried my stool to the door, settled myself in a sheltered corner where the air could reach me, but not the rain, and fell to wondering where George could have gone, and why he should not have waited till the time appointed. That he had left in haste was clear—not because his hat remained behind, for he might have a cap with him—but because he had left the book open, and the gas lighted. Perhaps one of the workmen had met with some accident, and he had been summoned away so urgently that he had no time to think of anything; perhaps he would even now come back presently to see that all was right before he went home to his lodgings. Turning these things over in my mind, I grew drowsy, my thoughts wandered, and I fell asleep.

I cannot tell how long my nap lasted. I had walked a great distance that day, and I slept heavily; but I awoke all in a moment, with a sort of terror upon me, and, looking up, saw George Barnard sitting on a stool before the oven door, with the firelight full upon his face.

Ashamed to be found sleeping, I started to my feet. At the same instant, he rose, turned away without even looking towards me, and went out into the next room.

'Don't be angry, George!' I cried, following him. 'None of the seggars are in. I knew the fires were too strong, and—'

The words died on my lips. I had followed him from the first room to the second, from the second to the third, and in the third—I lost him!

I could not believe my eyes. I opened the end door leading into the yard, and looked out; but he was nowhere in sight. I went round to the back of the baking-houses, looked behind the furnaces, ran over to the counting-house, called him by his name over and over again; but all was dark, silent, lonely, as ever.

Then I remembered how I had bolted the outer gate, and how impossible it was that he should have come in without ringing. Then, too, I began again to doubt the evidence of my own senses, and to think I must have been dreaming.

I went back to my old post by the door of the first baking-house, and sat down for a moment to collect my thoughts.

'In the first place,' said I to myself, 'there is but one outer gate. That outer gate I bolted on the inside, and it is bolted still. In the next place, I searched the premises, and found all the sheds empty, and the workshop-doors padlocked as usual on the outside. I proved that George was nowhere about, when I came, and I know he could not have come in since, without my knowledge. Therefore it is a dream. It is certainly a dream, and there's an end of it.'

And with this I trimmed my lantern and proceeded to test the temperature of the furnaces. We used to do this, I should tell you, by the introduction of little roughly-moulded lumps of common fire-clay. If the heat is too great, they crack; if too little, they remain damp and moist; if just right, they become firm and smooth all over, and pass into the biscuit stage. Well! I took my three little lumps of clay, put one in each oven, waited while I counted five hundred, and then went round again to see the results. The two first were in capital condition, the third had flown into a dozen pieces. This proved that the seggars might at once go into ovens One and Two, but that number Three had been overheated, and must be allowed to go on cooling for an hour or two longer.

I therefore stocked One and Two with nine rows of seggars, three deep on each shelf; left the rest waiting till number Three was in a condition to be trusted; and, fearful of falling asleep again, now that the firing was in progress, walked up and down the rooms to keep myself awake. This was hot work, however, and I could not stand it very long; so I went back presently to my stool by the door, and fell to thinking about my dream. The more I thought of it, the more strangely real it seemed, and the more I felt convinced that I was actually on my feet, when I saw George get up and walk into the adjoining room. I was also certain that I had still continued to see him as he passed out of the second room into the third, and that at that time I was even following his very footsteps. Was it possible, I asked myself, that I could have been up and moving, and yet not quite awake? I had heard of people walking in their sleep. Could it be that I was walking in mine, and never waked till I reached the cool air of the yard? All this seemed likely enough, so I dismissed the matter from my mind, and passed the rest of the night in attending to the seggars, adding fresh fuel from time to time to the furnaces of the first and second ovens, and now and then taking a turn through the yards. As for number Three, it kept up its heat to such a degree that it was almost day before I dared trust the seggars to go in it.

Thus the hours went by; and at half-past seven on Thursday morning, the men came to their work. It was now my turn to go off duty, but I wanted to see George before I left, and so waited for him in the counting-house, while a lad named Steve Storr took my place at the ovens. But the clock went on from half-past seven to a quarter to eight; then to eight o'clock; then to a quarter-past eight—and still George never made his appearance. At length, when the hand got round to half-past eight, I grew weary of waiting, took up my hat, ran home, went to bed, and slept profoundly until past four in the afternoon.

That evening I went down to the factory quite early; for I had a restlessness upon me, and I wanted to see George before he left for the night. This time, I found the gate bolted, and I rang for admittance.

'How early you are, Ben!' said Steve Storr, as he let me in.

'Mr Barnard's not gone?' I asked, quickly; for I saw at the first glance that the gas was out in the counting-house.

'He's not gone,' said Steve, 'because he's never been.'

'Never been?'

'No: and what's stranger still, he's not been home either, since dinner yesterday.'

'But he was here last night.'

'Oh yes, he was here last night, making up the books. John Parker was with him till past six; and you found him here, didn't you, at half-past nine?'

I shook my head.

'Well, he's gone, anyhow. Goodnight!'

'Goodnight!'

I took the lantern from his hand, bolted him out mechanically, and made my way to the baking-houses like one in a stupor. George gone? Gone without a word of warning to his employer, or of farewell to his fellow-workmen? I could not understand it. I could not believe it. I sat down bewildered, incredulous, stunned. Then came hot tears, doubts, terrifying suspicions. I remembered the wild words he had spoken a few nights back; the strange calm by which they were followed; my dream of the evening before. I had heard of men who drowned themselves for love; and the turbid Severn ran close by—so close, that one might pitch a stone into it from some of the workshop windows.

These thoughts were too horrible. I dared not dwell upon them. I turned to work, to free myself from them, if I could; and began by examining the ovens. The temperature of all was much higher than on the previous night, the heat having been gradually increased during the last twelve hours. It was now my business to keep the heat on the increase for twelve-more; after which it would be allowed, as gradually, to subside, until the pottery was cool enough for removal. To turn the seggars, and add fuel to the two first furnaces, was my first work. As before, I found number Three in advance of the others, and so left it for half an hour, or an hour. I then went round the yard; tried the doors; let the dog loose; and brought him back with me to the baking-houses for company. After that, I set my lantern on a shelf beside the door, took a book from my pocket, and began to read.

I remember the title of the book as well as possible. It was called *Bowlker's Art of Angling,* and contained little rude cuts of all kinds of artificial flies, hooks, and other tackle. But I could not keep my mind to it for two minutes together; and at last I gave it up in despair, covered my face with my hands, and fell into a long absorbing painful train of thought. A considerable time had gone by thus—maybe an hour—when I was roused by a low whimpering howl from Captain, who was lying at my feet. I looked up with a start, just as I had started from sleep the night before, and with the same vague terror; and saw, exactly in the same place and in the same attitude, with the firelight full upon him—George Barnard!

At this sight, a fear heavier than the fear of death fell upon me, and my tongue seemed paralysed in my mouth. Then, just as last night, he rose, or seemed to rise, and went slowly out into the next room. A power stronger than myself appeared to compel me, reluctantly, to follow him. I saw him pass through the second room—cross the threshold of the third room—walk straight up to the oven—and there pause. He then turned, for the first time, with the glare of the red firelight pouring out upon him from the open door of the furnace, and looked at me, face to face. In the same instant, his whole frame and countenance seemed to glow and become transparent, as if the fire were within him and around him—and in that glow he became, as it were, absorbed into the furnace, and disappeared!

I uttered a wild cry, tried to stagger from the room, and fell insensible before I reached the door.

When I next opened my eyes, the grey dawn was in the sky; the furnace-doors were all closed as I had left them when I last went round; the dog was quietly sleeping not far from my side; and the men were ringing at the gate, to be let in.

I told my tale from beginning to end, and was laughed at, as a matter of course, by all who heard it. When it was found, however, that my statements never varied, and, above all, that George Barnard continued absent, some few began to talk it over seriously, and among those few, the master of the works. He forbade the furnace to be cleared out, called in the aid of a celebrated naturalist, and had the ashes submitted to a scientific examination. The result was as follows:

The ashes were found to have been largely saturated with some kind of fatty animal matter. A considerable portion of those ashes consisted of charred bone. A semi-circular piece of iron, which evidently had once been the heel of a workman's heavy boot, was found, half fused, at one corner of the furnace. Near it, a tibia bone, which still retained sufficient of its original form and texture to render indentification possible. This bone, however, was so much charred, that it fell into powder on being handled.

After this, not many doubted that George Barnard had been foully murdered, and that his body had been thrust into the furnace. Suspicion fell upon Louis Laroche. He was arrested, a coroner's inquest was held, and every circumstance connected with the night of the murder was as thoroughly sifted and investigated as possible. All the sifting in the world, however, failed either to clear or to condemn Louis Laroche. On the very night of his release, he left the place by the mail-train, and was never seen or heard of there, again. As for Leah, I know not what became of her. I went away myself before many weeks were over, and never have set foot among The Potteries from that hour to this.

THE SAVING OF A SOUL

SIR RICHARD BURTON

At the castle of Weixelstein in Germany, strange noises were heard during the night for several years towards the end of the seventeenth century. But the origin of these same noises was a subject of vain research and speculation. After a time, a new serving-maid named Ankha Wnikhlaukha was taken on at the castle. On hearing these mysterious sounds she decided they were caused by a ghost and made up her mind to address this ghost.

It fell out like this. On 15th January 1648, a noise arose at night in the servant-wenches' room, as though someone were walking about clad in iron armour and clanking chains. The women being sorely frightened, some stable-hands were brought to sleep in the room. They were struck upon the head by an unknown hand, and one was like to die of terror.

The following evening, while the lights were still burning, a rapping was heard at the door of the room. But when they went to see what caused it, nothing was found. Presently those inside put out the lamps, and lay down to rest. Thereupon began a loud clatter; two serving-wenches, Marinkha and Mitza, were seized by the hair, but they could not make out anyone near them.

The whole account is strictly 'spiritualistic'. Ankha is the chosen medium, and nothing is done till she appears on the scene. The ghost will hardly answer the officious and garrulous steward: and has apparently scant respect for the reverend men who were called in. One of the latter somewhat justified the ghost's disdain by telling a decided fib. The steps by which the apparition changes from hot to cold, from weariness to energy, from dark to white robes, and from loud noises to mild, are decidedly artistic.

On 17th January nothing happened.

On the 18th the servant-wenches being in great fear, five others joined them. One, Hansche Juritschkno Suppan, put out the light when all had lain down, locked the door, and endeavoured to sleep. Thereupon arose a dreadful noise. After it had ended, Ankha, by the advice of those present, thus bespake the ghost:

'All good spirits, praise the Lord,'—such being the recognized formula throughout Germany for addressing apparitions.

The ghost answered: 'I also; so help me God, and Our Blessed Lady, and the holy Saint Anthony of Padua!'

Ankha resumed: 'What wantest thou, O good spirit?'

The ghost replied: 'I require thirty Masses.' It added: 'This castle was once mine,'—and it disappeared.

On 19th January the ghost was present, but nothing untoward occurred.

On the evening of the 20th, the servant-wenches being still affrighted, the steward, one Antoni Glanitsschinigg, and the man Hansche beforementioned, with six other persons, were in the chamber. When all lay down to rest, the steward locked the door and put out the lamp. The ghost at once came and violently dragged a chair backwards. Whereupon quoth

Antoni: 'I confess that I am a great sinner; nevertheless, I dare address thee, and ask thee, in God's name, what more dost thou want?'

To this question no answer was vouchsafed by the ghost, although the steward repeated it a second time and a third time. He then rose up and advanced towards the apparition, which was seen standing near the window, thinking to discover whether it was a true ghost, or some person playing a trick. It vanished, however, before he could lay hand upon it. The steward went out with one of the servant-wenches to fetch a light; and, whilst doing so, he heard the ghost speaking in the room he had left. When the lamp was brought, nothing was found. Then all those present knelt down and prayed. After their devotions, the light was extinguished, and the ghost reappeared, crying out, with weeping and wailing: 'Ankha! Ankha! Ankha! help me.'

The wench answered: 'How can I help thee, O good spirit?' Whereupon the ghost rejoined:

'With thirty Masses, which must be said at the altar of Saint Anthony, in the church of Jagnenz,'—which church is in the parish of Schaffenberg.

Jagnenz is a church in the valley of the Sapotka, a small stream which falls into the Save River, about half a mile west of Weixelstein. Schaffenberg is the hereditary castle of the well-known count of that name, while Wrunikh is another little church, remarkably pretty, near Weixelstein. Apparently the ghost served to 'run' Jagnenz against all its rivals.

Hearing those words from the ghost, the steward again inquired:

'O thou good spirit, would it not be better to get the Masses said more quickly by dividing them, part at Jagnenz, the other at the altar of Saint Anthony in Wrunikh?'

Whereto the ghost made an answer: 'No! Ankha! Ankha! Only at Jagnenz, and not at Wrunikh!' The steward continued: 'As this ghost refuseth to answer me, do thou, Ankha, ask it what and why it suffers.'

Then Ankha addressed it: 'My good spirit! Tell me wherefore thou dost suffer?' It replied: 'For that I unrighteously used sixty florins; so I, a poor widow body, must endure this penalty.'

Ankha further said: 'Who shall pay for these thirty Masses?'

The ghost rejoined: 'The noble master of the castle,' and continued: 'Ankha! Ankha! I am so weary, and dead-beat, and martyred, that I can hardly speak.'

Then cried the steward: 'My good spirit! When the thirty Masses shall have been said, come back and give us a sign that they have helped thee.' The ghost rejoined. 'Ankha, to thee I will give a sign upon thy head.'

Ankha replied: 'God have mercy upon me, that must endure such fright and pain!' But the ghost thus comforted her: 'Fear not, Ankha. The sign which I will show to thee shall not be visible upon thy head, nor shall it be painful.' It added: 'Ankha! Ankha! I pray thee, when thou enterest into any house, tell the inmates that one unjust farthing eats up twenty honest farthings.'

Then the ghost began to scratch the wench's cap, and she, in her terror, took to praying for help. The ghost comforted her, bade her feel no fear nor anxiety, took leave, and was seen no more that night.

Late on 21st January the ghost reappeared, and made a terrible noise with a chair in presence of the lord of the castle, Sigmund Wilhelm Freiherr, Baron von Zetschekher, and of two priests, Georg Schlebnikh and Lorenz Tsichitsch. Several others, men and women, were present, and nothing took place till the candles were put out. Whereupon the said Schlebnikh began to exorcize the apparition, beginning with the usual formula:

'All good spirits, praise the Lord.'

'I also,' replied the ghost.

It would not, however, answer any questions put to it by the priestly man, but began to speak with Ankha, saying: 'Ankha, help me!'

Ankha rejoined: 'My dear good spirit, all that lies in my power will I do for thee. Only tell me, my spirit, if the two Masses already said have in any way lessened thy pain.'

'Yea, verily,' answered the ghost.

'How many more Masses must thou still have?' Ankha continued.

'Thirty, less two,' was the response.

'My good spirit,' asked Ankha, 'tell me thy family name.'

'My name is Gallenbergerinn,' quoth the ghost.

The wench further asked for a sign of salvation when all the thirty Masses should have been said. The ghost promised to do so, and disappeared.

On the night of 22nd January, when the lights were put out, the ghost reappeared, passing through the locked door. This was in presence of Wolff Engelbrecht, Baron Gallen, of the lord of the castle, and of three priests, namely, Georg Schiffrer, curate of Laakgh, Georg Schlebnikh, and Lorenz. There were again several others. This time the ghost did not make a frightful noise as before, the reason being that eight Masses had been said. So at least it appeared from its address.

'Ankha, Ankha, I thank thee; I shall soon be released,' it said.

'O my good spirit,' the wench answered; 'dost thou feel any comfort after the eight Masses?'

'Yea, verily, my Ankha,' the apparition replied—and when asked how many more were required, answered: 'Two and twenty.'

As it had declared its family name, it was now prayed to disclose its Christian name, in order that the latter might be introduced into the Masses by the four reverends.

'My name is Mary Elisabeth Gallenbergerinn,' it said.

Further it was asked whether, being a Gallenberg, the thirty Masses should be paid for by the Lord of Gallenberg or by Zetschekher of Weixelstein.

'Zetschekher,' it ejaculated, without giving the baron's title, and added: 'A thousand, thousand, and a thousand thanks to thee, dear Ankha.'

'O my good spirit,' said Ankha, 'tell me what wrong didst thou with the sixty florins, that we may make restitution.'

The ghost replied: 'Ankha, this must I tell thee in secret,' upon which the wench begged that the matter might be disclosed in public, so that men would believe it, but the ghost answered: 'No, Ankha; in private.'

It then took leave and disappeared, promising to come back for three more evenings.

On 23rd January, the lord of the castle, with three priests, prayed at the altar of Saint Anthony of Jagnenz, and five more Masses were said. They all lodged that night with Georg Schlebnikh of Altenhoff, not far from the church. When the lamps were put out, Ankha was sitting on a chest, between two of the priests. Then, after rapping thrice, the ghost entered and pulled the hair of one of these reverends. He stood up from the chest, whereupon the ghost struck Ankha so violent a box on the ear that it sounded like a sharp hand-clap and could be heard all over the dwelling-place.

Lights were brought, and revealed the print of a left hand burnt in the coif on the right side of the wench's head. She was not hurt, but the cap remained heated for some time. Nothing else occurred that night.

On the evening of 24th January, after prayers by the priests, and the lamp being extinguished, the ghost rapped once and came in. As the wench again sat on the same chest between the priests, the curate of Laagkh felt his hair tugged, and he rose up.

At the same time Ankha exclaimed: 'Who is touching me so coldly?'

The priest, who was sitting near, said: 'Be not afraid, it is I.'

But this was not true. He wished to dispel her fright.

On 25th January when all the required Masses had been said at the altar of Saint Anthony of Jagnenz, the Lord of Weixelstein and the priests engaged in the ceremony returned to pass the night at the castle, and to receive the thanksgiving of the Saved Soul. While they were supping, the housemaid, carrying the children's food, was crossing the hall to the dining-room, when the ghost seized her arm.

She started back, and saw behind her the form of a woman robed in white. As the family were retiring to rest, the lord of the castle ordered two of his dependants, Christop Wollf and Mathew Wreschek, to pass the night with the serving-wenches in the haunted room.

As the lamps were put out, the ghost entered and rapped loudly on the table, saying: 'Ankha, now I am saved, and I am going to heaven.' The wench rejoined: 'O blessed soul, pray to heaven for me, for the noble master, the noble mistress, and all the noble family, and for all those who helped thee to attain thine eternal salvation,' whereto the ghost responded: 'Amen, amen, amen.' It then went towards Ankha, and privily told her the promised secret of her sin, strictly forbidding her to divulge it.

Finally, it should be noted that before all these happenings, Ankha had been to confession and partaken of holy communion.

All this was translated from the folios of the 'Honour of the Duchy of Carniola', written by Johann Weichard, Baron Walvasor, Lord of Wazemberg, and printed at Laibach in M.DC.LXXXIX.

THE BEARER OF THE MESSAGE

Fritz Hopman

During the winter of 1869, I entrusted my medical work for a while to two of my friends, and left Paris in order to attend the International Congress of Medicine at Moscow. The first sessions of the Congress were extremely interesting.

Famous men of the day exposed new theories and discussed new methods which have been quite forgotten since, and I entered, with the ardent enthusiasm of youth, into the discussions that followed these discourses.

On the third day of the Congress, a young Swedish professor had been talking of the treatment of epilepsy by 'mesmerism', as psychic medicine was called in those days. During the course of these interesting and stimulating debates I heard telepathy and the significance of dreams discussed by eminent men whom I could not but respect. Hitherto, I had considered such phenomena as inventions of the superstitious, but as I was on the way back to my hotel, I realized that the materialism of my young days had had a rude blow, and that it was time I revised my outlook on life.

That evening, the Governor of Moscow gave a dinner in honour of the delegates; it was an assembly of the most brilliant diplomatists and officers, of renowned scholars and beautiful women.

I was sitting next to a Dorpot surgeon, who knew French very well, and I was absolutely in my element. I was still at the age when all hero-worship had not been stifled, and I lived in the timid admiration that a young man must have experienced later, when he saw for the first time Pasteur, Lister, Metchnikoff or Virchou. To my romantic mind these great men seemed like stars in the firmament, totally superior beings.

Moreover, I was conscious that for the time being at least, even I was on an equal footing with the great men who were present.

Someone touched my arm gently. I was surprised to see a woman, whom I did not know, speaking to me in Russian. She was an intriguing creature, pale, supple and slight. The pallor of her face was remarkable, and lines of care marked it. Amid an assembly of such brilliant men and women she introduced an element of sadness and anxiety. It was as though a window had been opened, through which an icy wind blew, driving snow into the room.

As I did not understand Russian, I appealed to the surgeon, to whom I had been talking, for an explanation. He told me that the woman had heard that my treatment of affections of the heart was excellent, and that she wanted me to attend a relative of hers who was dangerously ill. Impelled by a cavalier spirit, I answered that I was ready to accompany her. It would mean missing the gala dinner, but that was one of the chief reasons that induced me to accept, for self-sacrifice is one of the foremost needs of youth. Moreover, my pride was flattered because I was chosen out of all that galaxy of great men. However, I asked no questions but took my hat and overcoat and set off.

I remember, as though it all happened yesterday, the sight I saw when I went towards the door of the palace with the woman who had spoken to me. At that moment, a girl in a white mantle came up the steps to the palace. The light, coming through the open doors, fell on her face. I can see all that now, but it is like a photograph yellow with age, like a relic of the past that survives only in an old man's memory.

We passed the row of vehicles, and we were fortunate in finding a troika, the ordinary vehicle used in the streets of Moscow, and drawn by three horses. While the woman was talking to the driver, I observed him by the light of a lantern. He had red cheeks, and rough, furrowed skin, a thick beard and an insignificant nose, as all Russians have.

We took our places in the troika, and passed through some streets that were brightened by lights from big shops. After that we came to great, deserted open spaces, where the outline of equestrian statues could be discerned.

In places the white domes of Russian churches stood out in startling contrast against the dark sky, giving a strange, weird effect. We met no one but a squadron of soldiers with guns and a poacher. After passing through the dim suburbs we reached the country, leaving behind us the light and noise of the old city.

But before long I became a prey to doubts and distrust, and I regretted the light and warmth of the palace I had so thoughtlessly left. I cursed my own credulity. The silence and monotony of the journey made me sink into a drowsy sleep. I felt detached sometimes as though I were alone in the sledge, sometimes as though I were old, very old.

I began to dread an attack of wolves, and I wished I had brought a revolver with me. I did not know what to think of my adventure, for in a country infested with secret societies anything might happen. Was I walking into some trap? Was I not suspected of Nihilism? Was I going to be robbed? But why not choose someone rich? I invented endless theories, and rejected them all.

I was almost asleep when we reached a little village, where lights were still burning in the windows of some of the houses.

The horses were foaming and panting when they stopped outside a kind of inn. The door opened, and I saw, through a cloud of tobacco smoke, the

151

dark form of a man in a tunic and high boots. We got out of the sledge, and I was glad to stretch my stiff legs. The driver was in conversation with the innkeeper, but the woman led me farther on in the darkness.

I had decided to defend myself to the best of my power if I were attacked. There was perfect silence all around us; as we made our way through the snow, we did not speak a word. I was greatly distressed, and my mind was full of the talk about the occult to which I had listened during the afternoon. I thought of the stories my nurse had told me, when she was putting me to bed; of spectres haunting newly opened graves, and I saw in my mind's eye, tombs, coffins, black-covered lanterns lit on grey days, and all the fantastic visions that have profaned the idea of death and made it hideous and terrifying.

Finally we reached the garden wall of a dark-looking country house. I rang, footsteps approached. I turned round thinking that the woman was going to speak. To my great horror and amazement, I found that she had disappeared. I was alone. I could not understand how she could have vanished so quickly and so silently, but I had not time to indulge in speculations, for the door opened, and I saw a girl standing before me.

I explained to her in French the purpose of my visit. She answered hesitatingly that I must have made a mistake, since all the members of the family were in good health. She asked me to go in and speak to her father, who spoke and understood French better than she did. I was in utter despair, but I followed her to a kind of study, where an old man was sitting in an arm-chair, beside an earthenware stove.

There was no need of a specialist to tell that he was suffering from some form of heart disease. His face was a bluish-purple, and his nose was red like a drunkard's. He held a cigarette in his hand, and it quivered each time his heart beat.

I greeted him, and explained again the reason of my visit. The old man looked at me over his spectacles and frowned. Evidently he didn't believe a single word of what I said, and he wanted to know my real intentions. To appease him and to explain my disturbing his peaceful dwelling at such an hour, I told him all the details of my adventure. He listened with eager attention to my story, and when I had finished, he said:

'I don't know what to think of it. In any case, you are wrong. There is no one ill here. But now you have taken so much trouble for nothing, I should like you to stay a while. You can't return to Moscow tonight. You will have to stay at the inn. I should be glad to offer you hospitality, but we do not receive visitors, and we have not many comforts to offer.'

He passed me a box of cigarettes and the daughter made me some tea with lemon and rum. Meanwhile, I constructed a theory, more or less unconsciously. I decided that the woman realized that the old man was suffering from heart disease, although he himself did not. She saw that the advice of a doctor was indispensable, and she had found a very cunning ruse to send him a doctor without being compromised herself.

I asked the old man if he was well. He smiled and said:

'I'm sixty-one years old, and I have never been laid up in bed. Of course, weakness comes with old age. I'm not as strong as I was, and I have asthma a little, but apart from that I am very well. No, doctor you can take it from me, there's not a rouble to be earned here.'

The conversation turned on the Congress and on life in Paris, about which he had read much. His daughter, a slight, shy girl, gazed at me with her deep, dark eyes, but took no part in the conversation. The father's conversation was witty and gay, and this surprised me in a hermit.

Probably my conversation brightened him, for he talked of his student days, of his youthful follies, and of the time when he was a young lawyer. For an hour he recalled his forgotten youth and talked of the good old times. Suddenly the lamp flickered as though it were about to go out.

Candles were brought, but the charm was broken, and I felt like a young husband who suddenly sees an ill omen. The clock was striking twelve when

I took my leave. The old man asked me to call the next day, and naturally I promised to do so. The daughter came with me to the door, and said:

'I'm so glad you have come, doctor, even though it was by error. Papa has not been so gay for many years. You must come back tomorrow. I wish we had a few more visitors. It would do him good.'

I had a kind of presentiment that I should find my silent companion on the road, but I saw no one. Lights were still burning in the inn, and when I entered the innkeeper was reading the newspaper to some men, who looked like peasants, wearing Russian tunics. They had long hair and long beards, sombre faces, and they all sat in the same position, with their chins in their hands.

The atmosphere of the inn was stifling and a cloud of tobacco smoke was rising slowly towards the ceiling. I made the innkeeper understand that I wanted a room for the night by gesticulating, and he took me to a room where there was a huge bed.

There were some pictures of saints of the Greek Church hanging on the whitewashed wall. The innkeeper brought candles and lit a big wood fire. I did not want to sleep, so I lit a cigar and sat in an armchair to think over the happenings of the evening.

I had just thrown the end of my cigar away when I heard footsteps on the stairs. I was terrified, for I was afraid it was a trap and that I was going to be robbed. But it was the innkeeper and the daughter of the old man with whom I had spent the evening. The girl seemed greatly excited, but she did not lose control of herself.

'How fortunate that you are here, doctor,' she said. 'Poor father had scarcely got into bed when he had a terrible attack. Perhaps he's had too much excitement tonight. I'm sorry to trouble you, but would you mind coming with me? Perhaps you could do something for him.'

The room into which she took me was lofty and uninviting; there was a sharp smell of eau de Cologne and of ammonia in the air. A lamp was burning on a table where there were the usual things one sees in a bed-room—hairbrush, razor, clock and a big tiepin with a cameo.

The last flame was dying out on the hearth. The curtains of the bed were drawn aside and an old servant was praying at the bedside, while another was sitting on a chair, weeping.

I listened for the old man's heartbeats, but there was not the slightest breath. Death had done its work, and the limbs were already growing stiff. I broke the news to the girl as gently as possible, but she had already under-stood, and mastered herself with a truly feminine energy.

While I was washing my hands and thinking of the adventures of the day, I noticed a framed oil painting. It was painted in 1830s style, and it showed a young woman with low-cut dress and flattened hair. Without the least doubt I recognized in her the mysterious companion who had sought me out in the hall of the palace at Moscow. My surprise was so great that I could not restrain a cry.

'Who is that?' I asked, pointing to the portrait. 'It is the woman who brought me here.'

The girl looked at me fixedly. Her upper lip was twisted in an expres-sion of incredulity, but seeing me look uneasy, she, too, grew pale.

'It's my mother,' she said. 'She died when I was born, twenty years ago.'

CANON ALBERIC'S SCRAP-BOOK

M. R. JAMES

St. Bertrand de Comminges is a decayed town on the spurs of the Pyrenees, not very far from Toulouse, and still nearer to Bagnéres-de-Luchon. It was the site of a bishopric until the Revolution, and has a cathedral which is visited by a certain number of tourists. In the spring of 1883 an Englishman arrived at this old-world place—I can hardly dignify it with the name of city, for there are not a thousand inhabitants. He was a Cambridge man, who had come specially from Toulouse to see St. Bertrand's Church, and had left two friends, who were less keen archaeologists than himself, in their hotel at Toulouse, under promise to join him on the following morning. Half an hour at the church would satisfy *them*, and all three could then pursue their journey in the direction of Auch. But our Englishman had come early on the day in question, and proposed to himself to fill a notebook and to use several dozens of plates in the process of describing and photographing every corner of the wonderful church that dominates the little hill of Comminges. In order to carry out this design satisfactorily, it was necessary to monopolize the verger of the church for the day. The verger or sacristan (I prefer the latter appellation, inaccurate as it may be) was accordingly sent for by the somewhat brusque lady who keeps the inn of the Chapeau Rouge; and when he came, the Englishman found him an unexpectedly interesting object of study. It was not in the personal appearance of the little, dry, wizened old man that the interest lay, for he was precisely like dozens of other church-guardians in France, but in a curious furtive, or rather hunted and oppressed, air which he had. He was perpetually half glancing behind him; the muscles of his back and shoulders seemed to be hunched in a continual nervous contraction, as if he were expecting every moment to find himself in the clutch of an enemy. The Englishman hardly knew whether to put him down as a man haunted by a fixed delusion, or as one oppressed by a guilty conscience, or as an unbearably henpecked husband. The probabilities, when reckoned up, certainly pointed to the last idea; but, still, the impression conveyed was that of a more formidable persecutor even than a termagant wife.

However, the Englishman (let us call him Dennistoun) was soon too deep in his notebook and too busy with his camera to give more than an occasional glance to the sacristan. Whenever he did look at him, he found him at no great distance, either huddling himself back against the wall or crouching in one of the gorgeous stalls. Dennistoun became rather fidgety after a time. Mingled suspicions that he was keeping the old man from his *déjeuner*, that he was regarded as likely to make away with St. Bertrand's ivory crozier, or with the dusty stuffed crocodile that hangs over the font, began to torment him.

"Won't you go home?" he said at last; "I'm quite well able to finish my notes alone; you can lock me in if you like. I shall want at least two hours more here, and it must be cold for you, isn't it?"

"Good heavens!" said the little man, whom the suggestion seemed to throw into a state of unaccountable terror, "such a thing cannot be thought of for a moment. Leave monsieur alone in the church? No, no; two hours, three hours, all will be the same to me. I have breakfasted, I am not at all cold, with many thanks to monsieur."

"Very well, my little man," quoth Dennistoun to himself: "you have been warned, and you must take the consequences."

Before the expiration of the two hours, the stalls, the enormous dilapidated organ, the choir-screen of Bishop John de Mauléon, the remnants of glass and tapestry, and the objects in the treasure-chamber, had been well and truly examined; the sacristan still keeping at Dennistoun's heels, and every now and then whipping round as if he had been stung, when one or other of the strange noises that trouble a large empty building fell on his ear. Curious noises they were sometimes.

"Once," Dennistoun said to me, "I could have sworn I heard a thin metallic voice laughing high up in the tower. I darted an inquiring glance at my sacristan. He was white to the lips. 'It is he—that is—it is no one; the door is locked,' was all he said, and we looked at each other for a full minute."

Another little incident puzzled Dennistoun a good deal. He was examining a large dark picture that hangs behind the altar, one of a series illustrating the miracles of St. Bertrand. The composition of the picture is wellnigh indecipherable, but there is a Latin legend below, which runs thus:

> *"Qualiter S. Bertrandus liberavit hominem quem diabolus diu volebat strangulare." (How St. Bertrand delivered a man whom the Devil long sought to strangle.)*

Dennistoun was turning to the sacristan with a smile and a jocular remark of some sort on his lips, but he was confounded to see the old man on his knees, gazing at the picture with the eye of a suppliant in agony, his hands tightly clasped, and a rain of tears on his cheeks. Dennistoun naturally pretended to have noticed nothing, but the question would not away from him, "Why should a daub of this kind affect anyone so strongly?" He seemed to himself to be getting some sort of clue to the reason of the strange look that had been puzzling him all the day: the man must be a monomaniac; but what was his monomania?

It was nearly five o'clock; the short day was drawing in, and the church began to fill with shadows, while the curious noises—the muffled footfalls and distant talking voices that had been perceptible all day—seemed, no doubt because of the fading light and the consequently quickened sense of hearing, to become more frequent and insistent.

The sacristan began for the first time to show signs of hurry and impatience. He heaved a sigh of relief when camera and notebook were finally packed up and stowed away, and hurriedly beckoned Dennistoun to the western door of the church, under the tower. It was time to ring the Angelus. A few pulls at the reluctant rope, and the great bell Bertrande, high in the tower, began to speak, and swung her voice up among the pines and down to the valleys, loud with mountain-streams, calling the dwellers on those lonely hills to remember and repeat the salutation of the angel to her whom he called Blessed among women. With that a profound quiet seemed to fall for the first time that day upon the little town, and Dennistoun and the sacristan went out of the church.

On the doorstep they fell into conversation.

"Monsieur seemed to interest himself in the old choir-books in the sacristy."

"Undoubtedly. I was going to ask you if there were a library in the town."

"No, monsieur; perhaps there used to be one belonging to the Chapter, but it is now such a small place——" Here came a strange pause of irresolution, as it seemed; then, with a sort of plunge, he went on: "But if monsieur is *amateur des vieux livres,* I have at home something that might interest him. It is not a hundred yards."

At once all Dennistoun's cherished dreams of finding priceless manuscripts in untrodden corners of France flashed up, to die down again the next moment. It was probably a stupid missal of Plantin's printing, about 1580. Where was the likelihood that a place so near Toulouse would not have been ransacked long ago by collectors? However, it would be foolish not to go; he would reproach himself for ever after if he refused. So they set off. On the way the curious irresolution and sudden determination of the sacristan recurred to Dennistoun, and he wondered in a shamefaced way whether he was being decoyed into some purlieu to be made away with as a supposed rich Englishman. He contrived, therefore, to begin talking with his guide, and to drag in, in a rather clumsy fashion, the fact that he expected two friends to join him early the next morning. To his surprise, the announcement seemed to relieve the sacristan at once of some of the anxiety that oppressed him.

"That is well," he said quite brightly—"that is very well. Monsieur will travel in company with his friends; they will be always near him. It is a good thing to travel thus in company—sometimes."

The last word appeared to be added as an afterthought, and to bring with it a relapse into gloom for the poor little man.

They were soon at the house, which was one rather larger than its neighbours, stone-built, with a shield carved over the door, the shield of Alberic de Mauléon, a collateral descendant, Dennistoun tells me, of Bishop John de Mauléon. This Alberic was a Canon of Comminges from 1680 to 1701. The upper windows of the mansion were boarded up, and the whole place bore, as does the rest of Comminges, the aspect of decaying age.

Arrived on his doorstep, the sacristan paused a moment.

"Perhaps," he said, "perhaps, after all, monsieur has not the time?"

"Not at all—lots of time—nothing to do till tomorrow. Let us see what it is you have got."

The door was opened at this point, and a face looked out, a face far younger than the sacristan's, but bearing something of the same distressing look: only here it seemed to be the mark, not so much of fear for personal safety as of acute anxiety on behalf of another. Plainly, the owner of the face was the sacristan's daughter; and, but for the expression I have described, she was a handsome girl enough. She brightened up considerably on seeing her father accompanied by an able-bodied stranger. A few remarks passed between father and daughter, of which Dennistoun only caught these words, said by the sacristan, "He was laughing in the church," words which were answered only by a look of terror from the girl.

But in another minute they were in the sitting-room of the house, a small, high chamber with a stone floor, full of moving shadows cast by a wood-fire that flickered on a great hearth. Something of the character of an oratory was imparted to it by a tall crucifix, which reached almost to the ceiling on one side; the figure was painted of the natural colours, the cross was black. Under this stood a chest of some age and solidity, and when a lamp had been brought, and chairs set, the sacristan went to this chest, and produced therefrom, with growing excitement and nervousness, as Dennistoun thought, a large book, wrapped in a white cloth, on which cloth a cross was rudely embroidered in red thread. Even before the wrapping had been removed, Dennistoun began to be interested by the size and shape of the volume. "Too large for a missal," he thought, "and not the shape of an antiphoner; perhaps it may be something good, after all." The next moment the book was open, and Dennistoun felt that he had at last lit upon something better than good. Before him lay a large folio, bound, perhaps, late in the seventeenth century, with the arms of Canon Alberic de Mauléon stamped in gold on the sides. There may have been a hundred and fifty leaves of paper in the book, and on almost every one of them was fastened a leaf from an illuminated manuscript. Such a collection Dennistoun had hardly dreamed of in his wildest moments. Here were ten leaves from a copy of Genesis, illustrated with pictures, which could not be later than A.D. 700. Further on was a complete set of pictures from a Psalter, of English execution, of the very finest kind that the thirteenth century could produce; and, perhaps best of all, there were twenty leaves of uncial writing in Latin, which, as a few words seen here and there told him at once, must belong to some very early unknown patristic treatise. Could it possibly be a fragment of the copy of Papias "On the Words of Our Lord," which was known to have existed as late as the twelfth century at Nîmes?* In any case, his mind was made up; that book must return to Cambridge with him even if he had to draw the whole of his balance from the bank and stay at St. Bertrand till the money came. He glanced up at the sacristan to see if his face yielded any hint that the book was for sale. The sacristan was pale, and his lips were working.

"If monsieur will turn on to the end," he said.

So monsieur turned on, meeting new treasures at every rise of a leaf; and at the end of the book he came upon two sheets of paper, of much more recent date than anything he had yet seen, which puzzled him considerably. They must be contemporary, he decided, with the unprincipled Canon Alberic, who had doubtless plundered the Chapter library of St. Bertrand to form this priceless scrap-book. On the first of the paper sheets was a plan, carefully drawn and instantly recognizable by a person who knew the ground, of the south aisle and cloisters of St. Bertrand's. There were curious signs looking like planetary symbols, and a few Hebrew words, in the corners; and in the north-west angle of the cloister was a cross drawn in gold paint. Below the plan were some lines of writing in Latin, which ran thus:

"*Responsa 12mi Dec. 1694. Interrogatum est: Inveniamne?*
Responsum est: Invenies. Fiamne dives? Fies. Vivamne

---

* We now know that these leaves did contain a considerable fragment of that work, if not of that actual copy of it.

invidendus? Vives. Moriarne in lecto meo? Ita." (*Answers of the 12th of December, 1694. It was asked: Shall I find it? Answer: Thou shalt. Shall I become rich? Thou wilt. Shall I live an object of envy? Thou wilt. Shall I die in my bed? Thou wilt.*)

"A good specimen of the treasure-hunter's record—quite reminds one of Mr. Minor-Canon Quatremain in 'Old St. Paul's,' " was Dennistoun's comment, and he turned the leaf.

What he then saw impressed him, as he has often told me, more than he could have conceived any drawing or picture capable of impressing him. And, though the drawing he saw is no longer in existence, there is a photograph of it (which I possess) which fully bears out that statement. The picture in question was a sepia drawing at the end of the seventeenth century, representing, one would say at first sight, a Biblical scene; for the architecture (the picture represented an interior) and the figures had that semi-classical flavour about them which the artists of two hundred years ago thought appropriate to illustrations of the Bible. On the right was a King on his throne, the throne elevated on twelve steps, a canopy overhead, lions on either side—evidently King Solomon. He was bending forward with outstretched sceptre in attitude of command; his face expressed horror and disgust, yet there was in it also the mark of imperious will and confident power. The left hall of the picture was the strangest, however. The interest plainly centred there. On the pavement before the throne were grouped four soldiers, surrounding a crouching figure which must be described in a moment. A fifth soldier lay dead on the pavement, his neck distorted, and his eyeballs starting from his head. The four surrounding guards were looking at the King. In their faces the sentiment of horror was intensified; they seemed, in fact, only restrained from flight by their implicit trust in their master. All this terror was plainly excited by the being that crouched in their midst. I entirely despair of conveying by any words the impression which this figure makes upon anyone who looks at it. I recollect once showing the photograph of the drawing to a lecturer on morphology—a person of, I was going to say, abnormally sane and unimaginative habits of mind. He absolutely refused to be alone for the rest of that evening, and he told me afterwards that for many nights he had not dared to put out his light before going to sleep. However, the main traits of the figure I can at least indicate. At first you saw only a mass of coarse, matted black hair, presently it was seen that this covered a body of fearful thinness, almost a skeleton, but with the muscles standing out like wires. The hands were of a dusky pallor, covered, like the body, with long, coarse hairs, and hideously taloned. The eyes, touched in with a burning yellow, had intensely black pupils, and were fixed upon the throned King with a look of beast-like hate. Imagine one of the awful bird-catching spiders of South America translated into human form, and endowed with intelligence just less than human, and you will have some faint conception of the terror inspired by this appalling effigy. One remark is universally made by those to whom I have shown the picture: "It was drawn from the life."

As soon as the first shock of his irresistible fright had subsided, Dennistoun stole a look at his hosts. The sacristan's hands were pressed upon his eyes; his daughter, looking up at the cross on the wall, was telling her beads feverishly.

At last the question was asked, "Is this book for sale?"

There was the same hesitation, the same plunge of determination that he had noticed before, and then came the welcome answer, "If monsieur pleases."

"How much do you ask for it?"

"I will take two hundred and fifty francs."

This was confounding. Even a collector's conscience is sometimes stirred, and Dennistoun's conscience was tenderer than a collector's.

"My good man!" he said again and again, "your book is worth far more than two hundred and fifty francs, I assure you—far more."

But the answer did not vary: "I will take two hundred and fifty francs, not more."

There was really no possibility of refusing such a chance. The money was paid, the receipt signed, a glass of wine drunk over the transaction, and then the sacristan seemed to become a new man. He stood upright, he ceased to throw those suspicious glances behind him, he actually laughed or tried to laugh. Dennistoun rose to go.

"I shall have the honour of accompanying monsieur to his hotel?" said the sacristan.

"Oh no, thanks! It isn't a hundred yards. I know the way perfectly, and there is a moon."

The offer was pressed three or four times, and refused as often.

"Then, monsieur will summon me if—if he finds occasion; he will keep the middle of the road, the sides are so rough."

"Certainly, certainly," said Dennistoun, who was impatient to examine his prize by himself; and he stepped out into the passage with his book under his arm.

Here he was met by the daughter; she, it appeared, was anxious to do a little business on her own account; perhaps, like Gehazi, to "take somewhat" from the foreigner whom her father had spared.

"A silver crucifix and chain for the neck; monsieur would perhaps be good enough to accept it?"

Well, really, Dennistoun hadn't much use for these things. What did mademoiselle want for it?

"Nothing—nothing in the world. Monsieur is more than welcome to it."

The tone in which this and much more was said was unmistakably genuine, so that Dennistoun was reduced to profuse thanks, and submitted to have the chain put round his neck. It really seemed as if he had rendered the father and daughter some service which they hardly knew how to repay. As he set off with his book they stood at the door looking after him, and they were still looking when he waved them a last good night from the steps of the Chapeau Rouge.

Dinner was over, and Dennistoun was in his bedroom, shut up alone with his acquisition. The landlady had manifested a particular interest in him since he had told her that he had paid a visit to the sacristan and bought an old book from him. He thought, too, that he had heard a hurried dialogue between her and the said sacristan in the passage outside the *salle à manger*; some words to the effect that "Pierre and Bertrand would be sleeping in the house" had closed the conversation.

All this time a growing feeling of discomfort had been creeping over him—nervous reaction, perhaps, after the delight of his discovery. Whatever it was, it resulted in a conviction that there was someone behind him, and that he was far more comfortable with his back to the wall. All this, of course, weighed light in the balance as against the obvious value of the collection he had acquired. And now, as I said, he was alone in his bedroom, taking stock of Canon Alberic's treasures, in which every moment revealed something more charming.

"Bless Canon Alberic!" said Dennistoun, who had an inveterate habit of talking to himself. "I wonder where he is now? Dear me! I wish that landlady would learn to laugh in a more cheering manner; it makes one feel as if there was someone dead in the house. Half a pipe more, did you say? I think perhaps you are right. I wonder what that crucifix is that the young woman insisted on giving me? Last century, I suppose. Yes, probably. It is rather a nuisance of a thing to have round one's neck—just too heavy. Most likely her father has been wearing it for years. I think I might give it a clean up before I put it away."

He had taken the crucifix off, and laid it on the table, when his attention was caught by an object lying on the red cloth just by his left elbow.

Two or three ideas of what it might be flitted through his brain with their own incalculable quickness.

"A penwiper? No, no such thing in the house. A rat? No, too black. A large spider? I trust to goodness not—no. Good God! a hand like the hand in that picture!"

In another infinitesimal flash he had taken it in. Pale, dusky skin, covering nothing but bones and tendons of appalling strength; coarse black hairs, longer than ever grew on a human hand; nails rising from the ends of the fingers and curving sharply down and forward, grey, horny and wrinkled.

He flew out of his chair with deadly, inconceivable terror clutching at his heart. The shape, whose left hand rested on the table, was rising to a standing posture behind his seat, its right hand crooked above his scalp. There was black and tattered drapery about it; the coarse hair covered it as in the drawing. The lower jaw was thin—what can I call it?—shallow, like a beast's; teeth showed behind the black lips; there was no nose; the eyes, of a fiery yellow, against which the pupils showed black and intense, and the exulting hate and thirst to destroy life which shone there, were the most horrifying features in the whole vision. There was intelligence of a kind in them—intelligence beyond that of a beast, below that of a man.

The feelings which this horror stirred in Dennistoun were the intensest physical fear and the most profound mental loathing. What did he do? What could he do? He has never been quite certain what words he said, but he knows that he spoke, that he grasped blindly at the silver crucifix, that he was conscious of a movement towards him on the part of the demon, and that he screamed with the voice of an animal in hideous pain.

Pierre and Bertrand, the two sturdy little serving-men, who rushed in, saw nothing, but felt themselves thrust aside by something that passed out between them, and found Dennistoun in a swoon. They sat up with him that night, and his two friends were at St. Bertrand by nine o'clock next morning. He himself, though still shaken and nervous, was almost himself by that time, and his story found credence with them, though not until they had seen the drawing and talked with the sacristan.

Almost at dawn the little man had come to the inn on some pretence, and had listened with the deepest interest to the story retailed by the landlady. He showed no surprise.

"It is he—it is he! I have seen him myself," was his only comment; and to all questionings but one reply was vouchsafed: "Deux fois je l'ai vu; mille fois je l'ai senti." He would tell them nothing of the provenance of the book, nor any details of his experiences. "I shall soon sleep, and my rest will be sweet. Why should you trouble me?" he said.*

We shall never know what he or Canon Alberic de Mauléon suffered. At the back of that fateful drawing were some lines of writing which may be supposed to throw light on the situation:

> "*Contradictio Salomonis cum demonio nocturno.*
> *Albericus de Mauleone delineavit.*
> *V. Deus in adiutorium. Ps. Qui habitat.*
> *Sancte Bertrande, demoniorum effugator, intercede pro me miserrimo.*
> *Primum uidi nocte 12^{mi} Dec. 1694: uidebo mox ultimum.*
> *Peccaui et passus sum, plura adhuc passurus. Dec. 29, 1701.*"*

---

* He died that summer; his daughter married, and settled at St. Papoul. She never understood the circumstances of her father's "obsession."

* I.e., The Dispute of Solomon with a demon of the night Drawn by Alberic de Mauléon. *Versicle.* O Lord, make haste to help me. *Psalm.* Whoso dwelleth (xci.).

Saint Bertrand, who puttest devils to flight, pray for me most unhappy. I saw it first on the night of Dec. 12, 1694: soon I shall see it for the last time. I have sinned and suffered, and have more to suffer yet. Dec. 29, 1701.

The "Gallia Christiana" gives the date of the Canon's death as December 31, 1701, "in bed, of a sudden seizure." Details of this kind are not common in the great work of the Sammarthani.

I have never quite understood what was Dennistoun's view of the events I have narrated. He quoted to me once a text from Ecclesiasticus: "Some spirits there be that are created for vengeance, and in their fury lay on sore strokes." On another occasion he said: "Isaiah was a very sensible man; doesn't he say something about night monsters living in the ruins of Babylon? These things are rather beyond us at present."

Another confidence of his impressed me rather, and I sympathized with it. We had been, last year, to Comminges, to see Canon Alberic's tomb. It is a great marble erection with an effigy of the Canon in a large wig and soutane, and an elaborate eulogy of his learning below. I saw Dennistoun talking for some time with the Vicar of St. Bertrand's, and as we drove away he said to me: "I hope it isn't wrong: you know I am a Presbyterian—but I—I believe there will be 'saying of Mass and singing of dirges' for Alberic de Mauléon's rest." Then he added, with a touch of the Northern British in his tone, "I had no notion they came so dear."

The book is in the Wentworth Collection at Cambridge. The drawing was photographed and then burnt by Dennistoun on the day when he left Comminges on the occasion of his first visit.

THE STORY OF MEDHANS LEA

E. AND H. HERON

The following story has been put together from the account of the affair given by Nare-Jones, sometime house-surgeon at Bart's, of his strange terror and experiences both in Medhans Lea and the pallid avenue between the beeches; of the narrative of Savelsan, of what he saw and heard in the billiard-room and afterwards; of the silent and indisputable witness of big, bullnecked Harland himself; and, lastly, of the conversation which subsequently took place between these three men and Mr Flaxman Low, the noted psychologist.

It was by the merest chance that Harland and his two guests spent that memorable evening of the 18th of January, 1899, in the house of Medhans Lea. The house stands on the slope of a partially-wooded ridge in one of the Midland Counties. It faces south, and overlooks a wide valley bounded by the blue outlines of the Bredon hills. The place is secluded, the nearest dwelling being a small public-house at the cross roads some mile and a half from the lodge gates.

Medhans Lea is famous for its long straight avenue of beeches, and for other things. Harland, when he signed the lease, was thinking of the avenue of beeches; not of the other things, of which he knew nothing till later.

Harland had made his money by running tea plantations in Assam, and he owned all the virtues and faults of a man who has spent most of his life abroad. The first time he visited the house he weighed seventeen stone and ended most of his sentences with 'don't yer know?' His ideas could hardly be said to travel on the higher planes of thought, and his chief aim in life was to keep himself down to seventeen stone. He had a red neck and a blue eye, and was a muscular, inoffensive, good-natured man, with courage to spare, and an excellent voice for accompanying the banjo.

After signing the lease, he found that Medhans Lea needed an immense amount of putting in order and decorating. While this was being done, he came backwards and forwards to the nearest provincial town, where he stopped at a hotel, driving out almost daily to superintend the arrangements of his new habitation. Thus he had been away for the Christmas and New Year, but about the 15th January he returned to the Red Lion, accompanied by his friends Nare-Jones and Savelsan, who proposed to move with him into his new house during the course of the ensuing week.

The immediate cause of their visit to Medhans Lea on the evening of the 18th inst. was the fact that the billiard table at the Red Lion was not fit, as Harland remarked, to play shinty on, while there was an excellent table just put in at Medhans Lea, where the big billiard-room in the left wing had a wide window with a view down a portion of the beech avenue.

'Hang it!' said Harland, 'I wish they would hurry up with the house. The painters aren't out of it yet, and the people don't come to the Lodge till Monday.'

'It's a pity, too,' remarked Savelsan regretfully, 'when you think of that table.'

Savelsan was an enthusiast in billiards, who spent all the time he could spare from his business, which happened to be teabroking, at the game. He was the more sorry for the delay, since Harland was one of the few men he knew to whom it was not necessary to give points.

'It's a ripping table,' returned Harland. 'Tell you what,' he added, struck by a happy idea, 'I'll send out Thoms to make things straight for us tomorrow, and we'll put a case of syphons and a bottle of whisky under the seat of the trap, and drive over for a game after dinner.'

The other two agreed to this arrangement, but in the morning Nare-Jones found himself obliged to run up to London to see about securing a berth as ship's doctor. It was settled, however, that on his return he was to follow Harland and Savelsan to Medhans Lea.

He got back by the 8.30, entirely delighted, because he had booked a steamer bound for the Persian Gulf and Karachi, and had gained the cheering intelligence that a virulent type of cholera was lying in wait for the advent of the Mecca pilgrims in at any rate two of the chief ports of call, which would give him precisely the experience he desired.

Having dined, and the night being fine, he ordered a dogcart to take him out to Medhans Lea. The moon had just risen by the time he reached the entrance to the avenue, and as he was beginning to feel cold he pulled up, intending to walk to the house. Then he dismissed the boy and cart, a carriage having been ordered to come for the whole party after midnight. Nare-Jones stopped to light a cigar before entering the avenue, then he walked past the empty lodge. He moved briskly in the best possible temper with himself and all the world. The night was still, and his collar up, his feet fell silently on the dry carriage road, while his mind was away on blue water forecasting his voyage on the S.S. *Sumatra*.

He says he was quite halfway up the avenue before he became conscious of anything unusual. Looking up at the sky, he noticed what a bright, clear night it was, and how sharply defined the outline of the beeches stood out against the vault of heaven. The moon was yet low, and threw netted shadows of bare twigs and branches on the road which ran between black lines of trees in an almost straight vista up to the dead grey face of the house now barely two hundred yards away. Altogether it struck him as forming a pallid picture, etched in like a steel engraving in black, and grey, and white.

He was thinking of this when he was aware of words spoken rapidly in his ear, and he turned half expecting to see someone behind him. No one was visible. He had not caught the words, nor could he define the voice; but a vague conviction of some horrible meaning fixed itself in his consciousness.

The night was very still, ahead of him the house glimmered grey and shuttered in the moonlight. He shook himself, and walked on oppressed by a novel sensation compounded of disgust and childish fear; and still, from behind his shoulder, came the evil, voiceless murmuring.

He admits that he passed the end of the avenue at an amble, and was abreast of a semi-circle of shrubbery, when a small object was thrust from the shadow of the bushes, and lay in the open light. Though the night was peculiarly still, it fluttered and balanced a moment, as if windblown, then came in skimming flights to his feet. He picked it up and made for the door, which yielded to his hand, and he flung it to and bolted it behind him.

Once in the warmly-lit hall his senses returned, and he waited to recover breath and composure before facing the two men whose voices and laughter came from a room on his right. But the door of the room was thrown open, and the burly figure of Harland in his shirt-sleeves appeared on the threshold.

'Hullo, Jones, that you? Come along!' he said genially.

'Bless me!' exclaimed Nare-Jones irritably, 'there's not a light in any of the windows. It might be a house of the dead!'

Harland stared at him, but all he said was: 'Have a whisky-and-soda?'

Savelsan, who was leaning over the billiard table, trying side-strokes with his back to Nare-Jones, added:

'Did you expect us to illuminate the place for you? There's not a soul in the house but ourselves.'

'Say when,' said Harland, poising the bottle over a glass.

Nare-Jones laid down what he held in his hand on the corner of the billiard table, and took up his glass.

'What in creation's this?' asked Savelsan.

'I don't know; the wind blew it to my feet just outside.' replied Nare-Jones, between two long pulls at the whisky-and-soda.

'*Blown* to your feet?' repeated Savelsan, taking up the thing and weighing it in his hand. 'It must be blowing a hurricane then.'

'It isn't blowing at all,' returned Nare-Jones blankly. 'The night is dead calm.'

For the object that had fluttered and rolled so lightly across the turf and gravel was a small battered, metal calf, made of some heavy brass amalgam.

Savelsan looked incredulously into Nare-Jones' face, and laughed.

'What's wrong with you? You look queer.'

Nare-Jones laughed too; he was already ashamed of the last ten minutes.

Harland was meantime examining the metal calf.

'It's a Bengali idol,' he said. 'It's been knocked about a good bit, by Jove! You say it blew out of the shrubbery?'

'Like a bit of paper, I give you my word, though there was not a breath of wind going,' admitted Nare-Jones.

'Seems odd, don't yer know?' remarked Hark carelessly. 'Now you two fellows had better begin; I'll mark.'

Nare-Jones happened to be in form that night, and Savelsan became absorbed in the delightful difficulty giving him a sound thrashing.

Suddenly Savelsan paused in his stroke.

'What the sin's that?' he asked.

They stood listening. A thin, broken crying could heard.

'Sounds like green a plover,' remarked Nare-Jones chalking his cue.

'It's a kitten they've shut up somewhere,' said Harlan.

'That's a child, and in the deuce of a fright, too,' said Savelsan. 'You'd better go and tuck it up in its little bed Harland,' he added, with a laugh.

Harland opened the door. There could no longer be any doubt about the sounds; the stifled shrieks and thin whimpering told of a child in the extremity of pain and fear.

'It's upstairs,' said Harland. 'I'm going to see.'

Nare-Jones picked up a lamp and followed him.

'I'll stay here,' said Savelsan, sitting down by the fire.

In the hall the two men stopped and listened again. It is hard to locate a noise, but this seemed to come from upper landing.

'Poor little beggar!' exclaimed Harland, as he bounded up the staircase. The bedroom doors opening on the square central landing above were all locked, the keys being on the outside. But the crying led them into a side passage which ended in a single room.

'It's in here, and the door's locked,' said Nare-Jones. 'Call out and see who's there.'

But Harland was set on business. He flung his weight against the panel, and the door burst open, the lock ricocheting noisily into a corner. As they passed in, the crying ceased abruptly.

Harland stood in the centre of the room, while Nare-Jones held up the light to look round.

'The dickens!' exclaimed Harland exhaustively.

The room was entirely empty.

Not so much as a cupboard broke the smooth surface of the walls, only the two low windows and the door by which they had entered.

'This is the room above the billiard-room, isn't it?' said Nare-Jones at last.

'Yes. This is the only one I have not had furnished yet. I thought I might—'

He stopped short, for behind them burst out a peal of harsh, mocking laughter, that rang and echoed between the bare walls.

Both men swung round simultaneously, and both caught a glimpse of a tall, thin figure in black, rocking with laughter in the doorway, but when they turned it was gone. They dashed out into the passage and landing. No one was to be seen. The doors were locked as before, and the staircase and hall were vacant.

After making a prolonged search through every corner of the house, they went back to Savelsan in the billiard-room.

'What were you laughing about? What is it anyway?' began Savelsan at once.

'It's nothing. And we didn't laugh,' replied Nare-Jones definitely.

'But I heard you,' insisted Savelsan. 'And where's the child?'

'I wish you'd go up and find it,' returned Harland grimly. 'We heard the laughing and saw, or thought we saw, a man in black—'

'Something like a priest in a cassock,' put in Nare-Jones.

'Yes, like a priest,' assented Harland, 'but as we turned he disappeared.'

Savelsan sat down and gazed from one to the other of his companions.

'The house behaves as if it was haunted,' he remarked, 'only there is no such thing as an authenticated ghost outside the experiences of the Psychical Research Society. I'd ask the Society down if I were you, Harland. You never can tell what you may find in these old houses.'

'It's not an old house,' replied Harland. 'It was built somewhere about '40. I certainly saw that man; and, look to it, Savelsan, I'll find out who or what he is. That I swear! The English law makes no allowance for ghosts—nor will I.'

'You'll have your hands full, or I'm mistaken,' exclaimed Savelsan, grinning. 'A ghost that laughs and cries in a breath, and rolls battered idols about your front door, is not to be trifled with. The night is young yet—not much past eleven. I vote for a peg all round and then I'll finish off Jones.'

Harland, sunk in a fit of sullen abstraction, sat on a settee, and watched them. On a sudden he said:

'It's turned beastly cold.'

'There's a beastly smell, you mean,' corrected Savelsan crossly, as he went round the table. He had made a break of forty and did not want to be interrupted. 'The draught is from the window.'

'I've not noticed it before this evening,' said Harland, as he opened the shutters to make sure.

As he did so the night air rushed in heavy with the smell of an old well that has not been uncovered for years, a smell of slime and unwholesome wetness. The lower part of the window was wide open and Harland banged it down.

'It's abominable!' he said, with an angry sniff. 'Enough to give us all typhoid.'

'Only dead leaves,' remarked Nare-Jones. 'There are the rotten leaves of twenty winters under the trees and outside this window. I noticed them when we came over on Tuesday.'

'I'll have them cleared away to-morrow. I wonder how Thoms came to leave this window open,' grumbled Harland, as he closed and bolted the shutter. 'What do you say—forty-five?' and he went over to mark it up.

The game went on for some time, and Nare-Jones was lying across the table with the cue poised, when he heard a slight sound behind him. Looking round he saw Harland, his face flushed and angry, passing softly— wonderfully softly for so big a man, Nare-Jones remembers thinking— along the angle of the wall towards the window.

All three men unite in declaring that they were watching the shutter, which opened inwards as if thrust by some furtive hand from outside. At the moment Nare-Jones and Savelsan were standing directly opposite to it on the further side of the table, while Harland crouched behind the shutter intent on giving the intruder a lesson.

As the shutter unfolded to its utmost the two men opposite saw a face pressed against the glass, a furrowed evil face, with a wide laugh perched upon its sinister features.

There was a second of absolute stillness, and Nare-Jones' eyes met those other eyes with the fascinated horror of a mutual understanding, as all the foul fancies that had pursued him in the avenue poured back into his mind.

With an uncontrollable impulse of resentment, he snatched a billiard ball from the table and flung it with all his strength at the face. The ball crashed through the glass and through the face beyond it! The glass fell shattered, but the face remained for an instant peering and grinning at the aperture, then as Harland sprang forward it was gone.

'The ball went clean through it!' said Savelsan with a gasp.

They crowded to the window, and throwing up the sash, leant out. The dank smell clung about the air, a boat-shaped moon glimmered between the bare branches, and on the white drive beyond the shrubbery the billiard be could be seen a shining spot under the moon. Nothing more.

'Whatwasit?' asked Harland.

' "Only a face at the window," ' quoted Savelsan with an awkward attempt at making light of his own scare. 'Devilish queer face too, eh, Jones?'

'I wish I'd got him!' returned Harland frowning. 'I'm not going to put up with any tricks about the place, don't yer know?'

'You'd bottle any tramp loafing around,' said Nare-Jones.

Harland looked down at his immense arms outlined in his shirt-sleeves.

'I could that,' he answered. 'But this chap—did you hit him?'

'Clean through the face! Or, at any rate, it looked like it,' replied Savelsan, as Nare-Jones stood silent.

Harland shut the shutter and poked up the fire.

'It's a cursed creepy affair!' he said. 'I hope the servants won't get hold of this nonsense. Ghosts play the very mischief with a house. Though I don't believe in them myself,' he concluded.

Then Savelsan broke out in an unexpected place.

'Nor do I—as a rule,' he said slowly. 'Still, you know it: a sickening idea to think of a spirit condemned to haunt the scene of its crime waiting for the world to die.'

Harland and Nare-Jones looked at him.

'Have a whisky neat,' suggested Harland, soothingly. 'I never knew you taken that way before.'

Nare-Jones laughed out. He says he does not know why he laughed nor why he said what follows.

'It's this way,' he said. 'The moment of foul satisfaction is gone for ever, yet for all-time the guilty spirit must perpetuate its sin—the sin that brought no lasting reward, only a momentary reward experienced, it may be, centuries ago, but to which still clings the punishment of eternally rehearsing in loneliness, and cold, and gloom, the sin of other days. No punishment can be conceived more horrible. Savelsan is right.'

'I think we've had enough about ghosts,' said Harland, cheerfully, 'let's go on. Hurry up, Savelsan.'

'There's the billiard ball,' said Nare-Jones. 'Who'll go fetch?'

'Not I,' replied Savelsan promptly. 'When that—was at the window, I felt sick.'

Nare-Jones nodded. 'And I wanted to bolt!' he said emphatically.

Harland faced about from the fire.

'And I, though I saw nothing but the shutter, I—hang it!—don't yer know—so did I! There was panic in the air for a minute. But I'm shot if I'm afraid now,' he concluded doggedly, 'I'll go.'

His heavy animal face was lit with courage and resolution.

'I've spent close upon five thousand pounds over this blessed house first and last, and I'm not going to be done out of it by any infernal spiritualism!' he added, as he took down his coat and pulled it on.

'It's all in view from the window except those few yards through the shrubbery,' said Savelsan. 'Take a stick and go. Though, on second thoughts, I bet you a fiver you don't.'

'I don't want a stick,' answered Harland. 'I'm not afraid—not now— and I'd meet most men with my hands.'

Nare-Jones opened the shutters again; the sash was low and he pushed the window up, and leant far out.

'It's not much of a drop,' he said, and slung his legs out over the lintel;

180

but the night was full of the smell, and something else. He leapt back into the room. 'Don't go, Harland!'

Harland gave him a look that set his blood burning.

'What is there, after all, to be afraid of in a ghost?' he asked heavily.

Nare-Jones, sick with the sense of his own newly-born cowardice, yet entirely unable to master it, answered feebly:

'I can't say, but don't go.'

The words seemed inevitable, though he could have kicked himself for hanging back.

There was a forced laugh from Savelsan.

'Give it up and stop at home, little man,' he said.

Harland merely snorted in reply, and laid his great leg over the window ledge. The other two watched his big, tweed-clad figure as it crossed the grass and disappeared into the shrubbery.

'You and I are in a preposterous funk,' said Savelsan, with unpleasant explicitness, as Harland, whistling loudly, passed into the shadow.

But this was a point on which Nare-Jones could not bring himself to speak at the moment. Then they sat on the sill and waited. The moon shone out clearly above the avenue, which now lay white and undimmed between its crowding trees.

'And he's whistling because he's afraid,' continued Savelsan.

'He's not often afraid,' replied Nare-Jones shortly; 'besides, he's doing what neither of us were very keen on.'

The whistling stopped suddenly. Savelsan said afterwards that he fancied he saw Harland's huge, grey-clad shoulders, with uplifted arms, rise for a second above the bushes.

Then out of the silence came peal upon peal of that infernal laughter, and, following it, the thin pitiful crying of the child. That too ceased, and an absolute stillness seemed to fall upon the place.

They leant out and listened intently. The minutes passed slowly. In the middle of the avenue the billiard ball glinted on the gravel, but there was no sign of Harland emerging from the shrubbery path.

'He should be there by now,' said Nare-Jones anxiously.

They listened again; everything was quiet. The ticking of Harland's big watch on the mantelpiece was distinctly audible.

'This is too much,' said Nare-Jones. 'I'm going to see where he is.'

He swung himself out on the grass, and Savelsan called to him to wait, as he was coming also. While Nare-Jones stood waiting, there was a sound as of a pig grunting and rooting among the dead leaves in the shrubbery.

They ran forward into the darkness, and found the shrubbery path. A minute later they came upon something that tossed and snorted and rolled under the shrubs.

'Great Heavens!' cried Nare-Jones, 'it's Harland!'

'He's breaking somebody's neck,' added Savelsan, peering into the gloom.

Nare-Jones was himself again. The powerful instinct of his profession—the help-giving instinct—possessed him to the exclusion of every other feeling.

'He's in a fit—just a fit,' he said in matter-of-fact tones, as he bent over the struggling form; 'that's all.'

With the assistance of Savelsan, he managed to carry Harland out into the open drive. Harland's eyes were fearful, and froth hung about his blue puffing lips as they laid him down upon the ground. He rolled over, and lay still, while from the shadows broke another shout of laughter.

'It's apoplexy. We must get him away from here,' said Nare-Jones. 'But, first, I'm going to see what is in those bushes.'

He dashed through the shrubbery, backwards and forwards. He seemed to feel the strength of ten men as he wrenched and tore and trampled the branches, letting in the light of the moon to its darkness. At last he paused, exhausted.

'Of course, there's nothing,' said Savelsan wearily. 'What did you expect after the incident of the billiard ball?'

Together, with awful toil, they bore the big man down the narrow avenue, and at the lodge gates they met the carriage.

Some time later the subject of their common experiences at Medhans Lea was discussed amongst the three men. Indeed, for many weeks Harland had not been in a state to discuss any subject at all, but as soon as he was allowed to do so, he invited Nare-Jones and Savelsan to meet Mr Flaxman Low, the scientist, whose works on psychology and kindred matters are so well known at the Metropole, to thresh out the matter.

Flaxman Low listened with his usual air of gentle abstraction, from time to time making notes on the back of an envelope. He looked at each narrator in turn as he took up the thread of the story. He understood perfectly that the man who stood furthest from the mystery must inevitably have been the self-centred Savelsan; next in order came Nare-Jones, with sympathetic possibilities, but a crowded brain; closest of all would be big, kindly Harland, with more than one strong animal instinct about him, and whose bulk of matter was evidently permeated by a receptive spirit.

When they had ended, Savelsan turned to Flaxman Low.

'There you have the events, Mr Low. Now, the question is how to deal with them.'

'Classify them,' replied Flaxman Low.

'The crying would seem to indicate a child,' began Savelsan, ticking off the list on his fingers; 'the black figure, the face at the window, and the laughter are naturally connected. So far I can go alone. I conclude that we saw the apparition of a man, possibly a priest, who had during his lifetime illtreated a child, and whose punishment it is to haunt the scene of his crime.'

'Precisely—the punishment being worked out under conditions which admit of human observation,' returned Flaxman Low. 'As for the child the sound of crying was merely part of the *mise-en-scène*. The child was not there.'

'But that explanation stops short of several points. Now about the suggestive thoughts experienced by my friend Nare-Jones; what brought on the fit in the case of Mr Harland, who assures us that he was not suffering from fright or other violent emotion; and what connection can be traced between all these things and the Bengali idol?' Savelsan ended.

'Let us take the Bengali idol first,' said Low. 'It is just one of those discrepant particulars which, at first sight, seem wholly irreconcilable with the rest of the phenomena, yet these often form a test point, by which our theories are proved or otherwise.' Flaxman Low took up the metal calf from the table as he spoke. 'I should be inclined to connect this with the child. Observe it. It has not been roughly used; it is rubbed and dinted as a plaything usually is. I should say the child may have had Anglo-Indian relations.'

At this, Nare-Jones bent forward, and in his turn examined the idol, while Savelsan smiled his thin, incredulous smile.

'These are ingenious theories,' he said; 'but we are really no nearer to facts, I am afraid.'

'The only proof would be an inquiry into the former history of Medhans Lea; if events had happened there which would go to support this theory, why, then—But I cannot supply that information since I never heard of Medhans Lea or the ghost until I entered this room.'

'I know something of Medhans Lea,' put in Nare-Jones. 'I found out a good deal about it before I left the place. And I must congratulate Mr Low on his methods, for his theory tallies in a wonderful manner with the facts of the case. The house was long known to be haunted. It seems that many years ago a lady, the widow of an Indian officer, lived there with her only child, a boy, for whom she engaged a tutor, a dark-looking man, who wore a long black coat like a cassock, and was called "the Jesuit" by the country people.

'One evening the man took the boy out into the shrubbery. Screams were heard, and when the child was brought in he was found to have lost his reason. He used to cry and shriek incessantly, but was never able to tell what had been done to him as long as he lived. As for this idol, the mother probably brought it with her from India, and the child used it as a toy, perhaps, because he was allowed no others. Hullo!' In handling the calf, Nare-Jones had touched some hidden spring, the head opened, disclosing a small cavity, from which dropped a little ring of blue beads, such as children made. He held it up. 'This affords good proof.'

'Yes,' admitted Savelsan grudgingly. 'But how about your sensations and Harland's seizure? You must know what was done to the child, Harland—what did you see in the shrubbery?'

Harland's florid face assumed a queer pallor.

'I saw something,' replied he hesitatingly, 'but I can't recall what it was. I only remember being possessed by a blind terror, and then nothing more until I recovered consciousness at the hotel next day.'

'Can you account for this, Mr Low?' asked Nare-Jones, 'and there was also my strange notion of the whispering in the avenue.'

'I think so,' replied Flaxman Low. 'I believe that the theory of atmospheric influences, which includes the power of environment to reproduce certain scenes and also thoughts, would throw light upon your sensations as well as Mr Harland's. Such influences play a far larger part in our everyday experience than we have as yet any idea of.'

There was a silence of a few moments; then Harland spoke:

'I fancy that we have said all that there is to be said upon the matter. We are much obliged to you, Mr Low. I don't know how it strikes you other fellows, but, speaking for myself, I have seen enough of ghosts to last me for a very long time.

'And now,' ended Harland wearily, 'if you have no objections, we will pass on to pleasanter subjects.'

THE PASSING OF EDWARD

RICHARD MIDDLETON

I found Dorothy sitting sedately on the beach, with a mass of black sea-weed twined in her hands and her bare feet sparkling white in the sun. Even in the first glow of recognition I realised that she was paler than she had been the summer before, and yet I cannot blame myself for the tactlessness of my question.

'Where's Edward?' I said; and I looked about the sands for a sailor suit and a little pair of prancing legs.

While I looked, Dorothy's eyes watched mine enquiringly, as if she wondered what I might see.

'Edward's dead,' she said simply. 'He died last year, after you left.'

For a moment I could only gaze at the child in silence, and ask myself what reason there was in the thing that had hurt her so. Now that I knew that Edward played with her no more, I could see that there was a shadow upon her face too dark for her years, and that she had lost, to some extent, that exquisite carelessness of poise which makes children so young. Her voice was so calm that I might have thought her forgetful had I not seen an instant of patent pain in her wide eyes.

'I'm sorry,' I said at length, 'very, very, sorry indeed. I had brought down my car to take you for a drive, as I promised.'

'Oh! Edward *would* have liked that,' she answered thoughtfully; 'he was so fond of motors.'

She swung round suddenly and looked at the sands behind her with staring eyes.

'I thought I heard—' She broke off in confusion.

I, too, had believed for an instant that I had heard something that was not the wind or the distant children or the smooth sea hissing along the beach. During that golden summer which linked me with the dead, Edward had been wont, in moments of elation, to puff up and down the sands, in artistic representation of a nobby, noisy motor-car. But the dead may play no more, and there was nothing there but the sands and the hot sky and Dorothy.

'You had better let me take you for a run, Dorothy,' I said. 'The man will drive, and we can talk as we go along.'

She nodded gravely, and began pulling on her sandy stockings.

'It did not hurt him,' she said inconsequently.

The restraint in her voice pained me like a blow.

'Oh, don't, dear, don't!' I cried. 'There is nothing to do but forget.'

'I have forgotten, quite,' she answered, pulling at her shoelaces with calm fingers. 'It was ten months ago.'

We walked up to the front, where the car was waiting, and Dorothy settled herself among the cushions with a little sigh of contentment, the human quality of which brought me a certain relief. If only she would laugh or cry! I sat down by her side, but the man waited by the open door.

'What is it?' I asked.

'I'm sorry, sir,' he answered, looking about him in confusion, 'I thought I saw a young gentleman with you.'

He shut the door with a bang, and in a minute we were running through the town. I knew that Dorothy was watching my face with her wounded eyes; but I did not look at her until the green fields leapt up on either side of the white road.

'It is only for a little while that we may not see him,' I said; 'all this is nothing.'

'I have forgotten,' she repeated. 'I think this is a very nice motor.'

I had not previously complained of the motor, but I was wishing then that it would cease its poignant imitation of a little dead boy, a boy who would play no more. By the touch of Dorothy's sleeve against mine I knew that she could hear it too. And the miles flew by, green and brown and golden, while I wondered what use I might be in the world, who could not help a child to forget. Possibly there was another way, I thought.

'Tell me how it happened,' I said.

Dorothy looked at me with inscrutable eyes, and spoke in a voice without emotion.

'He caught a cold, and was very ill in bed. I went in to see him, and he was all white and faded. I said to him, "How are you, Edward?" and he said, "I shall get up early in the morning to catch beetles." I didn't see him any more.' 'Poor little chap!' I murmured.

'I went to the funeral,' she continued monotonously. 'It was very rainy, and I threw a little bunch of flowers down into the hole. There was a whole lot of flowers there; but I think Edward liked apples better than flowers.'

'Did you cry?' I said cruelly.

She paused. 'I don't know. I suppose so. It was a long time ago; I think I have forgotten.'

Even while she spoke I heard Edward puffing along the sands: Edward who had been so fond of apples.

'I cannot stand this any longer,' I said aloud. 'Let's get out and walk in the woods for a change.'

She agreed, with a depth of comprehension that terrified me; and the motor pulled up with a jerk at a spot where hardly a post served to mark where the woods commenced and the wayside grass stopped. We took one of the dim paths which the rabbits had made and forced our way through the undergrowth into the peaceful twilight of the trees.

'You haven't got very sunburnt this year,' I said as we walked.

'I don't know why. I've been out on the beach all the days. Sometimes I've played, too.'

I did not ask her what games she had played, or who had been her play-friend. Yet even there in the quiet woods I knew that Edward was holding her back from me. It is true that, in his boy's way, he had been fond of me; but I should not have dared to take her out without him in the days when his live lips had filled the beach with song, and his small brown body had danced among the surf. Now it seemed that I had been disloyal to him.

And presently we came to a clearing where the leaves of forgotten years lay brown and rotten beneath our feet, and the air was full of the dryness of death.

'Let's be going back. What do you think, Dorothy?' I said.

'I think,' she said slowly, 'I think that this would be a very good place to catch beetles.'

A wood is full of secret noises, and that is why, I suppose, we heard a pair of small quick feet come with a dance of triumph through the rustling bracken. For a minute we listened deeply, and then Dorothy broke from my side with a piercing call on her lips.

'Oh, Edward, Edward!' she cried; 'Edward!'

But the dead may play no more, and presently she came back to me with the tears that are the riches of childhood streaming down her face.

'I can hear him, I can hear him,' she sobbed; 'but I cannot see him. Never, never again.'

And so I led her back to the motor. But in her tears I seemed to find a promise of peace that she had not known before.

Now Edward was no very wonderful little boy; it may be that he was jealous and vain and greedy; yet now, it seemed as he lay in his small grave with the memory of Dorothy's flowers about him, he had wrought this kindness for his sister. Yes, even though we heard no more than the birds in the branches and the wind swaying the scented bracken; even though he had passed with another summer, and the dead and the love of the dead may rise no more from the grave.

AN UNSOLVED MYSTERY

E. Owens Blackburne

About the close of the eighteenth century, the life of Dublin was at its zenith; the Ranelagh Gardens were the resort of the beaux and belles of the day; the Parliament was held in College Green; and its members had their town residences in Dublin, and lived there for a considerable portion of the year.

One of the members, an illustrious Irish nobleman who had spent some portion of his youth in Italy, was a man of cultivated taste and refinement. Upon his return to Dublin, he conceived the idea of inviting over some Italian artists to decorate the walls and ceilings of his residence after the Florentine manner. He carried out his idea, and the ornamentations of Charlemont House bear witness to the taste and skill of the decorators. Other noblemen employed these artists; the present Royal Irish Academy House, then a noble, private residence, is similarly decorated, also several other city mansions in several of the leading streets and squares.

When Dublin decreased in importance after the Act of Union in 1801, and was no longer the centre of fashion for the Irish nobility, its splendid private residences gradually decayed; and wealthy burghers and Dublin's proverbially professional aristocracy now inhabit them. Many of the houses yet retain their curious, rare old decorations, and of one of these residences, situated in a leading square, we would more especially speak.

A large, stately, gloomy-looking house, with a ponderous hall-door, studded with iron nails, like the door of a cathedral. High, narrow windows with Italian jalousies. The grass grows in the interstices of the high, steep steps, now fast falling away. The rusty iron railings have become loosened in their stone settings, and seem as though a good push would hurl them into the mouldering, vault-like areas. Entering the hall, a damp, earthy smell greets the intruder—for, intruder must anyone be considered who ventures into that region of ghostliness. The wide, flagged, echoing hall, the broad, dark, oak-panelled staircase, lead to chambers awful in their oppressive sense of loneliness and utter desolation. Cobwebs festoon the painted walls; queer, crawling creatures hold high holiday on the once polished floors; but not even the squeak of a rat of mouse breaks the solemn, death-like stillness which pervades this old, deserted mansion.

> *'Over all there hung a cloud of fear,*
> *A sense of mystery the spirit daunted,*
> *And said, as plain as whisper to the ear,*
> *"The house is haunted." '*

Twenty-five years ago this house was tenanted by Miss Steele, an eccentric old lady, who, dying suddenly at the advanced age of ninety-one, her property—including this house and furniture—came into the possession of a married grand-niece living in Kildare, whom she had never seen. The season in Dublin was just commencing about the time that all preliminary law-matters connected with the property were being settled, and the heiress, Mrs Nugent, acting upon the advice of her lawyer, resolved to let the house furnished. The furniture, although antique, was handsome; especially that of the drawing-room. The walls and ceilings of this apartment were superbly ornamented in the Florentine style. Arabesques on a pale blue ground adorned the ceilings; the panels of the walls were painted with groups of figures of rare pieces of still-life; whilst from the moudlings which separated these panels, sprang figures which, bending downwards, held the candelabra lighting the apartment. The furniture was in keeping with the architecture —of inlaid wood, heavy with gilding and upholstered in amber satin; it was of that stately and old-world type which suggested the days of minuets, apple-blossom sacques, cherry-coloured satin petticoats, and high-heeled shoes. A spindle-legged spinet stood near the fireplace, wherein was no grate, but great brass dogs. The fireplace was tiled with the queer little Dutch tiles that came over with the tulips in the days of William and Mary. These tiles bore a succession of Adams and Eves, of Cains and Abels, and other scriptural characters, who looked sadly out of place amongst the nymphs, and satyrs, and similar profanities which surrounded the chamber.

The house was no sooner advertised, than it was immediately taken by an officer then quartered in Dublin. Being a man of taste, Colonel Comyers would not allow the house to be remodeled in any way. Mrs Comyers, too, was a woman who liked novelty, and she triumphantly pictured to herself what a delightful sensation her antique-looking drawing-room would create when well lighted up and filled with a fashionable mob. A pretty, piquante little woman, she was enthusiastically charmed, enchanted, with her Irish residence. One day, about the beginning of October, she moved into it, with her two infant children, and two servants that she had brought from England—a cook and a nurse. For the first night she had no other servants in the house.

Upon the first evening of Mrs Comyers's arrival, her husband was obliged to spend the day and night from home. She amused herself by wandering about the old house, prying into musty cabinets and cupboards, looking with wondering and admiring eyes upon the rare old Venetian glass and egg-shell china, which seemed almost too fine and too delicate for use. About half-past six o'clock, as she sat in the drawing-room, the nurse entered, saying that it was necessary for her to go out to buy some things urgently required. The woman respectfully asked her mistress if she would go up to the nursery to the children should she hear them cry.

'Certainly, Nurse. I suppose you will not be very long away?'

'I cannot say, madam. I do not know Dublin.'

'Then I think Cook had better go with you—she has been here before. I dare say no one will call this evening.'

'Thank you, madam,' and the nurse left the room. Presently, Mrs Comyers heard the hall-door closed, and the two women's footsteps echoing down the steps.

A quarter of an hour—twenty minutes passed. The doors between the drawing-room and the nursery, two flights higher up, were left open, so that Mrs Comyers could hear every sound. The evening was fast closing in, and she experienced a strange feeling of loneliness, and began to regret her foolish impulse in allowing both servants to go out. She laid down the book she had been reading, and presently one of the children gave a cry.

The mother started from the couch where she was reclining, and was about to go up to the nursery, when hurried footsteps on the stairs struck upon her ear.

'Oh! I need not go,' she said to herself; 'I suppose Cook has stayed at home, after all': and, having by this time reached the door, she indeed saw, by the waning light, the figure of an elderly woman turning the landing of the flight upstairs opposite to her. Mrs Comyers returned to her sofa. But the child's crying did not cease; and as she listened, it increased from a whining cry to a wail of terror. In alarm she started up and ran to the nursery. The eldest boy, a child of three years old, was sitting up in bed, shrieking; but the cook was nowhere to be seen.

In vain Mrs Comyers tried to pacify the child. 'Freddy,' she asked, 'did not Cook come up to you?'

But the child only sobbed the more convulsively; so much so, that the mother refrained from asking any further questions. Softly singing to him, he was soon asleep again, and she stole quietly from the room. It was almost dark, yet she distinctly saw, walking a few steps before her, the figure of the woman which she yet believed to be the cook.

'Why, Cook, I thought you had gone out with Nurse.'

The figure had just reached the bottom of the flight of stairs; it turned slowly round, revealing the face of an old woman with a white cap-border closely crimped around her puckered-up, leering face. A gruesome, weird light seemed to surround her, so that Mrs Comyers distinctly saw the shrivelled lips move, the bleared eyes gleam; and the shaky, skinny hand, which was raised and shaken menacingly at her. The figure then turned and ran swiftly down the stairs.

For a moment, Mrs Comyers was frightened; but, girding up her courage, she blamed herself for giving way to nervousness—persuading herself that it must be some person engaged by the cook. She walked slowly down the stairs, her heart beating violently, and called out, courageously:

'My good woman, who are you; and what is your business here?'

For answer, a chuckling laugh resounded throughout the echoing old house. The clatter of many feet was heard upon the stairs; still, the brave little woman hardly quailed. But what was she to do? She was too terrified to venture after the figure. Just then, there was a knock at the hall-door, and, with a sense of relief, she hastened down to open it. The two women-servants entered.

'Cook,' said Mrs Comyers, 'did you leave anyone in the house during your absence?'

'No, madam.'

'Well, you had better go and look in the kitchen, for some woman went down the stairs just now.'

Lights were speedily procured, and every inch of the basement storey was unavailingly searched. The doors were then secured, and as Mrs

Comyers saw the servants were rather frightened, she wisely refrained from entering into any particulars concerning either the manner of the figure, or the strange noises which she had heard.

The next day she related the circumstance to her husband, who laughed at her nervous fancies, and practically suggested that a close eye be kept on the area gate. The weeks flew by, and the affair seemed to be almost forgotten; until one evening, as Colonel and Mrs Comyers sat alone in the dining-room, the sound of many footsteps was heard in the drawing-room overhead, and a plaintive air was played upon the old spinet. They listened, amazed, for a minute, and at length Mrs Comyers said:

'Henry, I am sure it is that—that thing!'

'You little goose!' he exclaimed, laughing. 'Stay where you are, and I'll go and see.'

He bounded up the stairs—there was a hurried shuffling of feet: the music ceased, and he soon returned. The scene he had witnessed he could not relate to his nervous, delicate wife. Therefore, to avoid being questioned, he said, with an assumption of gaiety:

'Mabel, congratulate me! I have at last seen your mythical old woman!'

Mrs Comyers shivered, and nestled into her husband's sheltering arms, as she whispered, faintly: 'Yes, I know you have seen her, for I saw her go before you out of the room.'

They could not account for the phenomenon, and naturally were diffident about mentioning it to anyone. Thus the time passed on until Christmas.

With the Christmas-time, there arrived a nephew of Colonel Comyers. Clever, handsome, merry Val Wycherley: a young doctor who had just taken out his diploma. He had passed a brilliant examination, and before again resuming work, had come to spend a few weeks in Dublin, for the purpose of resting his overtasked brain. It was agreed that he should not be told anything about the mysterious old woman.

On Christmas Day a number of friends were expected to dine. There was also to be an evening party; therefore, in order to save trouble, Mrs Comyers had had the dining-table arranged early in the afternoon, and then locked the door. She was very proud of her daintily-arranged table: she had tastefully disposed the quaint-coloured and gilt Venetian glass, and the rare old china belonging to the house. Groups of shepherds and shepherdesses holding cornucopias filled with glistening holly, interspersed with its own bright red berries and the snowy white ones of those of the mistletoe, were placed at intervals along the table.

About five in the afternoon, as Colonel Comyers and his nephew were sauntering home round the square, a sudden and heavy shower came on. They walked fast, but by the time they arrived at the hall-door they were thoroughly drenched. Colonel Comyers immediately went into his dressing-room on the first landing, inviting his nephew to follow; but that free-and-easy young gentleman preferred taking off his wet boots in the hall.

'Here, Bridget!—Mary!—Whoever you are, take these boots, like a good girl,' said he, addressing a woman standing in the shade at the top of the kitchen-stairs.

An aged woman, habited in an old-fashioned black gown, with a white handkerchief pinned across her bosom, approached him. He threw the boots to her, and, to his horror, *they went through her!* and then the figure vanished! Val being a doctor, his practical thought was, 'By Jove! My head must be in a precious queer state! A bad lookout for me and Christmas fare in prospective. I had better say nothing however, or these good folk may think I am completely off my head.'

He walked slowly up the stairs, and on the first landing again was the figure. It preceded him step by step, but Val did not feel frightened; as before, ascribing the vision to purely physical causes acting upon a brain which he felt was overtasked. Although a medical man, it did not occur to him to apply the unfailing test of pressing one eye so as to throw out of the parallel focus with the other. If the object be the result of hallucination, it is seen still and simply; if actual vision, it is seen double. The figure entered the drawing room. Val mechanically followed it; and there, what a seen met his eye!

On the polished oaken floor near the fireplace lay the body of a young and beautiful foreign-looking woman rich dressed. There were wounds about her neck half-concealed by her long raven-black hair. A tall, dark-complexioned man stood near, holding a long, thin Venetian stiletto, while beside him stood the old woman, who laughed a fearful laugh, as she spurned the body with her foot!

As she laughed, the vision faded, and Val Wycherley left the drawing-room, uneasy for his brain. At the door he was met by Mrs Comyers who insisted upon his coming down to see her pretty dinner-table. Colonel Comyers was also one of the privileged, and the proud young housekeeper unlocked the dining-room door, when lo!—all the exquisite old china and glass lay in fragments upon the floor! The tablecloth was pulled away, and all the pretty decorations ruthlessly destroyed! In a recess near the fireplace stood a dark foreign-looking man and the old woman, both of whom laughed devilishly, and then vanished! The scene was witnessed by the three. Mrs Comyers fainted in her husband's arms. A serious nervous illness followed, and as soon as it was practicable she was removed from the house.

Val Wycherley recounted his experiences in the drawing-room, and Colonel Comyers admitted that he had witnessed the same scene. Of course they left the house, but refrained from making the reason public, beyond telling the proprietors; who, naturally, did not credit it. But tenant after tenant left, scared away by strange noises and appearances, and the house fell gradually into its present state of decay: not even a caretaker could be induced to remain in it.

The main facts of the preceding story are perfectly true, and were related to the writer by Mrs Nugent's daughter, the present proprietress of the ill-fated house.

THE HORRORS OF SLEEP

EMILY BRONTË

Sleep brings no joy to me,
Remembrance never dies,
My soul is given to mystery,
And lives in sighs.

Sleep brings no rest to me;
The shadows of the dead
My wakening eyes may never see
Surround my bed.

Sleep brings no hope to me,
In soundest sleep they come,
And with their doleful imag'ry
Deepen the gloom.

Sleep brings no strength to me,
No power renewed to brave;
I only sail a wilder sea,
A darker wave.

Sleep brings no friend to me
To soothe and aid to bear;
They all gaze on, how scornfully,
And I despair.

Sleep brings no wish to fret
My harassed heart beneath;
My only wish is to forget
In endless sleep of death.

STREETS OF THE CITY
TONY RICHARDS

The first thing Marshall Harris noticed as he rounded the corner of Lexington and 23rd was the bright red wash of light across the entire street. Three squad cars and a black police sedan were parked outside the entrance to the Hotel *Fiorella*, where Harris had lived these past eight years. And, as he watched, an ambulance pulled up, two paramedics disgorged themselves and hustled their furled stretcher through the hotel's revolving doors. A huge crowd was already gathering, the few police outside were trying to hold them back, but all that Harris could see were the lights, the bright red strobing beacons on the cars. They swept across the buildings, lit the pavements with their flame. And it was just as though some small section of hell had been transplanted outside the hotel. Harris came untensed, shifted the bag of groceries from his right arm to his left and, despite his forty-one years, sprinted across the busy street and began to push his way through the crowd.

By the time that he was thirty-five, Marshall Harris had realized that he would never direct a show on Broadway. It had taken him, perhaps, another year to adjust to that fact, to realize that he had not *failed* in any way, but simply that his talent lay in other fields of theatre, less glamorous and less well-paid for sure, but noble nonetheless. Nobility had become his corner-stone in life. He drank little, smoked a pipe, and never doped at all. His physique was good, his appearance immaculately groomed without becoming dandyish. The clothes he wore were calm and unpretentious, young but not *too* young. At that time of life, in that profession, with that lack of pure financial success, most other men would have become embit-tered and seedy. Marshall Harris was neither, and it earned him respect from everyone from his fiancée Patty to the kids in the little theatre on Mercer where he was currently directing an updated version of Ibsen's *An Enemy of the People.* He had stopped rehearsals at six-thirty that day, show-ered and changed by seven, and suddenly, instead of going back to the hotel, decided he wanted to eat kosher that evening. If he had gone straight back, he reflected later, then he might actually have been able to do some-thing. But he walked to his favourite deli on Delancey Street, spent forty minutes chatting to the proprietor, and caught the IRT uptown almost an hour late. He jogged up the subway steps at 23rd and Park, and headed east, towards the bright red lights.

By the time he reached the inner circle of the crowd, the word was going round that somebody was dead. A uniformed cop moved forward to stop Harris from progressing farther, but the director snapped that he lived here, sidestepped, and went on through. There were more uniforms in the hotel lobby. A young man, plainclothes, was interviewing the desk porter. Ignoring the lift, Harris took the steps two at a time up to the second floor. And it was there, in corridor 212–236, outside his own room, that the main body of policemen was clustered. It was there that something terrible had taken place.

His first thought was of Patty. She might have dropped by unexpectedly, found him not there, let herself into his room. She might have waited there alone. And in this city . . . Harris ran, bursting through the reinforced-glass fire doors, groceries still tucked under his arm as though he were a quarter-back breaking with the ball. He had rammed, actually rammed, past two plainclothes detectives before he realized his mistake. His own door, 224, was shut. It was the room immediately adjacent that was the centre of attention.

The white-emulsioned inside of door 225 was splattered up and down with blood. It was still quite fresh, had not begun to darken yet, and its colour reminded Harris of the whirling lights out on the street. He stepped forward gingerly until he had an unobstructed view of the room.

They had not covered up the body yet. The police photographer was still at work, and the glare of his flashbulb brought the butchered corpse into sudden and obscene relief. The torso had been laid wide open, gutted like a fish. Every limb was hacked at; there were fingers missing from the hands. And the face—one eye missing, hardly any lower jaw at all. Only the long and tangled mass of blood-stained, mousy hair testified that this had been a human being once, a girl.

Mousy hair.

Harris had seen that kind of hair before, stained and tangled in that self-same way, attached to a corpse that had been mutilated in an identical manner. A young girl. A very pretty, very sweet young girl who had lived and died a whole lifetime ago. And though Harris had never once for-gotten, he had managed to sublimate the memory till now. Standing in front of that open, dripping door, he could hold it down no longer, and it came rushing out of his subconscious, crashed down on him like a wave. Mousy hair. Mousy, mousy, mousy hair.

His knees buckled and he slumped against the far wall of the corridor. The bag of groceries slipped from his grasp. Pastrami, bagels, haimishe pickles and cheese blintzes spilled across the rug. They went unnoticed, because at that moment Marshall Harris's mind went far away from him, and all of human sanity was lost.

She was waiting for him, in that place beyond the world and thought and time. She had not aged at all in twenty-one long years. Her long, mousy hair was bright and freshly-washed, and cut into a style that had been all the fashion two decades ago. Darkness and void surrounded her, but in the far, far distance Harris could make out the glow of myriad lights, sodium lamps, as though the dark streets of the city somehow threaded through this limbo land. She smiled at him, but there was no love in her smile any more. And her expression seemed to say: This is only the beginning. There is more and worse to come . . .

When he returned, he was sitting bolt upright against the wall, like an old derelict gone rigid from booze. The oldest of the plainclothes men was squatting down in front of him, popping the groceries back into the paper bag. His badge, clipped to the front of his coat, identified him as Lieutenant James Carrera, Homicide Division, and he looked vaguely annoyed. He was, Harris realized, one of the men he had rammed into in his headlong dash.

Carrera looked up sharply as Harris opened his eyes.

'You OK? You gonna be sick?'

'No, I . . . I think I'm all right now.'

'It's OK by me, either way. You know, the intern was sick when he saw that mess. I always thought those guys had stomachs made of lead.' Carrera laughed; the corners of his eyes did funny crinkly things, humourless things. 'I'm gonna have'ta ask you a few questions.'

It all went down in the Lieutenant's small black book, all the details that Harris could muster from his blood-fogged mind. Firstly about himself, his name, age, occupation, what he had been doing for the past hour and who could verify those facts. And then about the girl. Her name was Shirley DeVane. She had moved in six months ago from Cleveland, Ohio. She was a 'gipsy,' a chorus girl, and she had settled here, so long a walk from Broadway, because the hotel offered reduced rates to theatricals, and because she couldn't stand the YWCA or the all-women's hotels, and because somebody had told her, when she first arrived, that the East Side was safer than the West. It was a generalization for which she had paid dearly.

'Did she have many friends?'

'A few, I think. I didn't know her that well.'

'Any enemies?'

'I doubt it. She was a nice kid.'

'When was the last time you saw her, Mr Harris?'

'Just . . .' It seemed hard to believe. '. . . this morning. I bumped into her on the stairs.'

'Did she seem troubled in any way? Upset?'

'No, quite the opposite. She'd just landed a job in the new Sondheim musical. She was pretty well over the moon.'

Carrera snapped his notebook shut. 'OK, that's all for now. Thank you for your co-operation, Mr Harris.' He stood up and helped Harris to his feet, handed him the paper bag. 'It looks like a routine case. She disturbs an intruder in her room. The guy panics, goes berserk.'

'*That* berserk?'

'It happens. But we have to make sure.'

The two paramedics, sick-looking themselves, were carrying the body out. It was thankfully covered up, but a lock of mousy hair had fallen out from under the red blanket, dangled in full view. Harris turned away.

Carrera had lumbered halfway back down the corridor before Harris's shout brought him to a halt.

'Lieutenant? Can I ask you a question?'

The detective turned, nodded cautiously. 'Sure.'

'Was the girl . . . was she . . . assaulted?'

It was as if all the suspicion for all the crimes in New York City fell on

Harris right then. The look that the Lieutenant gave him seemed compounded of pure surprise and sheer anger, with lots of native instinct and experience thrown in. A dark-eyed, knowing look from a man who'd just realized Marshall Harris was far more involved than he was letting on. 'Yes, Mr Harris,' Carrera said slowly. 'Yes, she was.' He seemed on the verge of enquiring why Harris had asked that particular question, but his experience and instinct drew him short, and he simply grimaced, turned back round, and lumbered on. He looked back once, from the glass fire doors, and then was gone.

In his own room, with the door locked tight and the bolt and the chain on, Harris dumped the groceries into the wastepaper basket, drew all the blinds and threw himself out full-length on the bed. He lay quite still there, in a semi-darkness that gradually deepened to neon-slivered black. He lay there for hours. Some time around nine, his bedside phone rang persistency a dozen times, then stopped, and rang again. He did not even bother to reach across to answer it, though he knew that it was probably Patty calling him. They were due to get married early next month, and he loved her dearly. But he could not get that girl out of his mind.

And the worst thing was, he was afraid even to sleep. Rigid terror filled him every time he began to doze. For Marshall Harris knew that, in his impending dreams, *she* would be waiting for him. She, with her mousy hair.

It was well past midnight when Harris decided to get some coffee. He got up slowly, stiffly, from the bed, made some vague attempt to straighten out the wrinkles in his clothes, then unlocked his door and peered out. His gaze was returned blearily by a uniformed policeman sitting on a hard chair outside 225. Harris ignored the cop, unsure whether to acknowledge him or not, and wandered down the corridor still dangling the room keys from his hand.

The *Fiorella,* like most of New York's older hotels, had seen more glamorous days. The ghosts of the Gatsby era still wheeled and tinkled through its dimly-lit halls; the whole building was saturated with the memory of the Charleston and bright chatter and cocaine. Perhaps Dorothy Parker had once partied here. Perhaps James Thurber and his wife had sipped martinis in one of the sumptuous suites. Those days were long gone, but it remained a friendly place. No sterile modern decor here, no plastic and no chrome. Like Marshall Harris, the hotel retained its nobility.

And then there was the ground-floor coffee shop.

It was empty of customers when Harris wandered in. That pleased him. He liked, late at night, to sit at the far corner of the counter so that he could swivel around on his stool and watch Lexington Avenue through the big, velvet-draped window in the wall. From a distance, and through glass, the streets of the city were beautiful after dark. He sat, he swivelled, watched. Down at the far end, behind the counter, Rahsaan began fixing him a cup of Sanka, unasked.

'Coffee please, Rass,' Harris said. He would need the caffeine to keep him away from sleep.

The big Black man nodded and complied, then came limping along the back of the counter with the cup in his steadier hand. Harris winced inwardly every time he saw that limp, that tremble. Rahsaan Kirk Ali had once been a top amateur sprinter, hundred yards, one of the best. A row of honours on the top shelf behind the counter testified to that. There were shields and cups and medals and, most prized of all, a two-foot-high silver-plated figurine of an athlete in full pantheresque flight. That had been Rahsaan ten years ago until a speeding car had broken him completely, finished any promise of a full professional career. He set the cup down carefully, then leaned against the counter out of breath.

'Buh-bad business with that girl tuhday.'

'Uh-huh, very bad.'

'She wuz only a kid. Who the hell'ud go'n do a thing like that?'

'The police reckon it was a burglar.'

'Yeah, makes sense in this damn town.' He wiped his mouth uncomfortably.

'Her folks must know buh now. Shee-it! Ah keep thinkin', what if it was one'a mine, man? What if it was one'a mine?'

Harris had no answer to that. He sat, and sipped his coffee.

'Y'know,' the Black man continued, 'ah wish ah'd bin on up theyuh. If ah'd've only heard her scream, ah'd've *nailed* that bastard. May not be so strong as ah use'ta be, may not be so fast, but ah'd've had a damn good *go.*'

And he sincerely meant it; it was not just brag. And something heavy churned around in Harris's gut. Here was a man who was a virtual cripple, who had trouble carrying a cup of coffee ten yards up a bar, and yet who would still face an armed lunatic willingly to save a young girl's life. Harris would have liked to imagine he would do the same, but his own past denied that. Most emphatically.

'Goodnight, Rass,' he said, making no attempt to conceal the sharpness in his tone. He set the half-empty cup down on the counter, walked out of the coffee shop as fast as dignity allowed, still feeling the man's amazed stare on his neck.

Seven minutes after he had left, three scrawny white youths slouched into the shop, held Rahsaan up at knife-point and proceeded to raid the till. Just as they were leaving, almost as an afterthought, they took the two-foot silver trophy down from the shelf and beat the man to death with it. Nobody heard him scream, least of all Marshall Harris. And by one o'clock that morning, the squad cars and the black sedan were back outside the hotel. The streets of the city were once more awash with red.

Room 224 went away from Harris, and the void and the darkness returned. She was there, still smiling, and her hair was blowing in an insubstantial breeze that came from the direction of the sodium streetlights. And on that breeze there came a noise, the sound of tinkling laughter . . .

He was tired and puffy-eyed when he met Patty the next morning, some-what less well-groomed than usual, somewhat less noble, somewhat slouched. She seemed surprised at first, until, over ham and eggs in the small diner just off Gramercy Park, he started to recount the story of the two concurrent murders. He was near to tears. An old Italian waitress who had been slathering the opposite, empty table with a dishcloth stopped to listen, stare, and Patty, noticing her, slammed five dollars onto the Formica, grabbed Harris by the arm and hustled him out of there. They wandered for an hour through the quiet streets of the teens, talking softly, staving off the pangs of fear with words layered on words. And Harris told her every-thing. Except about the past. Except about the mousy hair.

Patty was a stunning brunette, six years his junior. She worked with hand-icapped children in the slums of the barrio, and if Harris respected her just as much as he loved her, he felt that was *right,* that was *important,* that respect. He hoped she felt the same for him. And he hoped he would never give her cause to lose it. He was not about to start now. A wind had sprung up from the south, blowing in from the Upper Bay. It caught the old newspapers and the discarded candy wrappers and the dust, set the window frames in the sur-rounding blocks to rattling, and Harris faced right into it and straightened, stiffened like a lofted sail. He smiled. The old nobility was back.

'How about we find somewhere where we won't be disturbed?' he said.

'How about my place?'

The smile turned to an open grin.

Rehearsals began again that afternoon, and Harris approached them with all the confidence he'd ever known. He had been through a bad time of bloodshed and haunted guilt-ridden dreams, and the mere act of passing through unscathed had left him stronger. Marshall Harris: a pair of glowing, watching eyes in the darkness beyond the footlights, a voice so certain that it could not be ignored. He absorbed himself, completely.

And he stopped rehearsals half an hour early, perplexed and annoyed.

Jaqueline Sarn was one of the most talented young actresses he'd ever had the pleasure of working with. He had cast her in the role of Petra, Stockmann's daughter, and she had played that small part with a degree of honesty and grace astonishing to watch. Until today, when she muffed her lines and stuttered and looked so self-conscious it could make you scream.

He took her to one side after the others were gone, and asked her, gently, what was wrong. And heard an old, old story. She had been on the little theatre circuit for six years now. She had tried for bigger productions, been turned down with those flimsy excuses commercial directors apply when a kid is so good that she might upstage the bigger names. And she was sick to death of it. She *knew* she had the wherewithal, she *knew* that she could make it, and if New York wouldn't take her then perhaps Hollywood might. Even if it meant working commercials and TV. Even if it meant hanging out at Schwab's with all the silicone-puffed starlets, waiting for the right producer to come along. She had sunk the last of her savings in a Greyhound ticket to L. A., had sat up all night clutching the damned thing, trying to decide whether to tear it up or not. Harris talked to her quietly, just as Patty had talked to him, weighing up the pros and cons, the chances and the risks. It was an idiotic scheme in his opinion, but he kept that to himself; the girl was old enough to run her own life. The only concrete advice he could offer was that she could get a refund on the ticket if she forewent the symbolic act of ripping it to shreds. She seemed satisfied. He had helped.

While Harris was taking his customary shower, Jaqueline Sarn got her things together and wandered out of the back door of the theatre—straight into the arms of a wild-eyed, unknown man. She was assaulted on the spot, then brutally murdered with what proved to be, when the police found it in a nearby dustbin later, a fifteen-inch meat cleaver. The killer was escaping just as Harris turned the water off. He stepped out, dripping, onto the latex mat, feeling uncomfortable all of a sudden. There was a sharp chill on the air. He felt as though he were being watched. He turned around twice, satisfied himself that he was alone in the cubicle, and then glanced at himself in the mirror. Staring over his right shoulder, reflected in the steamy glass, was a young woman, a girl. Smiling. Mousy hair. Twenty-one years dead.

Lieutenant James Carrera sat on the edge of the bed in Harris's room, gazing at the broken man who occupied the armchair opposite. Harris had been trembling long before the detective arrived; he was not near to stopping yet. His hands were clenched one around the other till the knuckles had gone white. Only the eyes were invisible, lost in pools of shadow. Carrera did not particularly care to see those eyes.

He pulled the notebook out again, toyed with it but did not open it.

'I'd have you under suspicion,' he commented, 'except you've got perfectly good alibis for two of the killings. Forensics can disprove you did the last.'

Harris looked up. 'Fine.' He did not sound convinced.

'But I know one thing,' the Lieutenant continued. 'Somehow, you're the focus for these three deaths. Each one came in close contact with you; each one was murdered shortly after in an abnormally brutal manner. I think you're the key to all this, Mr Harris. And I'm damned if I know why. Like'ta tell me?'

'Perhaps some lunatic is doing this.' He was clutching at straws; he knew it. 'A madman, out to hurt me by getting at people I know.'

'Uh-uh, it's not one man.'

'*What?*'

'We caught Shirley DeVane's killer, *two hours* before Jackie Sarn got hers. Found him blind drunk in an alley, mumbling how sorry he was. A bagsnatcher, Mr Harris. A petty, small-time thief who'd faint at the sight of his own blood. He doesn't know why he did it. He has no history of violence,

213

no psychiatric record. And yet, dig this, he claims he heard voices telling him to kill the girl. One voice, specifically. A young woman's voice.'

'Oh my God!'

'What was that?'

'I said, oh my *God!* Will you leave me alone?'

Carrera stayed where he was. 'The fingerprints on the trophy and the meat cleaver don't match up. That's three *separate* killers, Mr Harris. All centred around you.'

'Get out of here!'

'Make me.' And the swipe came at Carrera from nowhere; just a blur where Harris had been sitting, and then that clenched fist sweeping in from the left corner of his vision. The Lieutenant caught Harris's wrist before the blow was landed, and the two were locked like that for a second, fury against will, before Harris went limp. Carrera shoved him back into the chair, then began talking quickly and evenly. 'It's not going to end with those three people, Mr Harris. I know that in my bones. You know it too. And there's something you're not telling me. Why won't you let me help?'

'It happened a long time ago. I don't think it's any use to you.'

'Well, let me be the judge of that.'

Harris rubbed his hands against his checks, as though the motion would erode some of his weariness and fear. 'OK,' he whispered. 'All right, you win.' But he would not look at Carrera.

'Kris and I were going to be married. It was summer, the beginning of the sixties, and it seemed like a good time. We'd both just graduated from the High School of Performing Arts, and we'd got part-time jobs in one of the big restaurants on Fifth. I was a waiter, she was a waitress; we worked the evening shift. That night . . . we knocked off around one and headed for my apartment on 94th. We took a short cut across the Park—it was supposed to be safe in those days. And then *they* showed up.'

His face began to cloud.

'Remember those street gangs we used to have?'

Carrera nodded. He had pounded a beat in the South Bronx from '54 through to '57. He remembered the street gangs only too well.

'There were six of them, way off their turf. God knows what they were doing there! They were all drunk or stoned on something, and they began to chase us. We ran, of course, and I thought Kris was right beside me till I heard them laugh. She'd fallen over. She was wearing those damn stupid little stiletto heels and she'd been too scared to take them off. I stopped and I looked back and . . . they were all around her.' His hands covered his eyes, concealing far more than mere tears. 'I looked at them. They were huge. They were all armed. And I didn't know what to do. A guy's supposed to defend his girl, right? A guy's supposed to risk everything for someone he loves. It *says* so in every book and movie that you've ever read or seen. And yet to go back into that mob was to die. And I . . . didn't . . . want . . . to die.'

His words had become long, husking sobs by now, barely coherent at all. Carrera sat there waiting, eyes like frosted glass, till the man had calmed down.

'I ran,' Harris told him. 'Don't ask me where, just anywhere away from there. I was so ashamed and confused I didn't even try to get help. I must have passed a squad car, God knows how many phone boxes. But I just ran, and kept on running. I huddled in an alley until dawn, and then I pulled together enough courage to go to my folks' home. They'd been looking for me, frantic. The cops had been dredging the lake for me. When I told them where I'd been . . . the looks on their faces . . .

'I went down to the morgue. I wanted to see her one last time. The gang . . . when they'd finished with her, they tore her apart like wild animals. They used knives, bike chains, broken bottles, even their hands. There was hardly any of her left. Her family was there. God, it was *terrible!*'

A long while later, when he had finished rocking back and forth, finished clutching himself, finished crying, Carrera said: 'Mr Harris, nobody would blame you for backing off, for not getting yourself killed too.'

'But I could have got help. I could have saved her if I'd only called the cops. I didn't even *try,* don't you understand?'

'OK, you made a big mistake. We're all entitled to one.'

'Even if it costs another life? Tell me, what kind of man just runs away and lets another human die? What kind of person does that and retains the right to live?'

'A lot of people do it these days, Mr Harris.'

'That makes it *better?* Cowardice by popular consent?'

'Perhaps that's the way we've all become.' Carrera was still toying with his notebook. 'I still don't understand. What's all this got to do with the killings?'

From somewhere in that room, Harris could hear the laughter. From somewhere in the room, Harris could feel that breeze. Sodium lamps twinkled at the periphery of his vision. Limbo land. Streets of the city. The Lieutenant could not hear or feel or see it, and Harris knew that he would never understand.

'I keep seeing her.'

'The girl? Kris?'

Harris nodded. 'She appears to me, in visions, dreams. She's been dead twenty-one years, and yet she's still out there somewhere. I sound crazy, don't I?'

'That's not for me to say,' Carrera replied, standing up. 'Have a drink and get some sleep. I'd be a little crazy too.'

'You aren't going to . . .'

'I'll check out the girl's family. That might give us a lead. But I deal in reality, Mr Harris, not in dreams.'

When he was gone, Harris crossed to his window and gazed down on Lexington. The streetlamps were hard at work down there, weaving their bright glow into the folds of night. But the light that they cast was not nearly enough.

It was in the papers the next morning. Lieutenant James Carrera, who only dealt in reality, had stopped a battered black Chevy on a routine investigation, walked round to the driver's door and asked the kid inside to show his licence. The kid had reached into the glove compartment, pulled out a Saturday night special and with two shots blown the lieutenant's brains out through the back of his skull.

When questioned later, the kid claimed he had heard a woman's voice telling him to do it, the voice of a young girl.

That had been the morning Harris was due to take Patty up to 47th Street to buy the ring. He had promised to pick her up at nine and when, by nine thirty, he had not moved from his room, she phoned him. He let it ring twelve, fifteen times before picking it up.

'Marsh, where *are* you? I've been sitting here for ages.'

His jaw moved, but he could not answer her.

'Marsh, are you all right?'

'One of the kids got killed yesterday,' he said. 'One of my actors.'

'Oh, no!'

'The cop who questioned me, he got killed too. That's four dead, all because of me.'

'Because of . . . what on earth are you talking about?'

He told her about Kris, about that summer from his long dead youth. Every lousy detail, to the last bright drop of blood, and he hoped that she forgave him. She sounded shocked and slightly stunned, but not less loving for all that. Then he told her about the visions and the dreams.

'Marsh, that can't be.'

'Can't, but is. Call it a ghost, call it a psychic manifestation of my guilt, call it anything, but it's *real,* and it's out to get me.'

'Stop talking like that. That's insane.'

Harris almost grinned. Like a torture victim does, in that rictus of a smile when the whips and the branding irons break through the wall that marks the outer limit of pure human pain. 'You want insane, I'll give you insane. Tell me, Patty. What's the one thing worse than dying?'

There was something wrong with the line, as if it had been crossed. A sound like a breeze blowing, a noise like someone laughing in the void.

'Nothing's worse than dying, Marsh.' She honestly believed that or she would have given up on her job long ago.

'You're wrong, so wrong. There is one thing. It's to live while everybody else dies. It's to be the immune carrier of some fatal disease. To stand back and watch while everyone you love, everyone you care for, everyone you talk to or open to or touch is cut to shreds, and then to have to live on with the memory of that. To know that it's your fault. To know there's nothing you can do, because you had your chance long ago and you blew it. She's worked it out well, Patty. She's had twenty-one long years.'

She seemed to be considering that, seemed to half-believe it. 'But even if it is true,' she said, 'why wait till now? Why wait so very long?'

It was the single thing he did not understand. It did not fit. He had been pondering the question since he had read about Carrera, and the answer would not come . . .

Until that moment. When he listened to her voice over the line, and heard the noise of laughter and of wind, and knew. Suddenly *knew!* Twenty-one years he had stumbled through life, setting up a noble pose, trying to forget. And, in all that time he had never found another girl like Kris, a woman he could love. Until he had met Patty. They were due to be married in a few weeks, just as he and Kris . . . The terror in him mounted to a fever point.

'Patty! Get off the phone!'

'I can't hear you! The line—!'

'Don't call me, don't try to see me, ever again! Forget about me, please!'

'I don't understand. Marsh, I'm coming round there, now!'

'I won't be here! I'm going where you'll never find me! Stay away, don't even try!'

She was crying, hurt and lost. God, if she only knew how small a pain that was.

'This is ridiculous, Marsh. I—' And she stopped dead. 'Hold on will you, please? There's someone pounding on the door.'

'No!'

The wind on the line caught his scream and hurled it back at him. He knew she had not heard it.

'Patty, don't answer it! Stay away from there!'

But there was no reply. She had already gone.

He heard the latch click back, heard it with such terrifying clarity he knew more than the phone had picked it up. As though the sound were being relayed through a void. He heard Patty begin to speak, then heard the first word muffled as something like a leather glove was pressed against her mouth. There was the scuffle of someone pushing somebody else backwards, and then the noise of the door shutting. The thump of her body against the rug. The sudden rip of cloth. A scream that never quite made it beyond her covered mouth.

Get help!

Call the police!

Harris hammered at the phone and nothing happened. *She* had called *him.* He could not clear the line.

There was a phone box in the lobby. It would take him two minutes to run there, many more minutes for the police to arrive. Too late. Twenty-one years too late. He'd had his chance; he would not get another.

And he sat, listening, transfixed. The assault was over. He could hear the knife go in for the first time, of many.

It was a century later when he heard the thud of sneakers, the reopening and the quick closing of the door. He was still as stone and bled completely dry. His eyeballs burned for lack of moisture.

Patty, somehow, was still breathing, making ragged, frothing sounds that had no human origin. He could hear her dragging herself across the rug to the phone, moving in short, seal-like flops as one of her crippled children might move. It took her a very long while.

'Pa—tty.'

'Marsh . . .' Her voice was no more than a graveyard whisper. 'Marsh. Help . . . me . . .'

The breeze came back, far stronger than before. It blew until it was a howling gale that deafened Harris, echoed through his room. And then, abruptly, it was gone. The line went very dead.

Marshall Harris sprang to his feet, bolted for the door and ran. Through the lobby, ignoring the doorman and the porter and the clerk. Down Lexington, east on 23rd. Running, running, just as he had run on that summer so long ago, not knowing where he was running, just anywhere, away. He dodged and ducked, trying desperately to avoid contact with any other person.

But there were crowds. He collided with a middle-aged executive, and saw a garishly painted Olds draw up beside the man and two young hoods step swaggeringly out. He brushed against an old woman walking into her apartment building, and saw a tall Black junkie draw a straight razor and follow her inside. There was no place to run, no place to ever hide.

The streets of the city were awash with blood.

IN THE DARK

Mary E. Penn

'It is the strangest, most unaccountable thing I ever knew! I don't think I am superstitious, but I can't help fancying that—'

Ethel left the sentence unfinished, wrinkling her brows in a thoughtful frown as she gazed into the depths of her empty teacup.

'What has happened?' I enquired, glancing up from the money article of *The Times* at my daughter's pretty, puzzled face. 'Nothing uncanny, I hope? You haven't discovered that a ghost is included among the fixtures of our new house?'

This new house, The Cedars, was a pretty, old-fashioned riverside villa between Richmond and Kew, which I had taken furnished, as a summer residence, and to which we had only just removed.

Let me state, in parenthesis, by way of introducing myself to the reader, that I, John Dysart, am a widower with one child: the blue-eyed, fair-haired young lady who sat opposite to me at the breakfast table that bright June morning: and that I have been for many years the manager of an old-established life insurance company in the City.

'What is the mystery?' I repeated, as Ethel did not reply.

She came out of her brown study, and looked at me impressively.

'It really is a mystery, Papa, and the more I think of it the more puzzled I am.'

'I am in the dark at present as to what "it" may be,' I reminded her.

'Something that happened last night. You know that adjoining my bed-room there is a large, dark closet, which can be used as a box- or store-room?'

'I had forgotten the fact, but I will take your word for it. Well, Ethel?'

'Well, last night I was restless, and it was some hours before I could sleep. When at last I did so, I had a strange dream about that closet. It seemed that as I lay in bed I heard a noise within, as if someone were knocking at the door, and a child's voice, broken by sobs, crying piteously, "Let me out, let me out!" I thought that I got out of bed and opened the door, and there, crouching all in a heap against the wall, was a little boy; a pretty, pale little fellow of six or seven, looking half-wild with fright. At the same moment I woke.'

'And lo, it was a dream!' I finished. 'If that is all, Ethel—'

'But it is not,' she interposed. 'The strangest part of the story has to come. The dream was so vivid that when I woke I sat up in bed and looked towards the closet door, almost expecting to hear the sounds again. Papa, you may believe me or not, but it is a fact that I *did* hear them, the muf-fled knocking, and the pitiful cry. As I listened, it grew fainter and fainter and at length ceased altogether. Then I summoned courage to get out of bed and open the door. There was no living creature in the place. Was it not mysterious?' she concluded. 'What can it mean?'

I glanced at her with a smile, as I refolded the paper and rose from my chair.

'It means, my dear, that you had a nightmare last night. Let me recom-mend you for the future not to eat cucumber at dinner.'

'No, Papa,' she interrupted. 'I was broad awake, and I heard the child's voice as plainly as I ever heard a sound in my life.'

'Why didn't you call me?'

'I was afraid to stir till the sound had ceased; but if I ever hear it again, I will let you know at once.'

'Be sure you do. Meantime, suppose you come into the garden,' I continued, throwing open the French windows. 'The morning air will blow all these cobwebs from your brain.'

Ethel complied, and for the present I heard no more of the subject.

Some days passed away, and we began to feel quite at home in our new quarters.

A more delightful summer retreat than The Cedars could hardly be imagined, with its cool, dusky rooms, from which the sunlight was excluded by the screen of foliage outside; its trellised verandah, overgrown with creepers, and its smooth lawn, shaded by the rare old cedar-trees which gave the place its name.

Our friends soon discovered its attractions and took care that we should not stagnate for want of society. We kept open house; lawn-tennis, garden-parties, and boating excursions were the order of the day. It was glorious summer weather, the days warm and golden, the nights starlit and still.

One night, having important letters to finish, I sat up writing after all the household were in bed. The window was open, and at intervals I glanced up from my paper across the moonlit lawn, where the shadows of the cedars lay dark and motionless. Now and then a great downy moth would flutter in and hover round the shaded lamp; now and then the swallows under the eaves uttered a faint, sleepy chirp. For all other signs and sounds of life I might have been the only watcher in all the sleeping world.

I had finished my task and was just closing my writing-case when I heard a hurried movement in the room above—Ethel's. Footsteps descended the stairs, and the next moment the dining-room door opened, and Ethel appeared, in a long, white dressing-gown, with a small night-lamp in her hand.

There was a look on her face which made me start up and exclaim:

'What is the matter? What has happened?'

She set down the lamp and came towards me.

'I have heard it again,' she breathed, laying her hand on my wrist.

'You have heard—what?'

'The noise in the box-room.'

I stared at her a moment in bewilderment, and then half-smiled.

'Oh, is that it?' I exclaimed, in a tone of relief. 'You have been dreaming again, it seems.'

'I have not been asleep at all,' she replied. 'The sounds have kept me awake. They are louder than the first time; the child seems to be sobbing and crying as if his heart would break. It is miserable to hear it.'

'Have you looked inside?' I asked, impressed in spite of myself by her manner.

'No, I dared not tonight. I was afraid of seeing—something,' she returned with a shiver.

'Come, we must get to the bottom of this mystery,' I said cheerfully, and taking up the lamp I led the way upstairs to her room.

As the door of the mysterious closet was level with the wall, and papered like it, I did not perceive it till Ethel pointed it out. I listened with my ear close to it, but heard not the faintest sound, and after waiting a moment, threw it open and looked in, holding the lamp so that every corner was lighted. It was a cramped, close, airless place, the ceiling (which was immediately below the upper staircase) sloping at an acute angle to the floor. A glance showed me that it contained nothing but a broken chair and a couple of empty boxes.

Slightly shrugging my shoulders, I closed the door.

'Your ghost is *vox et praeterea nihil*, it seems,' I remarked drily. 'Don't you think, Ethel, you may have been—'

Ethel held up her hand, motioning me to silence.

'Hark,' she whispered, 'there it is again! But it is dying away now. Listen—'

I complied, half-infected by her excitement, but within and without the house all was profoundly still.

'There—it has ceased,' she said at length, drawing a deep breath. 'You heard it, did you not?'

I shook my head. 'My dear Ethel, there was nothing to hear.'

She opened her blue eyes to their widest.

'Papa—am I not to believe the evidence of my own senses?'

'Not when they are affected by nervous excitement. If you give way to this fancy, you will certainly make yourself ill. See how you tremble! Come, lie down again, and try to sleep.'

'Not here,' she returned, glancing round with a shudder. 'I shall go to the spare chamber. Nothing would induce me to spend another night in this room.'

I said no more, but I felt perplexed and uneasy. It was so unlike Ethel to indulge in superstitious fancies that I began to fear she must be seriously out of health, and I resolved for my own satisfaction to have a doctor's opinion regarding her.

It happened that our nearest neighbour was a physician, whom I knew by repute, though was not personally acquainted with him. After breakfast, without mentioning my intention to my daughter, I sent a note to Dr Cameron, requesting him to call at his earliest convenience.

He came without delay: a tall, grey-bearded man of middle age, with a grave, intelligent face, observant eyes and sympathetic manner.

His patient received him with undisguised astonishment, and on learning that he had called at my request she gave me a look of mute reproach.

'I am sorry that Papa troubled you, Dr Cameron. There is really nothing whatever the matter with me,' she said.

And indeed at that moment, with flushed cheeks, and eyes even brighter than usual, she looked as little like an invalid as could well be imagined.

'My dear Ethel,' I interposed, 'when people take to dreaming startling dreams, and hearing supernatural sounds, it is a sign of something wrong with either mind or body—as I am sure Dr Cameron will tell you.'

The doctor started perceptibly. 'Ah—is that Miss Dysart's case?' he enquired, turning to her with a sudden look of interest.

She coloured and hesitated. 'I have had a strange—experience, which Papa considers a delusion. I daresay you will be of the same opinion.'

'Suppose you tell me what it was?' he suggested.

She was silent, trifling with one of her silver bangles.

'Please excuse me,' she said hurriedly, at length. 'I don't care to speak of it; but Papa will tell you.' And before I could detain her, she had hurriedly left the room.

When we were alone he turned to me enquiringly, and in a few words I related to him what the reader already knows. He listened without interruption, and when I had finished, sat for some moments without speaking, thoughtfully stroking his beard.

He was evidently impressed by what he had heard, and I waited anxiously for his opinion. At length he looked up.

'Mr Dysart,' he said, gravely, 'you will be surprised to learn that your daughter is not the first who has had this strange experience. Previous tenants of The Cedars have heard exactly the sounds which she describes.'

I pushed my chair back half-a-yard in my astonishment.

'Impossible!'

He nodded emphatically.

'It is a fact, though I don't pretend to explain it. These strange manifestations have been noticed at intervals for the last three or four years; ever since the house was occupied by a Captain Vandeleur, whose orphan nephew—'

'Vandeleur?' I interrupted. 'Why, he was a client of ours. He insured his nephew's life in our office for a large amount and—'

'And a few months afterwards, the child suddenly and mysteriously died?' my companion put in. 'A singular coincidence, to say the least of it.'

'So singular,' I acquiesced, 'that we thought it a case for enquiry, particularly as the ex-captain did not bear the best of characters, and was known to be over head and ears in debt. But I am bound to say that after the closest investigation nothing was discovered to suggest a suspicion of foul play.'

'Nevertheless there *had* been foul play,' was the doctor's reply.

'You don't mean that he murdered the boy! That pretty, fragile-looking little fellow—'

'No, he did not murder him, but he let him die,' Dr Cameron rejoined. 'Perhaps you were not aware,' he continued, 'that the little lad was somewhat feeble in mind as well as body? I attended him more than once, at Vandeleur's request, and found that among other strange fears and antipathies he had a morbid dread of darkness. To be left alone in a dark room for only a few minutes was enough to throw him into a paroxysm of nervous excitement. His uncle—who by the way, professed more affection for him than I could quite believe in, when I noticed how the child shrank from him—consulted me as to the best means of overcoming this weakness. I strongly advised him to humour it for the present, warning him that any mental shock might endanger the boy's reason, or even his life. I little thought those words of mine would prove his death warrant.'

'What do you mean?'

'Only a few days afterwards, Vandeleur locked him up all night in a dark closet, where he was found the next morning, crouching against the wall; his hands clenched, his eyes fixed and staring—dead.'

'Good heavens, how horrible! But no word of this was mentioned at the inquest?'

'No; and I did not hear of it myself till long afterwards, from a woman who had been Vandeleur's housekeeper, but was too much afraid of him to betray him at the time. From her, too, I learnt by what refined cruelty the poor little lad's nerves had been shaken and his health undermined. If the intention makes the deed, James Vandeleur was a murderer.'

I was silent a moment, thinking, with an uncomfortable thrill, of Ethel's dream. 'I wish I had never entered this ill-omened house!' I exclaimed at length. 'I dread the effect of this revelation on my daughter's mind.'

'Why need you tell her?' he questioned. 'My advice is to say nothing more about it. The sooner she forgets the subject the better. Send her away to the seaside; change of air and scene will soon efface it from her memory.'

He rose as he spoke, and took up his hat.

'What has become of Vandeleur?' I enquired. 'I have heard nothing of him since we paid the policy.'

'He has been living abroad, I believe—going to the dogs, no doubt. But he is in England now,' the doctor added: 'or else it was his "fetch" which I saw at your gate the other night.'

'At our gate!' I echoed in astonishment. 'What the deuce was he doing there?'

'He seemed to be watching the house. It was last Sunday evening. I had been dining with friends at Richmond, and on my way back, between eleven and twelve o'clock, I noticed a man leaning over the gate of The Cedars. On hearing footsteps he turned and walked away, but not before I had caught a glimpse of his face in the moonlight.'

'And you are sure it was he?'

'Almost certain—though he was greatly altered for the worse. I have a presentiment, do you know, that you will see or hear of him yourself before long,' he added thoughtfully, as he shook hands and went his way.

I lost no time in following his advice with regard to Ethel, whom I despatched to Scarborough, in charge of my married sister, a few days later.

I had taken a hearty dislike to The Cedars, and resolved to get it off my hands as soon as might be.

Until another tenant could be found however, I continued to occupy it, going to and from town as before.

One evening I was sitting on the lawn, smoking an after-dinner cigar, and re-reading Ethel's last letter, which quite reassured me as to her health and spirits, when our sedate old housekeeper presented herself with the information that 'a party' had called to see the house.

'A gentleman or a lady?' I enquired.

'A gentleman, sir, but he didn't give his name.'

I found the visitor standing near the open window of the drawing-room; a tall, gaunt man of thirty-five or thereabouts, with handsome but haggard features, and restless dark eyes. His lips were covered by a thick moustache, which he was nervously twisting as he stood looking out at the lawn.

'This house is to be let, I believe; will you allow me to look over it?' he asked, turning towards me as I entered.

His voice seemed familiar; I looked at him more closely, and then, in spite of the change in his appearance, I recognized Captain Vandeleur.

What could have brought him here, I wondered. Surely he would not care to return to the house, even if he were in a position to do so—which, judging from the shabbiness of his appearance, seemed very doubtful.

Half-a-dozen vague conjectures flashed through my mind as I glanced at his face and noticed the restless, hunted look which told of some wearing dread or anxiety.

After a moment's hesitation I assented to his request, and resolved to conduct him myself on his tour of inspection.

'I think I have met you before,' I said, feeling curious to know whether he recollected me.

He glanced at me absently.

'Possibly—but not of late years; for I have been living abroad,' was his reply.

Having shown him the apartments on the ground floor, I led the way upstairs. He followed me from room to room in an absent, listless fashion, till we came to the chamber which Ethel had occupied. Then his interest seemed to revive all at once.

He glanced quickly round the walls, his eyes resting on the door of the box-closet.

'That is a bath or dressing-room, I suppose,' he said, nodding towards it.

'No, only a place for lumber. Perhaps I ought to tell you that it is said to be haunted,' I added, affecting to speak carelessly, while I kept my eyes on his face.

He started and turned towards me.

'Haunted—by what?' he enquired, with a faint sneer. 'Nothing worse than rats or mice, I expect.'

'There is a tragical story connected with that place,' I answered, deliberately. 'It is said that an unfortunate child was shut up there to die of fear, in the dark.'

The colour rushed to his face, then retreated, leaving it deadly white.

'Indeed!' he faltered; 'and do you mean to say that he—the child—has been seen?'

'No, but he has been heard, knocking within, and crying to be let out. The fact is confirmed by every tenant who has occupied the house since—'

I stopped short, startled by the effect of my revelation.

My companion was gazing at me with a blank stare of horror which banished all other expression from his face.

'Good heavens!' I heard him mutter; 'can it be true? Can this be the reason why I was drawn back to the place in spite of myself?'

Recollecting himself, however, he turned to me, and forced his white lips into a smile.

'A mysterious story!' he commented, drily. 'I don't believe a word of it, myself, but I should hardly care to take a house with such an uncanny reputation. I think I need not trouble you any further.'

As he turned towards the door, I saw his figure sway as if he were falling. He put his hand to his side, with a gasp of pain, a bluish shade gathering over his face.

'Are you ill?' I exclaimed, in alarm.

'I—it is nothing. I have a weakness of the heart, and I am subject to these attacks. May I ask you for a glass of water?'

I left the room to procure it. When I returned I found that he had fallen upon the bed in a dead swoon.

I hastily despatched a servant for Dr Cameron, who happened to be at home, and came immediately.

He recognized my visitor at once, and glanced at me significantly. I rapidly explained what had happened, while he bent over the unconscious man, and bared his chest to listen to the heart-beats.

When he raised himself his face was ominously grave.

'Is he in danger?' I asked, quickly.

'Not in immediate danger, but the next attack will probably be his last. His heart is mortally diseased.'

It was nearly an hour before Vandeleur awoke, and then only to partial consciousness. He lay in a sort of stupor, his limbs nerveless, his hands damp and cold.

'It is impossible to remove him in this condition,' the doctor remarked; 'I fear he must stay here for the night. I will send you someone to watch him.'

'Don't trouble—I intend to sit up with him myself,' I replied, speaking on an impulse I could hardly explain.

He looked at me keenly over his spectacles.

'Should you like me to share your watch?' he enquired, after a moment.

'I shall be only too glad of your company, if you can come without inconvenience.'

He nodded. 'I must leave you now, but I will return in an hour,' he responded.

Three hours had passed away; it was nearly midnight. The night was oppressively close, and profoundly still. The bedroom window stood wide open, but not a breath of air stirred the curtains. Outside, all was vague and dark, for neither moon nor stars were visible.

Vandeleur still lay, half-dressed, on the bed, but now asleep. His deep, regular breathing sounded distinctly in the silence. Dr Cameron sat near the dressing-table, reading by the light of a shaded lamp. I, too, had a book, but found it impossible to keep my attention fixed upon it. My mind was possessed by an uneasy feeling, half-dread, half-expectation. I found myself listening nervously to fancied sounds, and starting when the doctor turned a leaf.

At length, overcome by the heat and stillness, I closed my eyes, and unconsciously sank into a doze. How long it lasted, I cannot tell, but I woke abruptly, and looked round with a sense of vague alarm. I glanced at the doctor. He had laid down his book, and was leaning forward with one arm on the dressing-table, looking intently towards the door of the box-room. Instinctively I held my breath and listened.

Never shall I forget the thrill that ran through my nerves when I heard from within a muffled knocking sound, and a child's voice, distinct, though faint, and broken by sobs, crying piteously: 'Let me out—let me out!'

'Do you hear?' I whispered, bending forward to my companion.

He inclined his head in assent and motioned me to be silent, pointing towards the bed. Its occupant moved uneasily, as if disturbed, muttering some incoherent phrases. Suddenly he pushed back his covering and sat upright, gazing round with a wild, bewildered stare.

The pitiful entreaty was repeated more violently, more passionately than before. 'Let me out, let me out!'

With a cry that rang through the room, Vandeleur sprang from the bed, reached the closet door in two strides and tore it open.

232

It was empty. Empty at least to our eyes, but it was evident that our companion beheld what we could not.

For a few breathless seconds he stood as if frozen, his eyes fixed with the fascination of terror on something just within the threshold; then, as if retreating before it, he recoiled step by step across the room till he was stopped by the opposite wall, where he crouched in an attitude of abject fear.

The sight was so horrible that I could bear it no longer.

'Are you dreaming? Wake up!' I exclaimed, and shook his shoulder.

He raised his eyes, and looked at me vacantly. His lips moved, but no sound came from them. Suddenly a convulsive shudder ran through him and he fell heavily forward at my feet.

'He has swooned again,' I said turning to my companion, who stooped and lifted the drooping head onto his knee.

After one glance, he laid it gently down again.

'He is dead,' was his grave reply.

And with Vandeleur's death my story ends, for after that night the sounds were heard no more.

The forlorn little ghost was at rest.

SHADOWS ON THE GRASS

STEVE RASNIC TEM

Mark had read about the accident in the paper a week ago, a terrible thing, how the young boy had been killed on the road that wound around the park while his mother watched from the grassy bend, still eating their picnic lunch, still stretched out beneath the tree even as her son was struck by the car.

The boy had been riding his brand-new bicycle, the paper said. The way Mark remembered it, it had been the first time. He was showing off for his mother.

It was easy for Mark to become obsessed with that kind of story. After finding out about such a tragic incident he felt compelled to read everything he could about the accident—buying up all editions of the city's three newspapers for the next several weeks, watching every TV newscast he could—seeking any additional information. He needed to know the woman's reaction, the feelings of relatives and schoolmates, the driver's reaction and those of his neighbours. He usually took the time to visit the scene, map it out, figure how it would look from every angle. He needed to visualize the incident in his own mind, in every detail, then take it apart and analyse it.

He was not a voyeur, although he had been accused of it, first by his ex-wife and then by a few police officers who caught him taking photographs one day. It was, simply, that Mark Simms was an unhappy man, but with no tragic memories of his own to account for such unhappiness. There was no sad past, no ghosts to haunt him.

Mark Simms was a reasonable man, and that lack of sad memory to explain his depressions was terribly, unacceptably unreasonable.

He had collected his first sad memory when he had gone into hospital to have his appendix removed. In the next bed there was an old man dying of cancer, a *father* dying of cancer, he soon discovered as men and women of varying ages came to visit the old man in his last days. Mark got to know the family very well on their visits, and questioned them thoroughly concerning their father—what it had been like growing up in his house, where he had taken them on vacations, if he had been understanding, if he had been a strict disciplinarian.

And slowly Mark acquired their memories of the old man. Their past became his own, and when the father died, it was his own father dying. He had acquired their grief.

He had been thunderstruck when the old man died, weeping for hours, and what had followed had been a week-long depression. But for the first time in Mark's life, there seemed to be a *reason* for the depression.

Mark parked his car at the side of the park road, a hundred yards or so away from the bend where the boy had been killed. He began walking swiftly, anxious to get to the spot at about the same time of day the accident had occurred, hoping to see the same shadows, the same mixture of light and dark on asphalt, grass and trees the little boy's mother had seen. Mark had never lost a child.

As he came around the bend he saw that there was a woman already on the grass beside the road, stretched out beneath the tree, apparently having a picnic. He felt profoundly let down, and was rapidly plotting some way to scare the woman off when he recognized her from her picture in the paper. It was the boy's mother.

He approached her slowly. She was an older woman, grey streaks in her light brown hair, although Mark wondered if that were a change since the accident. Her silver-blue eyes seemed to fade a bit when she looked up at him. She continued to hum to herself, as if she didn't know he was there. She sat on a bright purple quilt, a wicker basket by her side, and a young boy's red jacket with white-striped sleeves beside that.

Mark took off his hat. 'Ma'am, I'm sorry about your son.'

She turned her head slightly, her eyes turning a darker blue. 'You mean Bobby? Yes . . . he's gone off playing on his bicycle now, missed his lunch. But he'll be back . . . he gets hungry, you know.'

Mark stared at her, not knowing what to say. He'd never encountered this before. He lowered himself to the ground and sat beside her, touching her arm gently. 'Lady . . . your boy . . . he's dead . . .' He held his breath, wondering if telling her might be a mistake.

'He gets hungry . . .' she said more quietly than before. 'He'll be back real soon now.'

Mark leaned back on his elbows. He wasn't sure what he should do now, but was tempted to forget the whole thing and leave. He felt sorry for the woman, but she was obviously in no condition to discuss grief with him— she wasn't feeling any grief. The selfishness of the thought made him feel bad about himself, and made it difficult for him to leave just yet.

He gazed at the green and brown area around them. Long, thin shadows left by their forms seemed to ripple through the uneven grass. A darker shadow where the sun had fixed the trunk of the tree. Round shadows left by nothing Mark could figure. Round shadows moving . . .

Mark turned quickly to the road, but something shiny and metallic reflected the sun back into his eyes so that he couldn't see. He rubbed his eyes painfully, and then there was nothing in the road. He thought of a passing car, but he would have heard it.

'That boy . . .' the woman sighed, 'wouldn't even stop when I waved. Guess he's gonna go round just one more time.'

Mark stared down the road, but could see nothing. He rubbed his hands together nervously, then turned to the woman. 'Lady . . . maybe you better let me take you home. It's getting late and you shouldn't . . .'

'I've gotta wait for Bobby, mister. Can't leave him out here by himself. He'll be afraid . . .'

It seemed to be getting colder, the wind beginning to chill. Mark stood up and walked away from the woman, towards the interior of the park, wondering if he could find a police officer on patrol, or a phone box where he could call one. He felt sure the woman would stay out all night if he didn't get help.

About thirty feet away he stopped, hearing voices behind him. He turned around and looked at the woman. She was speaking softly, and the shadows seemed lighter, somehow, next to her. Like a silhouette the light had begun to erase. A round shadow against the rough tree trunk, a glimmer of reflecting metal, shadowed branches gesturing excitedly like a little boy's arms . . .

Mark ran to the woman. She turned and smiled. 'I let him go round with his new bike just one more time, but he'll be coming back for lunch real soon. Bobby's a good son, mister.'

'Lady . . .' He stopped. There was nothing he could do for her. He began to walk slowly down the road towards his car. He intended to call the authorities when he got home. He had some responsibility.

The sun was lower in the sky now, lower than the leafy branches that had blocked it so well, down behind the trunks and lower boughs—and the shadows in the grass had multiplied.

He had no poignant memories of his own, so he borrowed them from others. He'd had no tragic past.

The shadows rippled through the grass beside him, just off the narrow roadway, as the wind picked up. Legs and arms, hands and fingers, long thin fingers like greedy snakes . . . Mark imagined if he threw food there, picnic food, the grey hands would gobble it up.

He walked more swiftly as it began to rain, a drop at a time. He'd only wanted something to remember, some image to justify his sadness. The shadows ran. He could hear the crackle of raindrops on the fallen leaves, steadily increasing their pace until they sounded to him like roaring flames. He could see his car just ahead.

He could not remember hearing anything, but for some reason he turned his head, and the reflection off the chrome handlebars blinded him.

He screamed, and suddenly the loose, bent wheel was spinning past him. He started running towards his car, trying to outrun the wheel.

When he reached the door the bent wheel fell on its side. Mark looked down.

Underneath the blur of turning spokes there lay a shadow. Small and frantically pressing at the pedal. Almost like a small foot.

He opened the door and slipped into the car, starting the engine immediately. But then he found he couldn't leave. It was raining outside.

He wanted to take their grief and make it his own; he stole their memories. But he would not take responsibility for their ghosts. He would not. He began to move the car forward.

Then stopped. It was raining outside. He couldn't just leave.

He reached back and unlocked the door. Then he pushed it open into the rain.

He could barely see it in his rearview mirror. The stormy afternoon was almost too dark for shadows. But there was a slightly darker greyness suddenly at the edge of the door, then a new scent of wetness in the back seat. He closed the door and picked up speed.

Mark filled his nostrils with the smell of wet hair and jeans, soggy tennis shoes. He had never lost a child. He didn't want to miss any detail.

THE ROADS OF DONNINGTON

RICK KENNETT

A ghost hunter? Me?

It had been on the merest impulse that I'd visited my country cousins, Doug and his wife Cathy, in Donnington during my summer vacation one day in January. It was near dusk when I arrived at their weatherboard house on Wayne Close. I spotted Doug in his vegetable garden as I trundled my motorcycle up to his front gate. He regarded me first with surprise and alarm, then when I'd doffed my helmet, with relief. This caused me to feel not for the first time, a certain resentment of the media hype which fosters the 'thug' image of motorcyclists through stereotyping, ignorance and sensationalism. But I was soon to discover that this time my indignation was misplaced.

'It's odd that you of all people should turn up here and now Ernie,' Doug said as we sat down on his verandah. 'Odd. You of all people.'

'Eh? Is there a reward out for me or something?'

He laughed, but it seemed strained. 'You might well be the man to help . . .' He gave an embarrassed cough. 'Your Aunt Rose was telling me once that you're interested in all this psychic stuff.'

Yes, I knew what he meant. Most of my family thought I was slight of tilt and left of centre. 'Hardly an expert, Doug. All I've done is read Elliot O'Donnell, Hans Holzer and *Lord Halifax's Ghost Book*. That doesn't make a Harry Price.'

'That's as maybe, Ernie, but Harry Holzers aside, you're the only person I know who can help. You see Donnington is . . . well, haunted.'

If he'd said Donnington is drought bound or bush fin threatened I wouldn't have blinked. But a whole township haunted. My reaction to this was, 'Eh?'

Doug spread his hands, 'Say, Ernie, why don't you stay a few days and look into this thing? It's right up your alley.'

So now I was a specialist. 'In what way?'

'It rides a motorbike.'

'Ah! T. E. Lawrence.'

'C. B. Who?'

'No, T. E. Lawrence . . . Lawrence of Arabia. He cracked up on his bike in 1935, though it's said his ghost still rides through the country lanes of Dorset in England.'

'Well, that's what's happening here.' He paused to light up a smoke. I could guess how upset he was by the way the match trembled in his hand. 'Barry Rand was a distant cousin of Cathy's, though she was all the family he'd had since he was a kid. He used to live on the other side of town and visit here occasionally. About three weeks ago he ran off the road on his bike up at a bend in the hills called Devil's Elbow and was killed.' He stopped to take a drag on his cigarette. 'I was driving home from work last week when Barry roared past me in the main street. No mistake. It was Barry all right. I think others have seen him, too. They look at me strange—you know how country towns can be—and ask things like, "Did Barry have a brother?" or "Did you sell Barry's bike to someone in town?" My God, Ernie, I thought *you* were Barry when you pulled up.'

At this his hands began to tremble even more. I turned the conversation around to mundane matters of family, work and the weather. He appeared to calm down, though there still seemed a lingering tension in his manner. A few minutes later Cathy arrived home from shopping. Talking with her, it appeared she knew as much about the matter as Doug. Invitations to look into the mystery were repeated and accepted.

I hoped I would not regret it.

Barry's bike was stored in the garage. This, I thought, was a good place to start. Just before eight the next morning, just after Doug had left for work at the fruit cannery, Cathy and I wheeled Barry's machine out into the sunshine. It was the same make as my own trusty, rusty beast, though a bigger model. Except for a broken left-hand rear vision mirror and some scratches on the chrome it was in good condition.

'He was a good rider,' said Cathy.

'I can believe that.' I indicated the equal wear on the sides of the tyres and beneath the footpegs. He'd been skilled at fast, tight cornering—something that scares the hell out of me.

Opening the petrol cap I took the handle bars and shook the bike. Being a thin, small-framed bloke I found it awkward. I wasn't used to such a heavy machine.

'What are you doing?' Cathy asked.

'Had a notion to try starting her up, perhaps go for a spin.'

'Do you think you should?'

'Can't see any harm in it,' I replied, getting the impression I'd just uttered my own personal Famous Last Words.

So, reluctantly, Cathy fetched the keys to the bike, and after some vicious jumping up and down on the kick-starter, the machine finally fired. Five minutes later, cobwebs cleared and engine warmed, I took Barry Rand's motorcycle out into the street. After a few turns up and down

Wayne Close (once with Cathy as a nervous pillion passenger) I left that quiet side street and ventured out on the main road.

All I knew about ghost hunting consisted of wires across doors and flour on floors, thermometers, tape recorders and midnight vigils. But what could be done with a ghost so mobile? The only answer I could come up with was what I called my Focus Theory. Barry's motorcycle was real, tangible, and yet it was also part of the ghost. My idea was to patrol the roads on it in the hope of attracting its psychic counterpart. It seemed like a good idea, and I could think of nothing better. So for the next three days the bitumen went idly under my wheels as I travelled the length and width of Donnington. But not a sight nor sound nor smell of any ghost did I catch.

On the third day it rained.

I shouldn't have gone out that day. Wet-weather gear notwithstanding, I squelched through the front door at three-thirty that afternoon, tired and saddle-sore, determined to hand in my notice as Donnington's resident spook chaser. But there were other considerations beside the weather. Not only did I think the whole experiment was becoming futile, but I was sure some of the townspeople were now eyeing me askance. Except for Doug and Cathy, none of Donnington's population had anything more than perhaps a vague impression that their town might be haunted. Most probably pegged me as a 'crazy biker', aimlessly roaring up and down their roads all day, come rain or shine, scaring the livestock and generally acting suspicious. I was growing paranoid.

I passed the rest of that wet afternoon flipping through a couple of photo albums. This wasn't so much idle gawking as idle research. It had finally occurred to my road-weary brain that I wouldn't have known Barry Rand had I fallen over him. So I did some swotting. Barry, I found with uneasy surprise, had been a thin, small-framed fellow with short, sandy hair. He'd looked a lot like me.

• • •

It's said that things always look better in the sunshine. That's how I saw the fourth day; bright blue and shiny. Quitting faded from my mind and I took to the road once more. There were no clouds, no rain and no ghosts. I probably would've come home that night just as disappointed as on the previous nights had it not been for a disturbing event in the early afternoon.

It happened on the main street, outside the Donnington shopping centre. I'd just bought a new rear vision mirror to replace the one broken in Barry's fatal crash. Screwing it into place, I was about to adjust it to the correct angle when I spied in the glass a man staring at me from across the street. Even as I looked, his stare became a glare. Then, with barely a glance left or right, he stepped off the kerb, stalking across the road towards me.

If ever there was a case for reincarnation, this guy was the evidence. He looked like he'd been a bull-terrier in a previous existence. He stopped a few inches from my back wheel and bounced the toe of his boot off it.

'What's your game?' he said in a half-grunt.

'Eh?' It was all I could manage.

'What's your game?'

'What game? What are you talking about?'

'Just keep out of my way. Understand?'

I didn't, and I didn't have the chance to say so, for at that instant he stalked off down the street, got into a purple panel van and left with a squeal of tyres that dislodged the wax in my ears.

The fifth day was a near-repeat of the fourth. It was noon. I was in the main street, outside the shopping centre again. I'd just bought some lunch in a milk bar after yet another uneventful morning when I noticed somebody staring at me from across the street. But this time it wasn't a reincarnated bull-terrier. It was an old Aboriginal, grey-haired, grey-bearded and shabby, an utterly forgotten man. Half stepping, half falling from the pavement he zig-zagged his way towards me, in the process accomplishing a minor miracle in not becoming a bonnet ornament of a passing cattle truck. I jumped off the bike and helped him the rest of the way across the road. He laid a heavy arm over my shoulder and mumbled something on a beery breath which took a few seconds to realize had been, 'You wus allus a good fellah.'

I set him down on a bench outside the milk bar. He seemed about to collapse. But as I turned to leave he mumbled something else which, at that moment, didn't register with me. In fact it was one o'clock the next morning that I found myself wide awake with his words suddenly clear in my head:

'Did it hurt when he killed you?'

Breakfast was a bleary-eyed affair. Tactfully, neither Doug nor Cathy asked why I resembled someone who'd only slept half the night. Moreover, before the kettle had even started singing, *I* asked *them* about the old black man, and was informed piecemeal from Doug to Cathy, from Cathy to Doug, that he was a familiar figure around town who people called Black Jack. He had a part-time job at the fruit cannery, but could usually be found drinking at the back door of the Donnington Hotel, or sleeping it off either in the park or in his humpy in the hills at Devil's Elbow.

Devil's Elbow, scene of Barry Rand's death and a name that ran a shudder down my spine. Admittedly it should have been my first stop five days before. In fact I now realized I'd been avoiding going there. I seemed to have had a strange aversion for the place.

Telling myself I was shirking my responsibilities, I took a trip into the hills on that fine, warm morning, travelling along Mountain Road until I came to Devil's Elbow. As I'd imagined, it was an aptly named steep hairpin bend. There was a high embankment on one side, a scrubby gully on the other.

Finding Black Jack's humpy took some time. It was hidden amongst the trees on the high embankment, a home of corrugated iron, board and bark. The hut was empty save for some equally empty bottles and the cold ashes of a cook-fire. I wandered over to the edge of the embankment which over-looked the entire sweep of the bend. As I understood it, at the time of the accident the bike had landed in thick scrub while Barry, less fortunate, was thrown straight into a tree trunk. For fully five minutes I stood and watched the road, but nothing moved on it in all that time. It was a quiet place to live. It was a sad and lonely place to die.

When I returned to the bike, which I'd parked in the sun beside the humpy, I found the tank and handle bars were bitterly cold. The air about it was chill, fogging my breath into strange shapes, like faces. Starting the engine with a frantic kick, I belted back to Donnington as hard as I could go. But until I was well out of sight of Devil's Elbow I was conscious of a subtle pressure between my shoulder blades—the classic feeling of being watched.

Back in town I stopped at the pub and sank a large whisky, ignored the barman's comment of, 'What's the matter, mate? Looks like you've seen a ghost', sank another large whisky and walked out almost as sober as I'd walked in.

'Maybe we're getting into things we're not meant to understand.'

I glanced at Doug across the kitchen table. His face was as near expres-sionless as a face can get, yet I knew we were sharing a common emotion: a healthy fear of the unknown. 'You asked me, Doug. You said, "Why don't you stay a few days and look into this thing". Well I've looked and the way I see it, if we weren't meant to understand these things, they wouldn't happen.'

'I get the feeling we're meddling, Ernie.'

'Then if you'll excuse me, Doug, I'll go meddle down at the pub.'

Irritated by my cousin's attitude I left the house and walked the twenty-minute distance to the local hotel where there was lots of lively noise. That's what I felt I needed. Ghost hunting could get terribly morbid.

I'd been in the pub five minutes and had just finished my first pot. I glanced up to catch the barman's eye and caught a redheaded barmaid instead, staring at me rather darkly. She took my empty glass and started swabbing the bar in front of me with a washcloth.

'What are you doing here?' she asked. 'Why are you riding Barry's bike up and down all day?'

'Did you know him?'

'No . . . Yes. Yes, I knew him. Most people know most people around here.'

'Then you probably know Doug and Cathy Asher. I'm Doug's cousin, Ernie Pine. Barry was Cathy's cousin. I don't know if that made us related. Cousins-in-law, perhaps.'

The ice broke. She smiled, brushing back a red curl. 'Oh. You're visiting.'

'Doug asked me to stay over a few days. You've probably seen me rambling around, seeing the sights, taking little day tours.'

'Yes. You know, for a couple of days I thought . . . Say, what's the attraction for Mountain Road? I've seen you up there several times.'

The only time I'd been on Mountain Road was to visit Black Jack's humpy. So if she'd seen me there several times, she'd seen *me* there only once.

'Do you live up that way?'

'My parents have a farm a mile up from . . ."

'Devil's Elbow?'

'Yes,' she said, her smile fading. 'How did you know?'

'There's no such thing as ghosts,' I lied.

She almost squinted at me. 'Same again?'

'Please.'

I dug into my jeans for some coins. Behind me the bar door opened and a disturbingly familiar grunt of a voice said, 'Come on if ya comin', Margo. Can't wait all . . . . ing night.' The barmaid, Margo, said something in answer. Then I did a very stupid thing. I turned around and came face to fist with the reincarnated bull-terrier.

'Well, boy, it looks like you meddled pretty damn well,' said Doug as he drove me home.

I wasn't in the mood to appreciate irony. My nose had stopped bleeding, but I was still counting my teeth.

'Listen, Doug, I think I've got this thing figured out. Was Barry seeing a girl at the time of his death?'

'What? Oh, yes. I think so.'

'Margo the barmaid?'

'I think so.' We drove on another minute in silence before he added, 'You best leave her alone, Ernie. Paul Markby, your sparring partner and her new boyfriend, is a nasty piece of work.'

We turned into the driveway and pulled up at the front door where stood Cathy with admonitions and ointment. I took them both with a minimum of fuss then went to bed. I'd listened to and taken absolutely no notice of what Doug had said about Margo. I was determined to take a ride up into the hills in the morning, to visit a farm a mile above Devil's Elbow.

The day was warm and humid. The air smelled of oncoming rain. But for the moment the road was dry, and I took to it at ten that morning. There was no traffic around, and consequently I sped along as fast as the road would allow. But soon after turning off onto Mountain Road I saw up ahead, just rounding one of the many bends, another motorcycle. It was Barry Rand.

Truth to tell I wanted to throttle back there and then and be gone. But my right hand seemed to act of its own accord, grabbing bigger and bigger handfuls of throttle. I raced ahead and soon only a few bike lengths separated us. Then we merged.

It was only late morning, yet night was gently wrapping itself around me. I wanted to brake, to put the bike down in a spray of gravel. But I couldn't because I was no longer myself. I was no longer Ernie Pine. I was Barry Rand and this, suddenly, was the night he'd died.

It was then I noticed the rear view mirrors. While the right showed the road winding behind me into night, the left, the one I'd replaced some days ago, showed the same road winding behind me into late morning sunshine. I glanced at the right one again. There were lights there, two of them, describing little spiral galaxies in the vibrating mirror. In the left one the daylight road was empty.

I was travelling fast now, far faster than I would have thought safe for those bends. The lights behind were close. There was no mistaking their murderous intent. Crouching low and leaning hard right, Barry and I took a curve, feeling the road grind away at the footpegs, then leant hard left into the next turn, our knee nearly at ground level. Somewhere close behind car wheels squealed as they too hung on desperately to each curve. Then all at once I had control of the bike again. Barry was sitting in my skull. His riding skills were mine as was his memory. I saw in his mind's eye how he'd tried to lay the bike down in the path of the car as they'd hurtled into Devil's Elbow, how he'd tried to jump clear, how the car had suddenly surged forward, spinning him out into space, into eternity. Forewarned, I swerved as the car tried to ram. There was no time for another shot. Devil's Elbow was dead ahead.

There was a wail of brakes. It was what I'd been waiting for. I swerved in front of the car again, wrenched the handle bars around and laid the bike down in a shower of sparks. The rest became a blur as I flew over the edge of the road, out into empty space. From somewhere unknown came the scream of violent metal to metal contact. I caught a glimpse of two entwined machines plunging into the gully, of a purple door ripping open, of a figure flying towards the trees.

I was out on a limb when I came to rest, shaken but unhurt. The night was gradually dissolving around me, giving back the morning. But for a bare second, before reality returned, I thought I saw a dark figure, a bottle in its hand, sitting on the raised embankment across the road. But the image was fleeting. I will never be sure of it.

I climbed to the ground and soon found the bike. It was as mangled as if it'd been jammed under a car. I didn't find the car.

What is it about Death that makes an unquiet spirit of one man, yet sends millions more to silent graves?

I pondered this question through all the long, lonely miles along the highway home. I was even thinking on it as I left Donnington where, at the edge of town on a clear stretch of road, police were trying to calm an obviously distressed red-haired woman, while ambulance men removed from an undamaged purple panel van something that doesn't bear thinking about.

THE DAY THAT FATHER BROUGHT SOMETHING HOME

R. CHETWYND-HAYES

Alexander was seven years old and saw much that seemed to escape the perception of his elders, but this he took for granted as the natural order of things. Grannie, for example, had been very poorly for some time; merely sat in her chair by the fireside, looking frail and shrivelled, her transparent hands trembling slightly. She seemed totally unaware of the little old lady who was standing behind her chair. Alexander would have drawn her attention to this strange visitor, only he knew from experience such revelations were not accepted kindly.

'The boy gives me the willies,' Aunt Martha had remarked on one occasion, 'always talking about things that aren't there. Like that time he said he saw a dog following us down Powder Mill Lane.'

That was the day Grandad had died. Dropped dead in the woodshed while he was sawing wood.

'Fine imagination,' Father remarked complacently, 'takes after me.'

'Lies, I call it,' Mother said spitefully, 'and that is certainly like you.'

He thus came to accept that such manifestations were best left undeclared;

a secret shared by himself and Tobias. Now, it must be clearly understood that Tobias was to all outward appearances a dog—a short-haired, sturdy animal of doubtful ancestry, but Alexander knew, of course, he was nothing of the sort. Tobias was a man in a dog's body. Where this information came from he was not aware. Tobias had certainly never mentioned it, neither had Alexander given the matter serious thought. He had never even said to himself, 'Tobias is a man,' but one day, the one when they had both seen a man with a badly scarred face peering down over the banisters, Alexander had known it was so. The fact was not important; merely another item of information to add to his growing store of knowledge.

Tobias was not kindly disposed to the little old lady who stood behind Grannie's chair, for he eyed her with a wary look, even growled deep down in his throat, until Mother snapped:

'What's wrong with that dog?'

And Father asked: 'What's the matter, boy, eh?' Thereupon, Tobias wagged his tail ten to the dozen, as though suddenly remembering that this was part of the dog-act.

'How do you feel, Grannie?' Mother asked for the third time that day. They were almost the only words anyone ever addressed to Grannie, and she always responded with one word: 'Poorly.'

'You'll soon be up and around,' stated Father boisterously. 'Come spring and you'll be chasing rabbits over the common.'

Alexander saw the little old lady who stood behind Grannie's chair smile, then shake her head.

Next day Grannie died. She slumped in her chair, and Tobias howled, one long mournful howl, and Alexander watched Grannie come out of her body, rather like a chick breaking free from its egg. First a kind of mist poured out of Grannie's ears, nose and mouth. This twisted and pulsated until finally a second Grannie stood in front of the original; a perfect duplicate, right down to the carpet slipper that had a hole in the right toe. She looked weak, her little, faded blue eyes were narrow slits, and she swayed like a water fern when the river in full flood, and there was a silver-coloured cord still joining her to the slumped body in the old rocking-chair, and this, the little old lady broke, and tied one half into a knot, which disappeared into a point just above Grannie's bottom. Then she led Grannie away, one arm about her waist, out through the parlour doorway, and Alexander saw them pass the window. Tobias gave Alexander one eloquent look, and the boy said;

'Must have been her sister, the one she kept talking about.'

Then Tobias went to sleep, apparently relieved that the unwelcome visitor was finally out of the house, and he could now dream peacefully of the time when he walked on two legs.

Mother of course had to scream, and Aunt Martha ran in from next door, and there was a lot of crying, and much mutual comforting, tea drinking, and utterance of statements.

'She's better off,' said Mother after Father had removed what remained of Grannie, 'she's at peace now.'

'A good innings,' said Aunt Martha, 'you've got to admit, she had a good innings.'

'That poor boy.' With a stab of alarm Alexander realised he was the subject under discussion. 'He saw it all. He was alone and saw her die.'

And Mother surrendered to another storm of tears while Alexander watched a little man walk under Aunt Martha's chair, and daintily wend his way between her feet. He was not more than three inches high, clad in a little green suit and a tiny hat complete with a green feather. Alexander knew he lived with his family behind the wainscoting, and sometimes when the sun had set, and the firelight was making shadows dance a sombre reel across walls and ceiling, two minute children, so small they could have been little balls of fluff, came out to play hide-and-seek in the hearthrug.

Grannie, Grandad and the little old lady all turned up for the funeral. They were attired in respectable black as befitted the occasion, and as there was no room for them in the following cars, they clambered up on top of the hearse, where they sat in a neat row with their legs dangling over one side. There was room for all in the church, the visible mourners consisting of Father, Mother, and Aunt Martha, plus a distant cousin who no one knew, but had turned up with a sympathetic smile and an eye for the refreshments that were to follow the sad proceedings. This meant the three uninvited mourners could make themselves comfortable in the front pew on the opposite side of the aisle to the family proper, and Alexander watched them wide-eyed, which earned him a reproof from Father, who said, 'Keep your eyes to the front and be more respectful.'

While the vicar expounded the virtues of Grannie who had been a constant source of irritation to him during her lifetime, having disapproved of his 'high church' ways, the object of his discourse dabbed her eyes with a small black handkerchief, and Grandad blew his nose into a bright red one. However, when the misguided cleric genuflected three times before the altar, and moreover swung an incense burner over Grannie's coffin, she shook a clenched fist in his direction, and Alexander saw Grandad and the Great-Aunt pleading with her to practise more self-restraint.

The north wind stabbed the live mourners with icy fingers as they huddled round the graveside, and Grannie appeared to be completely overcome by the sight of her own interment, for she was escorted by her two companions away over the long, winter-bitten grass towards the lych-gate where they disappeared from view. Alexander knew he would not see them again until they returned for some later bereavement.

After the funeral, life soon sank to its normal level of ordinariness. Alexander went back to school where he was careful not to acquaint Miss Everhard, his current teacher, with the indisputable fact that a little black man sat on her right shoulder and shook with grotesque joy whenever she considered it needful to slap a small girl's leg. In no time at all, spring breathed gently over the bleak countryside, and daffodils raised their yellow trumpets to a benign sky. Alexander, accompanied by Tobias, went down to the secret place well hidden in Marline Wood, where together they watched the outdoor-little-people as they crept out from their warm nest under the giant oak to perform a joyful dance to the new sun.

But spring did not enter the house on top of the hill, and Alexander became aware of a cold something which had not yet assumed visible form, but lurked unseen in dark corners and the shadows on the landing. He knew, and this knowledge came to him uninvited, that someone in the house was the cause of this uneasiness. The little man and his family no longer came out from behind the wainscoting. Tobias wore a dejected air and whenever possible kept close to Alexander's side.

He found himself watching Father, and presently arrived at a surprising discovery. Father was not what he seemed. The big, jovial, rather silly man was a skin that hid someone quite different. Or perhaps not so much different, as older, with a face that was still familiar, but more deeply lined, which in turn hid a brain where swam thoughts, memories, emotions, that neither Mother nor Aunt Martha, nor even Alexander himself, had ever suspected. Sometimes, in the soft twilight, before it was banished by lamplight, Alexander detected a red glow surrounding Father's head. It was never still. It pulsated as though in time to his thoughts, sometimes it was pale pink, at others bright red, and it was then the cold 'something' was most evident. It filled the cosy room, came between Alexander and the roaring fire, made Tobias whimper, and Father's eyes became as window panes reflecting the images of passing clouds. Stormy, sun-tinted, black, lightning-slashed, and Alexander watched, wondered, but was never, never afraid.

He lay awake in the thick darkness and listened to the sounds of the sleeping house. The muted sigh of the poor lady who had died here many years ago, and was now creeping down the stairs to roam through the lower rooms, searching for something she would never find. The soft flutter of wings on his bedroom window panes—the soul of someone closely connected with the sighing lady who must now fly through the night as a bird, even as Tobias walked the earth as a dog. Just before he slid into sleep Alexander heard a low cry by his bedside, and he murmured sleepily: 'Go away,' and the man with the scarred face went back to the world from which he had strayed. Then the cold 'something', brought into being possibly by Father's dreams, invaded the room, but Alexander ignored it, just wrapped himself up more tightly in the bedclothes, and dreamed he was having tea with the little family behind the wainscoting.

Then one day Father brought something home with him, and the cold 'something' went away. Perhaps it had only been a pathfinder for the visible 'something', or maybe Father's thoughts, the red ones, had given it substance, so that now it was visible to Alexander's special vision.

Whatever the answer, and Alexander did not ponder on these matters, Father came into the parlour late one evening, and a great bearlike thing followed in his footsteps. It was all of seven feet tall; a rough, black fur covered the entire body from the neck downwards, and the face was jet-black with great red eyes that glittered strangely in the artificial light. A mass of black hair covered the head and framed the face, while the chin was hidden behind a thick, frizzy beard.

The evening meal was eaten in almost total silence, for although Mother could not see the Bear-Thing Father had brought home, it did seem she felt its presence. She watched Father from under lowered eyelids, and he toyed with his food, seemed oblivious to his wife and small son, and Tobias whimpered unhappily from his place on the hearth-rug.

But Alexander watched the Bear-Thing, and the Bear-Thing watched him, seeming unpleasantly aware it was visible to his special eyes. It moved nearer to Father as though stressing that he was its particular property, and no interference would be tolerated; then as Alexander made no movement, only continued to eat a slice of Swiss roll, a delicacy to which he was most partial, it relaxed slightly, even moved back a few steps and examined the room with interest.

The overmantel mirror attracted Its attention, and after a single glance at Father as though to make certain he was firmly anchored to his chair, It lumbered over to the fireplace, and Tobias fled with lowered tail and dilated eyes to a position of comparative safety behind the sofa.

'What are you staring at?' asked Mother, and her voice was hoarse with fear.

'Nothing,' Alexander replied and turned his attention to Father who was giving out scarlet thought-waves. After a while he thought it safe to look once again in the direction of the fireplace.

The Bear-Thing was pushing its head right into the mirror. Alexander stifled a giggle. It was clearly trying to fasten its fangs into the neck of its reflection. The reflected head retreated before that of the real one; red eyes glittered with grotesque hate, the bearded face grimaced, the mouth gaped, and Alexander wondered if the Bear-Thing supposed the mirror image to be a rival with designs upon its property. Then Father got up and the Bear-Thing pulled its head out of the mirror, and swung round with surprising speed. Before he reached the door It was by his side.

'Harry!' Mother was half out of her chair. 'What's wrong with you?'

'Me!' He stared at her in amazement, but his eyes reflected a terrible fear. 'What are you going on about? I'm tired that's all. I want to go to bed.'

'You haven't said a word all evening. And you haven't eaten a thing.'

The scarlet thoughts were like lightning flashes against black clouds.

'Bloody hell, woman, I can't be chattering like a bloody monkey all the time, can I? Leave me alone.'

He pulled the door open and rushed out with the Bear-Thing close behind. Mother remained at her place at the bottom of the table, the nagging worry rising from her head in the form of little green bubbles. Alexander thought they looked rather pretty, like decorations on a Christmas tree, then suddenly she began to cry, a terrible body shaking outburst that had nothing in common with her grief for Grannie's passing. Alexander said 'Mummie', and he tasted fear for the first time; it clung to his palate like nasty medicine. His voice broke through the wall of her anguish, for she stared at him with eyes that were fired by a sudden blast of terrible knowledge, and she sprung to her feet and rushed from the room.

Tobias came out from behind the sofa to push a cold nose into Alexander's hand, as he stared sadly into the fire.

'Why?' he asked after a while. 'Why?'

Tobias did not, could not, answer.

The murmur of voices was like the sound of sea breaking on some wild shore. Sometimes it was soft, pleading. At others, it rose up into a battle of accusation and denial, but only an occasional word, a rare sentence, filtered through the dividing wall.

'You're mad.'

'What have you done?'

'. . . tell . . .'

'. . . No . . . nothing . . .'

The Bear-Thing must be in there with them. Perhaps it was seated on the little upholstered bedside chair, or fighting its reflection in the dressing-table mirror, or maybe knowing its property to be safely in bed, it was roaming the house like a newly arrived cat, smelling out the dark corners, peering into cupboards, looking up chimneys.

'Shut up, blast you.'

Father's voice was a scream of dark agony, and Mother's sobs a low cry of never-ending pain. Presently their bedroom door opened and heavy footsteps went down the stairs. The front door slammed, to be followed by a period of strange peace, such as comes during a lull in a violent storm. The house was unnaturally quiet, for the Bear-Thing had frightened the sad ghosts into uneasy retirement.

The word rang round the town and out across the surrounding countryside like a monstrous clarion call.

MURDER.

It shrieked at Alexander from newspaper placards on his way to school, it tripped off the tongues of children when they collected together in groups in the playground, it was spat out by bright-eyed women as they gossiped over garden fences, it was vomited by drunken men as they lurched against walls on their way home from The Black Bull.

MURDER.

Drab, grey lives received their meed of colour. Fearful excitement rippled across the stagnant pool of urban existence, and the skies rained policemen. Words, sentences, harsh lust-ridden thoughts poured in from every direction, and only Alexander was unmoved. Faces became round blobs with mouths.

'No more than seventeen. Raped, strangled, she was.'

'When they catch him, he ought to be boiled in oil.'

'It's come so a respectable woman can't walk down the street in peace.'

Alexander memorised the letters on the newspaper placard. He tactfully put the question to Aunt Martha.

'Please, what is a S-E-X-M-O-N-S-T-E-R?'

'Never you mind,' Aunt Martha glared at him. 'You don't want to know about things like that at your age.'

But a little boy at school was more informative.

'Everybody knows that, stupid. It's a bloke who kisses a girl who don't want to be kissed, then does her in so she won't tell on him.'

Alexander was not satisfied.

'What's he want to kiss her for?'

The boy shrugged.

'Because he's batty.'

They came knocking at every door, mostly smart young men with polite smiles. They used such words as: 'Routine, co-operation, would you be so kind,' but their eyes searched every new face with a kind of terrible, hopeful expectancy.

Alexander listened behind the parlour door.

'I am sure, Sir,' the smart young man was saying, while his companion watched Father with an unblinking stare, 'you wish this dreadful business cleared up, and the chap responsible brought to justice.'

'Yes,' Father agreed loudly, 'I do indeed. Yes.'

'Quite so. Then I would like you to cast your mind back to the night of May the nineteenth.'

'That would be last Tuesday,' Father said brightly. 'Yes.'

'As you say, Sir, last Tuesday evening. Can you recall where you were between the hours of seven and ten o'clock?'

'I was at home. Yes. Watching telly.'

'Do you support this statement, madam?'

'What?'

Mother sounded as if she had been stung by a wasp.

'Can you verify . . . ? Was Mr Palmer home on Tuesday evening last between the hours of seven and ten o'clock?'

'Oh, yes. Yes, he was.'

There was a short silence and Alexander patted Tobias's head. The suave voice spoke again.

'He did not go out at any time?'

'Beg pardon?'

'I said; your husband did not leave the house at any time between the hours of seven and ten?'

'No. No, he was here all the time.'

'You are absolutely certain? If he did it does not mean we suspect he did anything—improper. We just want to know where he went.'

'No.' Mother's voice was a trifle too loud. 'He went nowhere. Was here all the time.'

'I see. Good. How old are you, Sir?'

'Forty-three.'

'Right.'

Alexander peered through the crack between the door and its lintel. The young man was writing in a small blue notebook; his companion was still watching Father.

'I think that's all.' The man put his notebook away, then turned and walked towards the door. Alexander and Tobias beat a hasty retreat. Suddenly the voice spoke again.

'Just one little thing. Can you remember what programme you saw on television?'

There was an undercurrent of relief in Father's voice, rather like that of an examination candidate who has been asked a question to which he knows the answer.

'Yes, there was an old film which started at seven-thirty—*Carry on Smoking* I think it was, then a quiz show—Scotty Masters' *History is Knocking At Your Door,* then the news . . .'

The man cut him short with a low laugh.

'Same old rubbish each week. Scarcely worth the trouble of paying for the *T.V. and Radio Times,* is it, Sir? Well, thank you for your co-operation.'

Father said: 'Not at all, pleased to be of help. Hope you catch him soon,' and the man replied: 'Don't worry, Sir, we will,' and the smell of fear was foul—like sour milk on a hot day.

When the men had gone, when the door was fast shut, and Alexander had crept back into the parlour, then, Mother removed the fixed smile from her face, loosened the muscles round eyes and mouth, so that her face crumbled like a balloon when the air has been let out, and she cried, and cried. And the face of Father was that of a man who has walked beyond hope, who has drunk deep from the cup of despair, and now sits in an ante-chamber of hell where human emotions cannot enter. The Bear-Thing stood behind him, its face was raised and wore an expression of pain-ecstasy, so that for a moment Alexander thought it looked strangely beautiful.

'Go to bed, Alec,' Father said, 'like a good boy.'

There was a lump in his throat, and a strange liquid feeling in his stomach, and he recognised pity although he could give it no name. Tobias rubbed his rough coat against Father's leg, and he whimpered softly, trying with all his might to explain the great riddle, but the unbreakable, and never-to-be-spoken-law, said he must always pretend to be a dog, and dogs do not explain, only hide bones and christen lamp-posts. So Alexander drew him away, and together they ascended the stairs to take refuge in his bedroom, where sleep and forgetfulness lay waiting.

The two men came back the following evening, and they brought with them a third man, a much older, heavier person, who was trying unsuccessfully to pretend he was someone's benign uncle. He shook Father's hand, seated himself, looked round the small room with extravagated ease, then rubbed his hands together as though he were Santa Claus paying his final visit on a cold Christmas Eve.

'Cosy, Mr Palmer. Nice place you've got here. Real cosy, eh, lads?'

The two young men nodded like puppets when the strings have been jerked.

'Cosy, Sir. Cosy.'

Father had to say something. 'You wanted to see me?'

Alexander, for the moment forgotten in his seat by the fireplace, watched the red thoughts flicker and smelt the stench of fear.

'What!' The big man looked painfully surprised. 'See you . . . ? Oh, yes.

There was one little matter, purely routine, a damn nuisance really, but we do have to follow up every lead. You do understand?'

He appealed to Father who could only nod.

'You're very kind, very considerate. Many people aren't. I wonder, would you mind going over your statement again? The one you gave to these two officers.'

'Statement?'

Father let the word slide out of his mouth, like a plum stone that has aggravated a bad tooth.

'Yes, Mr Palmer.' The big man's voice was now low, caressing, soothing, inviting confidences, secrets, that would be forever locked in his brain. 'Where were you between seven and ten o'clock on Tuesday evening last?'

'I've told them already,' Father insisted.

'Yes, I know. Dreadful pests aren't we? Just tell me, so I can get the record straight.'

'I was home all the evening, watching telly.'

'And you never left the house? Not even once?'

Father was looking for a pitfall, but the way ahead was dark, and he must go forward.

'No. No, not once.'

'Thank you, Mr Palmer. You've taken a weight off my mind. These two do a good job, but I like to get in on the act sometimes. Have to appear to be earning my keep. Eh?'

He laughed loudly, and the two young men tittered politely, and Father permitted himself a mild grimace, but Mother stared blankly at the big man, and pushed back a strand of hair with a trembling hand.

'I wonder, Mrs Palmer,' the big man was now pretending to be shy, afraid of overstaying his welcome, 'could we trouble you for a cup of tea? The boys and I have been at it since lunchtime, and we're parched. Eh, lads?'

'Parched,' said one.

'Dry as a bone,' said the other.

'Of course.' Mother was most reluctant to leave the room, but this appeal to her hospitality could not be ignored.

'And,' the big man went on, 'I should take this little chap with you. He looks tired. Long past his bedtime, I expect.'

'Come on, Alec.' Mother jerked her head slightly, and Alexander could do no more than follow her out of the room. At the doorway he looked back. The Bear-Thing was leaning against the far wall. It looked very sad.

In the kitchen Mother gripped Alexander's shoulders tightly. Her eyes were wild, her voice a harsh whisper.

'Go back. Listen behind the door. Listen.'

He went back to his former place behind the half-open door and applied his eye to the crack. He could see the big man's face; it was still benign.

'Before your good lady comes back, Mr Palmer, there is one little matter I would like to clear up. We have recently interviewed a certain maiden lady by the name of . . .' He consulted a little black book. '. . . yes, here we are, a Miss Sidgwick. A formidable old party, who apparently wanders round the common looking for what she calls evildoers. She means snogging couples, of course. Turfs out any she finds and gives 'em a lecture on the evil of their ways. Know her?'

Father shook his head.

'Really!' The big man registered surprise. 'I thought everyone in these parts knew Miss Sidgwick. Well, she appears to know you. In fact she says she saw you walking across the common on Tuesday night.'

'She lies,' Father gasped, 'lies.'

'I think that is a bit strong, Mr Palmer,' the big man shook his head. 'No, she's an oddity, a bit cracked, perhaps, but a respectable old body. Mistaken maybe.'

'Well, then,' Father grasped the offered straw, 'she was mistaken.'

'That then is your opinion, Mr Palmer? The lady was mistaken if she states she saw you on the common between the hours of seven and eight on Tuesday last?'

'Yes,' Father repeated, 'she was mistaken.'

Mother swept by Alexander with a loaded tray, and the big man insisted on helping her lay out the cups and saucers on the dining table. The two young men did not move.

'Some old crow says she saw me out on the common on Tuesday night,' Father informed Mother.

She said, 'Oh,' quite sharply.

'Mistaken identity,' pronounced the big man.

'I'll sue her for libel,' Father stated.

'Slander,' corrected the big man, 'libel is written, slander is spoken.'

'I'll sue her anyway,' Father insisted, 'I've got my good name to think of.'

'Shouldn't let it worry you,' the big man comforted, 'a lot of what we hear goes in one ear and out the other.' He chuckled. 'As a matter of fact, she slipped up rather badly on Tuesday night. There was one young couple snogging away in the long grass, and she saw neither hair nor hide of them. I think you know them, Mr Palmer, a Jack Binns and a Winnie Baun. They work at Garridges.'

'I know them,' Father admitted.

'I thought you must.' The big man took a dainty sip from his cup. 'Young Binns says he saw you running across the common at five minutes to eight.'

'He can't have,' Father protested weakly.

'That's what he says. In fact they both say so. Another case of mistaken identity, Mr Palmer?'

'These kids will say anything.' Father had backed to the wall, right up against the Bear-Thing. It placed its great paws on his shoulders as though trying to comfort him.

'True,' the big man nodded, 'very true. No sense of values. The country is going to the dogs.' He stared sadly at his teacup as though pondering on the wickedness of the rising generation. 'Do you know a Miss Eve Roberts, Mr Palmer?'

'No.'

Tears were running down the Bear-Thing's face.

'Or Miss Jane Gardner?'

'No, no.'

'Strange.' The big man looked up, his eyes cold. 'They both stated you made—how shall I put it? Unwelcome advances to them?'

'Lies. I am a respectable, married man. Ask anyone.'

'You would appear,' said the big man slowly, 'to be a much slandered man, Mr Palmer.'

'Well,' he got up, 'time's a'wasting, mustn't keep you good people up any longer. Thank you for the tea, Mrs Palmer. Please, we will let ourselves out.'

At the door he looked back, an apologetic smile parting his lips.

'I would think over our little chat, if I were you, Mr Palmer. Try to think out why five people should be so very—mistaken. I'll see you tomorrow. Oh, one last thing. Take my tip, don't go out tonight. You'll be quite safe. I'm leaving a couple of chaps outside to keep an eye on things. Goodnight.'

They left, but their darkness remained behind them, and the very walls of the house were sobbing with terror.

The scream pulled Alexander up from the pit of sleep and hurled him into a harsh reality, where, once the light was on, the room was a cold, cold place that was full of noise. The scream was repeated again, and the howl of a dog rose like a banshee's cry, also there was a loud banging on the front door, and the rising murmur of many voices.

Down in the hall Alexander saw the Bear-Thing. It was slumped against the wall, and there was a look of naked terror in its red eyes. Alexander walked by it and crept into the kitchen. Father had been very clever. He had his head inside a plastic bag, the one Mother used to take the washing down to the laundrette, and after removing one of the gas burners, had connected a rubber tube to the pipe. The other end was in the plastic bag, which was tied tightly round Father's neck with a length of string. His body was very, very dead.

There was the sound of breaking glass, and presently the big man entered, followed by the two smart young men. They pulled Mother to her feet and escorted her to the parlour where she sat in Grannie's old chair, rocking to and fro.

'I didn't mean to fall asleep,' she kept repeating, 'I didn't mean to fall asleep.'

'It's better this way,' the big man said, 'you must see, it's better this way.'

The Bear-Thing had come in and was eyeing him with growing interest.

'Pity, Sir,' one young man remarked wistfully, 'he was near breaking point.'

'He broke, lad,' the big man replied, 'broke. They always break.'

The two young men looked at their chief with undisguised admiration; the Bear-Thing with pronounced consideration.

'Get the doctor,' the big man ordered, 'dig out the old party from next door, the woman will need someone to take care of her. I'll make out my report.'

He left and the Bear-Thing went with him.

In the weeks which followed Alexander kept an eye open for Father, but he failed to materialise. Grannie, Grandad and Great-Aunt turned up for the funeral, and the sighing lady returned to her haunting. Also, after a decent interval, the little man and his family made themselves heard behind the wainscoating. But no Father, nothing out of the ordinary.

Then one day Tobias brought home a small kitten. It was not more than a few weeks old, and was sopping wet. Alexander dried it on the kitchen towel, then made a home for it in a handleless shopping basket, well-lined with one of Father's vests. It accepted a saucer of milk, then after a short nap, woke up in time to see Mother, looking so old, so grey, as she cleared the table. It mewed piteously.

Alexander took the small bundle of fur up onto his lap and fondled the velvet ears. He looked at Tobias. The man-who-had-to-pretend-to-be-a-dog nodded.

They both knew.

ABOUT THE EDITORS

R. Chetwynd-Hayes had a publishing career that lasted more than forty years. He produced thirteen novels, twenty-five collections of stories, and edited twenty-four anthologies. In 1989 both the Horror Writers of America and the British Fantasy Society presented him with Life Achievement Awards, and he was the Special Guest at the 1997 World Fantasy Convention in London. His stories have been adapted for film, television, radio and comic strips, and have been translated into numerous languages around the world. He died in 2001.

Stephen Jones is the winner of three World Fantasy Awards, four Horror Writers Association Bram Stoker Awards and three International Horror Guild Awards, as well as being a Hugo Award nominee and a sixteen-times recipient of the British Fantasy Award. One of Britain's most acclaimed anthologists of horror and dark fantasy, he has more than eighty books to his credit. You can visit his web site at www.herebedragons.co.uk/jones.